# THE ROYAL ASSASSIN

*Kit Scarlett Mysteries  
Book Two*

## Adele Jordan

*Also in the Kit Scarlett Series*
The Gentlewoman Spy
A Spy at Hampton Court

# THE ROYAL ASSASSIN

Published by Sapere Books.

24 Trafalgar Road, Ilkley, LS29 8HH

saperebooks.com

Copyright © Adele Jordan, 2022

Adele Jordan has asserted her right to be identified as the author of this work.
All rights reserved.

No part of this publication may be reproduced, stored in any retrieval system, or transmitted, in any form, or by any means, electronic, mechanical, photocopying, recording, or otherwise, without the prior written permission of the publishers.
This book is a work of fiction. Names, characters, businesses, organisations, places and events, other than those clearly in the public domain, are either the product of the author's imagination, or are used fictitiously.
Any resemblances to actual persons, living or dead, events or locales are purely coincidental.

ISBN: 978-1-80055-803-8

# CHAPTER 1

*Richmond-upon-Thames, England, 1584*

"I could be executed for this," Kit Scarlett muttered as she walked between the townhouses, heading toward one in particular. At the end of the road through the blackness, she could see the only house that didn't have candles or lanterns sitting in the windows. This far into the night, the timber and thatched structure was only made visible by the candles from the adjoining houses' windows.

Kit whipped the skirt of her heavy gown around her legs, trying to make it easier to walk. Its dark pink colour was bold even in the darkness with the silk falling heavily around the farthingale about her ankles, and the underskirt made of a white and pink pattern gleaming through an opening at the front. She repeatedly fidgeted, tugging at the skirt, longing for the hose she usually wore.

When she reached the front of the house, it took a while to find the door. Hidden between two timbers, it appeared to be fresh plaster work with a strip of extra wood to hide where a small door handle was carved into the oak. She glanced behind her, checking the cobbled street for any sign of being followed, but there was no one, only the dark shadows between the candles in the windows.

"Where is he?" she whispered in the air. She didn't have time to wait. She just had to hope he found the house on time, or she would have to complete the task alone.

Turning back to the door, she knocked in a pattern: two slow taps, three quick, and another slow. The door creaked open, and on the other side a thin narrow face peered through the gap to stare at her with a curled nose.

"Don't know you," the man said with a strong Sussex accent.

"I do not know you either. Is the mistress of the house home?" Kit asked, jerking her chin higher as she stepped toward the door. She adopted a formal countenance, one she had seen Sir Francis Walsingham's daughter take many times, even amending her accent to something more formal. The man's eyes flicked down to her gown, recognising the strong pink colour that only the upper classes were permitted to wear.

"Mrs Minnow is indisposed." He paused with his words, clearly adjusting his opinion of her.

"She is expecting me," Kit said pointedly.

The man's thin eyebrows shot up before he stepped back and opened the door fully.

Kit glanced behind her, wondering where in the darkness of the street the man she had been waiting for was hiding. She didn't have long to look, for the steward attending to the door cleared his throat, urging her impatiently forward into the house.

"Wait here." The man walked away with his lope so laboured and such a skinny body that Kit was rather reminded of a whippet as she watched him meander through the shadows. When she was certain he had disappeared far enough into the house, she turned to the door and slid the bolt backward, before opening it a slither.

Within her sleeve she had hidden a small, enamelled pin with a ruby set in the centre of a gold circle, gifted to her from Walsingham. She reached out and pressed the pin into the slats beyond the doorframe, so when the man she was waiting for approached, he would be able to find the door to the house. The light of a lantern would bounce off the ruby, exuding a sharp red dot of light. When she pulled the door closed, she was careful to leave the door unbolted, and walked a few steps away, determined not to draw attention to the door.

As the servant returned, behind him was an elderly lady with her white hair tucked beneath an even paler cap and a farthingale dress that was somewhat larger than Kit's, taking up the entire space of the small entrance hall and making the steward press himself as far against the wall as he could.

"Ah! You came."

"Mrs Minnow," Kit said, affecting the soft tones she had used with the woman ever since she had met her a few weeks before. It hadn't been easy, trying to convince the elderly woman to trust her, but once Mrs Minnow spied the crucifix Kit had worn around her neck for her benefit, she was convinced that Kit was a Catholic. "I am so happy to be here at last. Is all prepared?"

"It is indeed. You are the first to arrive. Eager, I can see." Mrs Minnow turned, encouraging Kit to follow her as she shooed the servant away. "We must be quick. I have heard the watchmen are out early tonight. I do not want to give them a reason to look through my windows."

Kit affected a smile until Mrs Minnow turned away, then she let the smile drop. It seemed so odd to her that this kind lady would harbour a man known to be not only a Jesuit priest, but a man who longed for the death of Her Majesty Queen Elizabeth.

"We must be quiet," Mrs Minnow murmured as she beckoned Kit to follow her, leading the way down the corridor with one candle.

"It is very dark here tonight," Kit spoke conversationally, though at all times she was glancing to the side, looking through open doors to hunt for one face in particular.

"We cannot risk discovery. We'll swing at the gallows for worshipping our God."

"That we will," Kit muttered as she followed Mrs Minnow up a thin spiral staircase.

Walsingham's plan still sat uneasy on Kit. Had she been caught this evening attending Mass, she would have been taken to the Tower herself, but it was a risk she had been ordered to take.

The two of them struggled with their large gowns and farthingales, having to turn them sideways to climb up the steps. It inhibited their progress, making the skirts slide along the wooden walls and gather splinters.

At the top of the steps, Mrs Minnow opened a small door they had to clamber through. Kit heaved with the dress, feeling rather like she was being pressed through the eye of a needle. Beyond, the room opened out into an attic. Kit smiled a little, scarcely able to believe her scheme had worked.

"When does Mass begin?" she asked Mrs Minnow.

"Soon." Mrs Minnow passed the candle into Kit's hands and encouraged her forward into the attic. "I must go and meet the last of our guests."

Kit waited for Mrs Minnow to retreat back down the staircase with the tiny door closing behind the older woman's skirts before her eyes surveyed the attic room. In the middle of the space, oak benches had been laid out like pews in a church, and at the far end of the room, a table had been set up like an altar. Beneath the low-lying timber beams, a tall golden crucifix was set on a pedestal, ostentatious in its jewelled design with the light of the candle in Kit's fingers bouncing off its precious stones.

Kit walked toward one of these benches, ready to wait for the priest to approach to perform the illegal Mass, when a small door caught her eye. So difficult to see, it was set into the wooden wall of the attic as a secret room.

Laying down the candle on the altar, Kit approached the door, glancing back to the staircase at every opportunity as she pressed her ear to the door. No words came from the other side, but there was someone moving around the space and making the floorboards creak beneath their feet.

"He's in there," Kit whispered to herself as she stood back. With no handle on the door, she began to feel around the wooden panels, pushing the bell-shaped sleeves that were rimmed with pearls past her elbows. There was a clean ridge between the wooden slats, one that she could just peel her fingers around. As the door creaked within her grasp, there was a voice in the corridor below, suggesting Mrs Minnow was coming back in her direction.

Kit hurried as she pulled on the door until it creaked beneath her grasp and swung open. She hastened inside, letting it fall back into place before turning her eyes on the room beyond.

This part of the attic was much smaller but flooded with candles. Without a single window, so much light had to have been deemed safe from discovery. Along two tables, there were vast lines of candles, leading to a small arched space within the chamber, toward a second chamber, beyond which footsteps continued then a chair cracked beneath someone's weight.

Kit tiptoed toward the sound, being careful to walk on the balls of her feet so that the wooden heels of her shoes didn't tap the floorboards. In the archway, she pressed her body against the timber, knowing it was futile to attempt to hide herself for long when wearing such a grand garment, but the figure beyond had his back to her regardless, unprepared for her entry.

Dressed head to toe in black and with a balding head, he was a rather frantic figure with his body moving back and forth and his hand jerking to and fro across the table in front of him. He was clutching a small quill, hurrying to write a letter and dipping the nib of the quill in an inkwell repeatedly. He was murmuring, soft sounds that Kit could just about hear as he read out what he was writing.

"...in the name of the Father, and of the Son..." He completed his prayer and sat back in his rickety chair, letting the candlelight bounce off his balding head.

Kit stepped forward, no longer fearful of letting the man hear her footsteps. He was what she had come for, the Jesuit priest. At the sound of her heel tapping the floorboard, he flinched, and flicked his head round, revealing a face with heavy jowls.

"Are you here for Mass?" he asked.

"Not quite, Father Montague," she said, stepping forward and reaching into a hidden pocket within her gown. She slid out a thin loop of rope, watching as the priest tipped his head with the light of the candles reflecting off his cheeks and turning them orange. "You are charged with holding illegal Masses."

"No, no..." he muttered, shaking his head the way a dog tried to shake off water as he stood to his feet. "Foolish woman, what do you think you are doing? You are interrupting the work of God!" He began to rant and rave, shouting so loudly that Kit knew it wouldn't be long before Mrs Minnow and her whippet-like steward would come searching for the two of them.

"You are defying the crown and law, Sir. I am to take you to prison."

"No. I will not let you do this!"

She chose not to respond to him again but reached forward, taking hold of his wrists with the rope. He was a lump of a figure, and he used his weight to pull against the rope, tipping so far back that he nearly fell onto the table flooded with candles.

"You will release me. I command it!"

"I do not listen to the commands of traitors." Kit was taller, and used her extra height to stand over him, pulling him off the table and spinning him away.

"No, no, you cannot do this!"

Kit pushed him toward the door, yet he attempted to retreat back to the table, reaching for it with his bound-up hands. She snatched them away again, tugging on the loose end of the rope that she used like a dog's lead.

"God will protect me from you. I know He will. Whatever punishment you will give me, He will keep me safe."

"I do not provide the punishment, Sir. I am only here for the arrest." Yet her words didn't seem to register, he shouted all the more, reaching out for the table and trying to kick it. "What are you...?" She trailed off, forcing him away from the table as she watched the candles shudder on the top, with the inkwell wobbling so much it was in danger of tipping over and spilling the ink across the letter he had been writing.

He wanted the letter, that was plain to see.

"No. Give that to me." Father Montague tried to reach past her to take it, his great arms coming up past her shoulder. She elbowed his arms, shoving him further back to snap up the letter and hold it to the candlelight, quickly reading the words of the unfinished letter.

"Give it to me!" Father Montague roared again. This time, his efforts were imbued with his anger, and as he reached for Kit, trying to take the paper from her hands, he knocked her backwards. She collided with the table and the candles toppled sideways off the surface. Most of the candles snuffed out instantly, but other flames grew greater, setting the rug that was beneath the table alight. "You will kill us all! It is the fire of God, come to take you."

"Oh, good Lord," Kit said tiredly, shoving the letter she had taken from him down into the pocket within her skirt as she took hold of Father Montague. "Save me from the ravings of Jesuit priests."

"How dare you!" He reached for her, trying to get to the pocket. Behind them, the rug became engulfed in fire. "Give me that letter. If you do not, we shall all die in the flames."

Kit lifted her foot, kicking Father Montague firmly in his gut. It was a hard manoeuvre, inhibited by the farthingale, but the extra wooden heel had more impact, sending him backward so that he landed on his rear with a heavy thud.

Kit dragged on the rope, pulling him out of the attic chamber like a lump of meat attached to twine. She grabbed a nearby smock from off a hook, throwing it over the flames. It covered the rug, the great swathing black material starving the flames and making them die. Yet smoke filled the air regardless from the few seconds of fire, making them both cough as they turned their heads away, moving through the darkness.

"You will face God's wrath for this!" Father Montague continued to bellow at her as she dragged him further into the next room, not trusting the smock to hold off the flames for good.

"You can condemn me to hell all you wish, Sir. You have still broken the law." She jerked him to his feet and pushed open the door, urging him into the main body of the attic where the false altar had been set up.

"You ... y-you will pay the price!" he cried restlessly, his rantings morphing into desperate stammers as his face turned purple.

"In the Tower, you can rave all you wish to." She pushed him forward through the room between the pew-like benches when he dug his heels in, refusing to go any further.

"Mrs Minnow will not let you take me away. This is her house."

"Mrs Minnow is under arrest for harbouring a Jesuit priest." Kit elbowed him in his waist, tugging him forward. Kit was so busy trying to make him move that she wasn't prepared for the way he spun round, whipping his elbow in her direction. "What the —" She had to bend down, bowing out of the way to avoid the blow. By the time she had recovered herself, he was running, heading toward the door. "Stop!" Kit cried, hurrying after him, but her farthingale inhibited her from running as fast.

Father Montague opened the door enclosing the spiral staircase, only to jerk back in surprise.

"Good evening, Father," a familiar voice said.

Father Montague was pushed backwards, staggering on his feet as a man stepped through the gap, grabbing hold of the rope Kit had tied around the priest's wrists.

"Iomhar." Kit stopped behind the two of them as Iomhar forced the priest under control. "I had him."

"Aye, so why was he about to escape?" Iomhar Blackwood said with a smile on his lips.

# CHAPTER 2

"Another Jesuit, another traitor." A gaoler whistled with the words as he led the way down the narrow passage of the prison.

Kit pushed Father Montague forward with Iomhar at her side. They directed the priest along the corridor, his figure illuminated by the burning torches pinned against the stone walls either side of them.

"I am not a traitor," Father Montague cried darkly. "In the eyes of God, when judgment day comes —"

"Aye, we know," Iomhar said with a sigh. "We have heard it before." His words only made Father Montague curse their names even more, invoking the power of God against them.

Kit said nothing as she steered the priest into the next cell whilst the gaoler held open the door. She merely watched as Iomhar unbound his wrists, and lifted some chains from the stone floor, ready to fix the priest in place. She delved into her pocket within the long gown, peeling out the letter that she had taken from the priest in the attic.

"What's the charge?" the gaoler asked as he fussed with the oak door to the cell.

"Holding Mass," Kit said, turning her eyes down to the letter.

"And conspiracy to kill the queen," Iomhar added, looking up from his task.

"We do not have evidence of that, only hearsay." Kit shook her head. It was how they had heard of the priest in the first place, whispers in the street that claimed there was a new plot to kill the queen, spearheaded by the Jesuits, with Father Montague leading the plans in London.

"Did ye find any evidence?" Iomhar asked.

Kit didn't answer as she unfurled the letter, finding some of the wet ink had imprinted on the blank side of the paper from when she had folded it up.

*My dear friend,*

*I need not tell you what good news this is, but this morning I received a letter from our contact in Rome. It is what we have long wished for. Gregorio Luca is coming. Within the week, he will be here*

The letter broke off abruptly from where she had interrupted Father Montague.

"Who is Gregorio Luca?" Her question made not only Father Montague recoil, but Iomhar pause in his work with the chains, lifting his face to her sharply with his green eyes almost orange in the candlelight. "What is it?"

"Is that what it says?" he asked. "Gregorio Luca?"

"Yes. Who is he?" She addressed her question to the priest alone.

"You will not take me, and you certainly will not take him." Father Montague spoke with passion, his words growing louder before he veered away from Iomhar. With one arm still loose from the chains, he held onto the wall behind him and kicked out with his feet against Iomhar, shoving him harshly in the chest, knocking him against the stone wall where one of the burning torches was fixed. An almighty grunt of pain echoed around the gaol as Iomhar knocked the torch to the ground.

Kit did not wait to see the injury for Father Montague was pulling at the one chain attached to his right wrist, trying to break free. She grabbed one of the daggers from her secret pocket, unaccustomed to hiding the weapon in a gown, and launched herself toward him, reaching round and pressing the blade to his throat to stop him from going any further.

His hand froze on the chains. "Y-you wouldn't…" He stammered out the words, his spine going rigid. "You would be spilling the blood of a man of God."

"You have just injured another man. What man of God could do that?" she said coolly. "Release the chains." He did as she asked. "Wrists together and turn around." He followed her instructions, giving her the time she needed to fasten the other wrist with the chains and glance over to Iomhar. He had a palm to his face and the skin around his eyes was contorted in pain. "Are you well?" she called to him.

He said nothing, but he opened his eyes and lowered his palm from his cheek. A knot tightened in Kit's stomach, seeing the extent of the burn caused by the candle. Already the skin was pursed with a harsh white raised line, around which his cheek was turning red. She hesitated with the chain, finding herself wanting to walk toward Iomhar to check he was well, but the priest made another attempt to escape. She elbowed him in the gut. He buckled forward and abandoned his attempt to flee.

"It is done," she said as she released the chains and walked to Iomhar. He turned his head away, hiding the injury as he stepped out of the gaol cell. "How bad is the burn?"

"It does not matter." He spoke hurriedly and turned to let the gaoler close the cell door. Kit followed Iomhar's hardened gaze, looking toward Father Montague through the iron bars set within the oak. He was crippled on the floor, winded and clutching his abdomen with his chained hands. "Any words in your defence?"

Father Montague spat on the cell floor, the white spittle landing between the cobbles.

"I think that is a no," Kit said as she spun away and nodded her head at the gaoler. He turned the key in the lock, fastening Father Montague in firmly. "Who is Gregorio Luca?" Kit asked again as Iomhar lead their path down the corridor of the gaol.

"That is a hard question to answer."

"What do you mean?"

"Because he is known by different men for different things." Iomhar lifted a hand to his burned cheek, wincing at the pain. "Aye, what I can say, he is a man not to be trusted on England's shores. Walsingham must hear of this."

"We'll report to him tomorrow."

"Nay, Kit. We report to him tonight."

The darkness was thick as Kit stepped out of the gaol. Iomhar followed, still talking to one of the gaolers.

Kit took no notice of the conversation for a minute as she was too busy stretching out her legs, relieved to be back in her hose and doublet with her hair tucked under her man's cap. The gown she had been wearing with the farthingale and corset was in a large bag slung over her shoulder, so long that the tapestry-like material almost touched the ground.

Free of the restraint of a gown, she walked about for a few minutes, tempted to throw the bag in the river nearby to be free of it for good. The gown may have been useful when it came to deceiving Catholics into letting her into their secret Masses, but she didn't have to like wearing them.

"Nay visitors for the priest. Aye?"

"As you wish." The gaoler nodded at Iomhar. "Any food?"

"Aye, keep him alive. Do not indulge him."

"Understood."

"Walsingham will want to talk to him. Within a few days would be my wager. I do not know if torture will be authorised or not."

The words made Kit stop walking and turn. She had often heard of torture being authorised by the queen at Walsingham's bequest, but the thought made her queasy. She had walked the Tower's corridors enough to hear screams that could only come from torture. Screams that left her cold.

Kit heard a sound through the darkness and looked away, peering down the road to try and see what the source of the noise could be.

"Did you hear something?" she asked, continuing her search of the road and looking away from Iomhar and the gaoler that were stood together.

"Probably a fox," the gaoler said. "We get lots of them around here. Almost as many foxes out here as there are Jesuits inside these walls."

Kit murmured in agreement, but she still stepped further away, peering down the road. With the torches only burning along the walls of Richmond gaol, the light bathed them in a small circle, casting the rest of the street into a darkness as impenetrable as the ocean.

"Kit?" Iomhar tried to call her attention back. "We need to see Walsingham. Tonight."

"We can't."

"Why?"

"Because we'd have to go to Barn Elms."

"Aye. What is wrong with that?"

She had no answer to give him though she turned her eyes back to him, making it clear with her gaze alone that she was not pleased about the idea.

Something whistled through the air. Kit knew that sound, she had heard it often enough for her body to cower down to the earth, dodging the bolt that flew through the darkness.

"Aaarrgh!" a roar of pain erupted as she lifted her head, just an inch to see that Iomhar had done the same as her, with his body flat to the cobbled ground.

"Crossbow," he said hurriedly. "Look for it."

She jumped to her feet, turning round in circles frantically, with the tapestry bag flicking behind her. The gaoler that had been standing with them had an arrow firmly lodged in his shoulder and was falling backwards, staggering away as he clutched at the wound.

"I have ye." Iomhar reached out to the gaoler, peeling him off the wall and dragging him toward the door of the gaol as blood poured from the wound, staining the gaoler's clothes within seconds.

Kit felt nauseous at the sight. She turned in the direction the arrow had to have come from, squinting into the darkness. She could see nothing at first except the swathes of black above the riverbank nearby, then she heard the familiar woosh.

"Another!" she cried. She dropped to the cobbles as Iomhar shoved the gaoler through the open door, shielding himself with the wood. As Kit pulled the bag over her face, the second arrow landed through it. Her body laid motionless as she stared up at the arrowhead poking through the tapestry bag. It seemed the gown with the thick horn corset and the heavy material of the skirt and farthingale had slowed down the bolt's progress.

"Kit!" Iomhar shouted for her, just as she threw off the bag, revealing the fletching sticking up in the air through the other side of the tapestry material.

"I'm unharmed," she called.

Above the arrow, she could just catch a glimpse of the gaoler falling within Iomhar's grasp toward the floor, turning pale as the blood drained from his face.

"Will he live?" Kit said to Iomhar.

Iomhar's jaw tightened, and he didn't answer her. "See if ye can see who shot the arrow. I need to stop the blood."

She nodded and leapt to her feet, running out of the light from the torches to ensure the attacker wouldn't have a clean shot again. The deeper she ran into the darkness, the more her eyes began to adjust. Beneath the clouds and across the top of the thatched houses nearby, she could see a figure scrabbling across the roofs, on his hands and knees, unable to run on his feet. The silhouette revealed there was a weapon in his hands, the looped front showing it was a crossbow.

Kit didn't shout to alert him to her presence. She hurried as softly as she could across the cobbles, running on her toes before she reached the edge of the houses and jumped up, taking hold of a timber beam beneath the thatched roof of the single-storey building and climbing up. It was a tricky climb, but by swinging her body round, using momentum she pulled herself onto the thatching and clambered up the straw, her boots slipping on the damp strands.

Ahead, she could see the silhouetted figure, with a quiver of arrows across his back and the crossbow still clutched in his palms. Kit tried more than once to move to her feet, but with the thatching too damp, it was impossible to walk on the straw without falling. Forced to follow on her hands and knees, she climbed up the thatching to the ridge of the roof, along which the man was crawling.

Creeping up on him, the sounds of her own feet and palms on the straw were muffled by his louder efforts. When she caught up, she reached out with her fingers, grabbing his ankle and tugging him down.

He yelped in surprise, falling onto his front on the ridge, before turning and lifting the crossbow in her direction, pulling on the lever to release the bolt that was pre-loaded. Kit didn't stare at the bolt for long before she released his ankle and rolled away, down the pitched roof and dodging the bolt entirely. With the incline, it was impossible to stop herself. She rolled all the way across the roof until she reached the very edge and stretched out with her hand, clinging onto the timber beam with her fingers as her legs swung in the air.

She winced at the pain of clinging on with just one arm and peered over the edge of the roof, just catching sight of the figure as he hurried toward the chimney on the far side of the building. He climbed onto the chimney, using the bricks to jump and vault over the gap between two houses.

"Well, you have to come down some time," Kit said with a small smile and let herself drop the last of the distance to the floor with her legs bending and absorbing the impact.

Following the path the figure took, she ran between the houses, using the candlelight spilling from people's windows to track his progress. When he reached the far side of the line of houses finding nothing but open air before him, he came to a halt, squinting downward and moving his arms like a windmill to stay standing.

Kit stopped at the bottom, watching, waiting for him to jump down. There was nowhere else for him to go. If he wanted to escape, then this was the way to do it. He would have to meet her again. She stepped back from the eaves of the house, the better to watch him. Only, he didn't come down. Instead, he reloaded the crossbow and aimed it straight at her.

Kit was forced to run forward, back under the eaves of the house where she collided with the wall. The bolt he released landed directly in the earth where she had been standing.

After a few seconds of silence, she peeked out again, ready to cower when he next lifted the crossbow, only, he was not there.

She backed up further, her eyes not only flitting across the one rooftop but the thatched roofs of all the adjoining houses. There was no sign of the figure and no sight of a crossbow. The only indication that the man had been there at all was the bolt in the earth behind her and the untidy straw on the roof.

"No. No!" Kit muttered aloud, circling the building as quickly as she could. It didn't take long to find loose straw, from where he had scrambled down the other side of the building, and hoof marks left behind in the soil. "God's wounds!" she said angrily as she stepped back, craning her neck to look down the dark road.

He had escaped.

# CHAPTER 3

"Iomhar?" Kit whispered as Iomhar looked up from where the gaoler was laid down in a spare cell with a physician bent over him. Kit didn't need to ask her question. The state of the gaoler's health was quite plain. Iomhar stood to his feet and walked to join her in the doorway where the bars usually stood.

"He escaped, did he not?"

"I should have had a crossbow myself," Kit muttered. "Maybe then I would have had a chance of catching him, rather than just carrying that gown."

"It may have saved your life, Kit."

"Maybe." She was reluctant to admit it as she turned back to the gaoler, whose eyes were fluttering as he stared at the ceiling, his chest rising and falling delicately and quickly like the flapping of a butterfly's wings. "Enough of my life, what of his?" she asked.

"He may live."

"May?" Kit asked in a harried whisper as she looked back to Iomhar.

"It is too early to tell." Iomhar stepped out of the room, urging her to follow with a flick of his head. "He's losing a lot of blood. The physician cannot be certain what is pierced beneath the skin. The archer may have caught the top of his lung."

Kit felt that swell of nausea another time and placed the back of her hand to her lips, willing the sensation to fade.

"Ye all right?"

"Yes." Kit hurriedly lowered her hand again.

"We will leave the physician to his work." Iomhar steered their path toward the exit of the gaol, stepping out again though warily this time, gazing at the street around them.

"We should have asked him to look at you. You need someone to see that burn," Kit said as she followed Iomhar out of the prison. Behind them, the walls stretched high on the side of the River Thames, the grey cobbled stone blending into the blackness of the night.

"I do not need a physician," Iomhar said with vigour as he walked forward, glancing around at the tops of the houses.

"He is gone. He fled on a horse. I don't think he is coming back."

"Hmm, perhaps not."

A grunt of pain made Kit look back to see Iomhar wiping the burn mark on his cheek. As he walked away down the track road toward the streets nearby, Kit hurried alongside him, barely able to see the burn the further they walked into the darkness away from the flaming torches of the prison.

As they reached the nearest street set between narrow timber houses, she took hold of his shoulder and tried to steer him in the opposite direction.

"Where are we going?" he asked, his voice raising a notch in volume.

"To see a physician. There will be another awake in town at this hour, I am sure."

"I just said nay." Iomhar snatched his shoulder out of her grasp. "We need to go this way." He turned and walked in the other direction.

"Why that way?" she asked, keeping her boots firmly placed on the ground beneath her, refusing to move forward.

"Because Barn Elms is this way, isn't it?" Iomhar said as though the point were obvious.

"Barn Elms?" Kit said, feeling her body stiffen at the words. "Why are you heading there?"

"Do ye not wish to speak to Walsingham? Strange." He paused long enough to glance back to her in the street, his silhouette barely visible in the darkness. "I would have thought ye eager to tell Walsingham what had happened as soon as possible. Ye usually are."

"You are insufferable," she muttered as her feet moved forward, reluctantly catching up with him.

"Gregorio Luca ... remember that name? It's too important to wait on, Kit." He gestured to her doublet where she had hidden the letter.

"It can wait until he is back in Seething Lane," Kit said.

"If we stay out for much longer, the watchmen will arrest us for being out at night. I do not fancy that. We are going to Barn Elms, Kit. Now." Iomhar hurried ahead down the road.

Kit didn't move to follow him straight away. She balled her hands into fists and stood her ground, staring at the earth beneath her feet that was torn up with cart tracks and horses' hoof marks.

It was a rule she had. She didn't go to Barn Elms, not since the day Sir Francis Walsingham's daughter, Lady Sidney, Franny as she was known then, had made it abundantly clear that Kit was not welcome in that house.

"Kit, are ye coming?" Iomhar called back to her.

She hastened to catch up to him. She had no wish to explain her thoughts to Iomhar, but that didn't mean she had to like this outcome either. "We could stay here in Richmond."

"So we can meet that stranger with a crossbow again? Nay, I do not think that a good idea."

"What do you mean?"

"Kit." Iomhar pulled gently on her arm, urging her to a stop. "What do ye think that man wanted?"

"Shooting gaolers at a prison? Let me guess, it takes no great skill of imagination, he probably wished to break out a friend and did not expect so much opposition."

"Hmm, maybe." Iomhar paused and looked back down the street in the direction of the gaol.

"What is it?"

"It's dark, isn't it?" he asked, turning back to her. "We were merely three figures dressed like men, basically appearing as silhouettes in that light."

"Oh." Kit shifted her weight between her feet as the realisation dawned. "You think he could have been shooting at any one of us."

"I do not know." Iomhar shook his head as he walked on. "All I know for certain, is that he cannot have been confident who he was firing at."

Kit followed him, thinking on the gaoler that was now fighting for his life. As they walked down the street, heading toward Barn Elms Manor and where it sat overlooking the Thames, Kit felt her buckskin boots striking the ground with increasing insistence, just so that she had something else to think about. The walk was but a short one, taking them away from the busyness of Richmond toward a quiet embankment. They were almost at the house when Iomhar spoke again.

"Ye going to tell me what is wrong?" he asked.

"No," she said, lifting her head up a little, enough to see a small smile twist the fresh burn mark on his cheek. "What's made you smile?"

"Ye'll open up to me someday."

"Do you want a wager on that? All at Barn Elms will be asleep by now. Is it not best we return in the day at least?" Kit was running out of objections as they walked up the driveway toward the manor house.

"I see plenty of candlelight through those windows, Kit. Aye, looks to me like they are still awake," Iomhar said.

As they reached the house, Kit strained to see its outline in the night. It was barely distinguishable from the blanket of trees behind it, other than the windows that were lit by candles.

She could remember well enough how it had looked when she had lived there as a child after Sir Francis Walsingham had unofficially adopted her. Tall and rather narrow, with red and white bricks accented with brown timber beams at every join, and topped with so many tall chimneys on the roof that they rather looked like the spindles on a hedgehog's back. Now, all was black, with a few windows blinking at them with flickering candlelight.

Iomhar had to knock a few times for them to be heard. Eventually, when the door opened and a head popped out, the steward's face was more than a little irked to be disturbed so late at night.

"This is a most indecent hour to call —"

"We work for Walsingham," Iomhar said, cutting him off midway through his lecture.

The steward looked between the two of them, his gaze restless, before his eyes settled on Kit and widened.

"Kitty?" he said.

"Kitty?" Iomhar repeated, clearly humoured at the idea of her old name.

"Good evening, Mr Withers," Kit said, recalling the old steward from long ago. His nose curled with the same objection to her that he used to wear. She shifted uncomfortably, remembering how few people in this house had been impressed to see Walsingham turn up with a foundling from the streets. "Are you willing to let us die of the cold on the front step or will you let us inside to see Walsingham?"

The steward didn't answer at first, but after a second of silence he pushed the door open further, leaving room for them to walk in. As they stepped into the entrance hall, Kit found her eyes lifting to survey the space. It was not as big as she remembered. When she was young, she was certain it had been cavernous, a corridor that a giant would have no trouble fitting through, yet now the dark wood-panelled walls seemed to close in on her, and the floorboards beneath her feet were narrow though they stretched far ahead, showing the other side of the corridor wasn't visible in the faint candlelight.

"Aye, for a minute," Iomhar stepped toward Kit and whispered in her ear, "I thought he was tempted to take ye up on your words and leave us out there to freeze."

"So did I," she said with a sigh, watching as her breath no longer clouded the air the way it had done outside. The door closed heavily behind them, making Kit flinch, something that did not go unnoticed by Iomhar, whose brows furrowed together.

"Wait here," Mr Withers ordered with clear instruction and collected a candle from a nearby sideboard. He walked away down the corridor, lighting the dark end of the hallway before he disappeared through a series of doors.

Kit felt the silence stretch out between her and Iomhar, though she was aware he was staring at her still.

"What?" she asked, looking up at him.

"Just wondering why ye do not like the place so much."

"That is my matter." She walked away from him in order to put some distance there.

Nearby on a wall there was a painting just about visible in the glow from the moon through the window. She strode toward it for something to do and busied herself with gazing at the picture. It was of Walsingham when he was younger, with his wife at his side and his daughter sat on his lap. Lady Sidney had been but a child at the time, barely four years old in the painting, with big wide eyes that purported innocence. Kit had to bite the side of her mouth to stop herself from scoffing at the painting.

The candle reappeared at the end of the hallway, only this time Mr Withers was not the only figure lit by its orb. There was a second person walking toward them and judging by the silhouette of the skirt and farthingale, it was most definitely not Walsingham. As the figure's face came into view, Kit stood her ground, feeling her buckskin boots plant themselves firmly against the floorboards.

"Well, this is an oddity," the familiar high-pitched voice of Lady Sidney called out as her gaze settled on Kit. She didn't even glance Iomhar's way. "You have not been here for many years."

"I follow orders given to me," Kit said as she folded her arms and stared back at Lady Sidney, unblinkingly. Lady Sidney's dark eyes were calculating. They lingered for a good while on the men's clothes Kit was wearing, but Kit refused to fidget under that stare. "We are here to see your father, Lady Sidney. He needs informing of our latest commission."

"That can wait until the morning," Lady Sidney said, lifting her chin higher.

"It cannot." Iomhar spoke for the first time and earned Lady Sidney's harsh gaze. "It is important."

"And my family's evening together is not important?" Lady Sidney said, narrowing her eyes at him. "That is presumptuous indeed."

"Aye, I rather think England's safety takes precedence over a few sips of wine and a lavish dinner." Iomhar's words made Kit smile, but it was a smile that did not go unseen by Lady Sidney.

"You said you follow orders, so you can follow mine and leave now." Lady Sidney gestured toward the door.

"We will not leave." Kit refused to move. "Your father's orders outweigh your own, my Lady. We need to speak to him and Iomhar here needs a physician."

Lady Sidney sighed, as if it were the greatest request in the world and looked toward Mr Withers. "Very well, find them a room they can stay in for the night, and call a physician. In the morning they can see my father."

"Thank ye," Iomhar said with a nod, but Lady Sidney did not return any pleasantry. She offered Kit one last glare before flicking her head away, tilting her chin high above her ruff and walking down the corridor with the skirt swishing around the farthingale as she moved.

Mr Withers beckoned them to follow the other way down the corridor as Iomhar stepped toward Kit and whispered in her ear.

"Something tells me she doesn't like us very much."

"Have you lost your sight? She adores us. I do believe I am the person she loves most in this world," Kit said in mockery, earning a soft laugh from Iomhar.

# CHAPTER 4

"Hold that tight to your face," the physician said as he placed a poultice to Iomhar's cheek later that evening. Iomhar winced but did as he was instructed.

"This hurts more than before," he mumbled.

Kit looked away, not liking the knot that developed in her stomach to see Iomhar in pain. She busied herself with lighting some candles, casting a flint in a tinder box and setting each tallow stick alight before placing them on sideboards and tables around the room. Lastly, she set a candle over the fireplace before bending down to her knees and urging the fire to life. In the winter chill that was quickly taking hold, even the plush room they were standing in had succumbed to the cold breeze that rattled through the gaps between the window and the frame, making her shiver.

"You have made the burn worse by scratching it," the physician's words made Kit look toward Iomhar, who found her gaze over the poultice. He offered her a mocking warning glare, telling her not to say anything.

She hid her smirk as she stood to her feet and looked to the candle she had placed on the mantelpiece. Behind it, there was a wide mirror, set in a brass frame that curved, mimicking grapevines, bordered with two cherubs along the base. The glass surface itself was warped slightly, speckled with age, but Kit could see her distorted reflection in the candlelight.

She took off her man's cap and shook out her hair, the short dark red locks hanging loose around her ears. The bronze-coloured eyes could have been brown in this faded light, staring at her over the high collar of the red doublet. She stepped back from the mirror and glanced down at the outfit, remembering the way Lady Sidney's eyes had settled on her clothes.

The red doublet was lined with brass buttons down the middle and edged on the side panels, with the material embroidered in golden leaves and flowers. Where the doublet flared across her hips, it met dark black baggy hose, the kind worn by the lower classes, that hugged her legs and allowed her to move easily. She smiled at the sight, rather glad she didn't have to wear the large gown that Lady Sidney had been wearing, with the skirt so long she must have struggled to walk without tripping.

When Iomhar grunted in pain, Kit looked away from the mirror, turning to see his face still crooked with pain.

"What is it in the poultice?" she asked, stepping toward the physician as he bent down to pack his small glass bottles away in his leather bag.

"Oak leaves and red clover with honey and egg whites," the physician said, making Iomhar grimace all the more and lift the poultice off his face.

"Why am I putting this on my face?" His voice was filled with disgust and wariness.

"Strangely enough, young man, I know what I'm doing when it comes to this," the physician said and pushed the poultice back toward his cheek. "Keep it there all night and it should reduce the swelling and the pain. You'll have a scar though."

"Another one," Kit murmured, earning Iomhar's gaze. He looked to her, his eyes not leaving her face for a minute. "How did you get that one?" she asked, pointing toward the white scar that was already sat on his right cheek, a little above this fresh burn mark.

"Ye tell me your secrets, Kit, and I'll tell ye my own." Iomhar's voice had deepened. Kit folded her arms and walked away, not liking the idea at all. "Do we have a bargain?"

"No," she called with a clear voice as she sat down in an armchair nearby, reaching her feet toward the fireplace to warm her toes.

"That should do the trick," the physician said as he stood to his feet and closed his leather satchel. Iomhar handed over a few coins before he stepped away. "Keep it there all night, yes?"

"Aye." Iomhar spoke rather unconvincingly.

"I'll see myself out." The physician nodded to the two of them and moved to the door. Kit thanked him another time before he stepped out into the corridor and closed the door behind him.

"So…" Iomhar's voice made Kit turn her eyes back toward him. "All the bed chambers there must be in this manor house, and the steward gives us this small sitting room to spend the night in."

"So it would seem." Kit sighed as she watched Iomhar frown over the poultice.

"Does that not seem a little odd to ye?"

"Something you should grow accustomed to, Iomhar, is that no one in this house likes me very much," she said with a yawn, tipping her head backwards. "I imagine if Mr Withers thought he could get away with making us sleep in the kitchen on the rug with the house dogs, he would have done so."

Iomhar sat forward in his chair, still pressing the poultice to his cheek though his eyes were alert. "Why do they not like ye?"

"Do you need to ask?" She motioned down to herself.

"What does that mean?" he asked, frowning.

"Who wants a wealthy man to bring a foundling off the streets home?" She tilted her head to the side. "They were not pleased." The pitying look Iomhar offered made her turn her head, not wishing to continue on the matter. "I have no wish to discuss it anymore —"

"Oh, believe me, we will discuss it again, but it's late and ye need your sleep."

"Me? You do not need sleep?" Kit asked, trying to stifle the yawn that took over her cheeks. He pointed to her, showing he had seen the yawn despite her best efforts.

"Sleep, Kit," he said, sitting back in the chair. "Tomorrow we can discuss why Walsingham's family dislike ye so much."

"No, tomorrow we can question why a Jesuit priest was writing about this Gregorio Luca fellow," Kit spoke with a firm tone. "If it has anything to do with Scorpio, then things could be graver than we thought."

"Hmm." Iomhar didn't argue, though he adjusted the poultice on his cheek a little more. "We haven't heard anything of her for a while. It does not bode well."

Kit moved in her seat, thinking on what he had said. Scorpio, the codename for Mary Stuart, the last Queen of the Scots. Kit had always thought it rather apt, the idea that she possessed a sting, rather like a scorpion, yet she waited patiently for her opportunity.

"You think she could be involved in another plot?" Kit asked slowly, watching Iomhar for a reaction. "With this Gregorio Luca?"

He didn't reply straight away, though he moved the poultice, buying time before answering.

"I do not know," he said eventually. "Yet she has to be involved in something, does she not? Whether it is a plot of her own doing, or something orchestrated by someone else.

Gregorio Luca is a name I know, Kit, and he is a foul man, staunchly Catholic. Aye, he sees any death justified if they are not Catholic. If he comes to these shores, I'd wager money he is here because of Scorpio."

Kit felt her hands tighten into fists, until her nails dug ridges into her skin. The last time someone had tried to place Mary Stuart on the throne, Her Majesty Queen Elizabeth had nearly met her death. Kit could still remember the fear of having to dive into the River Thames and pull the queen free from the watery depths before dragging her to land. The terror that had been in the queen's dark eyes was enough to make Kit's own hands tremble.

"Kit?"

"Yes?"

"Get some sleep," Iomhar said quietly.

"I am fine." Kit shrugged, trying to hide another yawn that made Iomhar lift an eyebrow.

"Sleep," he urged again. "Before ye pass out from exhaustion."

"You have developed a habit of telling me what to do, you know," Kit complained as she sat back in the chair and closed her eyes.

"Nay, it's not a habit of telling ye what to do, it's a habit of looking out for ye." His words made her snap her eyes open again, finding him staring at her with sincerity.

"I do not need anyone looking out for me, Iomhar."

"Well, that's a discussion we can save for another day as well," he whispered with a smile, though his eyes were shut as he spoke, as he yearned for some sleep.

Kit closed her eyes and tipped her head back, seeking sleep and an oblivion that would stop her thinking of his words.

# CHAPTER 5

*Kit was under water, trying her best to reach the surface, though it didn't matter how many times her small pudgy hands stretched out toward that surface, it seemed an interminable distance away. One of her small fingers broke through the water, touching air briefly, but then her body began to slip down with her finger sinking back under the water.*

*She glanced at her body, seeing what she was wearing. Her tiny form was dressed in some kind of heavy material, possibly expensive, with velvet panels on a little dress being dragged deeper into the water. She kicked her feet, but one foot was missing a shoe, revealing a white stocking that was turning grey and slipping off her foot.*

*Kit tried to swim again, the lack of breath making her body convulse. She frantically waved her arms above her head, trying to reach the surface, but she was slipping further and further down into water that was as black as night.*

*There was a figure above her, just as she had seen before, though this figure was warped by the moving water that was trembling thanks to her efforts to swim. The figure's face was in shadow, before it turned and walked away, leaving Kit to stare up at a bright blue sky above the water.*

*She began to panic, her lips opening and her mouth filling with water as she scrambled to be free, yet it was no good. No one was coming to help her, and she couldn't get out of the water alone. Her arms gave up, suspended limply above her head as she tried to cough out the water.*

*Something moved above the surface, something shadowy that stepped in the way of the bright sunlight, casting darkness over her face. Kit looked up through the water, peering at what was standing over her. It was a second figure, their face undiscernible. The figure was bending down toward her, reaching for her...*

"Kit!" The snapped word made Kit's eyes shoot open and she veered forward.

She grew aware of her feet planted firmly on the wooden floorboards beneath her and a hand on her shoulder. She pushed the hand off.

"Calm yourself!" Iomhar said loudly. She darted her head toward him, still trapped somewhere between sleep and wakefulness, realising that Iomhar was the one who had woken her up. She blinked a few times and looked around the room, seeing she was still seated in one of the two chairs either side of the fire that had burned wood into nothing but ash.

Her doublet was hanging loose over her legs from where she had used it as a blanket, leaving her in her shirt and trousers. Her boots were kicked to the side beside the fireplace where they were drying off from the previous evening's exploits.

"Ye were dreaming, Kit," Iomhar explained, sitting back in his chair. He had taken off his doublet too. The poultice that had been attached to his cheek had been removed, revealing the way the burn cut into the top of his trimmed beard in a harsh line.

"I know," Kit said, hanging her head forward. "Why did you wake me?"

"Because, quite frankly, the yelping sounds ye were making made ye sound possessed. Ye make all those tales people mutter about spirits lurking through our doors sound true."

"I was not yelping!" Kit snapped her head up to see Iomhar with raised eyebrows. His face fully visible in the dawn light that was streaming through the window.

"Seeing as I was the one woken up by your yelping, ye can take my word for it." He yawned and rubbed his eyes. "I think I would have preferred your snoring to that."

"How dare you," she said, finding a smile jumping to her lips. He began to make a snoring sound, loud and snorting, prompting Kit to grab the small cushion she had been resting her head on and throw it across the room at his face. It landed squarely on his nose, making him laugh before he winced at the burn on his cheek.

"What was your dream about?"

She opened her mouth and found the words dying on her lips. She wasn't sure which part of it was a dream and which a memory. She had seen the first figure walk away, leaving her beneath the water, in many dreams over the years, but that second figure was new. She had never seen them before. Was it possible it was real? Or had it been just the work of her imagination?

"Kit?" Iomhar said, his voice turning softer. "What is it?"

"Nothing." She snapped up the doublet, threading it quickly over her shoulders. "We need to talk to Walsingham, I'll find him."

"Ye're avoiding telling me things again."

"You do not need to know everything about me, Iomhar," she said as she buttoned up her doublet and pulled on her boots.

"Nay, but it may help."

"Help what?" she asked as she finished with the boots. He had no answer, but he smiled a little more. "Confusing man." She walked toward the door, eager to end the conversation. "I'm going to find Walsingham."

"Good luck trying to find him. Avoid his daughter if ye can. Something tells me she'd sooner kick ye out the door herself than let ye near her father."

"Look at that, you know her so well already and you have only met her twice." Kit walked out of the door, closing it softly behind her.

The moment she was outside she breathed deeply, needing a minute of privacy to think over the dream. She ran her hands through her short auburn hair, clinging to the curls as she walked down the corridor. She thought of the second figure above her in the water, trying hard to recall if there was anything discernible about who it could have been, but just like the first figure, it was shrouded in shadow, silhouetted against the sunlight.

"It was just a dream," Kit muttered to herself as she dropped her hands from her head and went in search of Walsingham.

The house did not seem so dark or cramped this morning with the early morning light streaming through lead-lined windows and bouncing over the mahogany panelled walls. Unable to remember her way around the building, Kit wandered to and fro, at first tracing her way to the front door, using the path she had taken the night before, after which she chose corridors at random, going in search of any sign of life.

In a particularly bright corridor, lit on two sides by windows, she heard the chink of cutlery against plates, suggesting someone was behind a closed door. She tapped on the slatted wood and waited for a response.

"Enter," the voice called.

Recognising it, Kit grimaced but opened the door anyway, swinging it wide to reveal a breakfast room with a long dining table filled with food stretched out before her. Frances, Lady Sidney, sat on one side. The lady looked up from her round pewter plate with a smile that quickly faltered into a frown. "Are you still here?" she asked.

"Yes." Kit kept her voice level as she responded to Lady Sidney's question. "I have not yet seen your father. Once I have seen him, I will leave."

Kit's words seemed to have little effect on Lady Sidney, who returned her focus to her plate, offering Kit just one wave of her hand, as if she were one of their house dogs to be dismissed.

"You can wait for him in that sitting room," Lady Sidney said, as she lifted her cutlery and began to cut up manchet bread into thick slices.

"I rather expect if I keep sitting there, I'll be there all day waiting for him. Am I right?" Kit's question prompted Lady Sidney to freeze. It had happened once before, years ago when Kit had come to see Walsingham at his house in Seething Lane and Lady Sidney had called too. Lady Sidney had promised to give a message to Walsingham that Kit wanted to see him, but the message was never passed on. Kit had spent the day waiting in the kitchen, plied with food by the housekeeper, Doris. By the end of it, Kit had burst out of the room, demanding on seeing him.

Kit was not going to allow such a thing to happen again.

"Why are you here?" Lady Sidney asked, placing the cutlery down on her plate with a clatter.

"I have told you. I am here to see your —"

"You know what I meant." Lady Sidney turned her dark eyes up to Kit, those eyes with no colour in them, like blackened ink on a sheet of parchment. "You are not supposed to come *here*. Not to this house. I made that perfectly plain."

"The last time you said such a thing you were a child. I like to think your mind has grown and we are past the days where you burnt my hair, just because you did not like me being here," Kit said, lifting her arms and folding them across her body. The corner of Lady Sidney's lips tilted up, smiling at the memory. "I am pleased to see the memory amuses you. The recollection of my head being turned upside down in a copper basin of water for an hour afterwards is a strong one for me. Certainly not an amusing one."

"You were hardly badly burnt." Lady Sidney waved a hand in dismissal.

"I believe I'm in a better position to know how I was." Kit was not going to be cowed by this woman. She was young compared to Kit, petulant, yet thought she knew more of the world from her place hidden away in stately houses.

"You promised not to come back here."

"I promised not to come back if I could help it." Kit held the woman's dark gaze. "I could not help it, and I like to think you would not try to burn me again. You are no longer the child who would do anything to have her father's attention."

Kit didn't care if the words were harsh, nor if Lady Sidney looked at her with a slackening jaw of surprise. They both knew what had passed in that house years ago, nothing more than a child's jealousy that her father had brought home another child to raise. That was all.

"This is the last time you will come here," Lady Sidney importuned harshly as she turned her head and picked up the cutlery again.

"Do you expect me to follow your instruction simply because you are Walsingham's daughter?"

"I could threaten you instead," Lady Sidney spoke with a sweet smile that would have looked better placed on a young girl who had been gifted marchpane and candied fruits, rather than a woman making a threat.

Kit took a step forward and gestured down to the weapons belt around her hips, enjoying the sight of seeing that delighted smile falter.

"What kind of threat would you like to make?" Kit asked tauntingly, knowing there was nothing Lady Sidney could do. Short of throwing another candle at her head, they both knew Lady Sidney would not take her jealousy so far as to ever fight Kit.

Something quivered in Lady Sidney's neck, a muscle that suggested she was swallowing around a sudden lump in her throat. Kit stepped back, pleased with her small triumph.

"You were an odd thing when he first turned up here with you, did you know that?" Lady Sidney snatched her gaze away, turning back to the plate. "Freckled thing, as though you'd caught the pox."

"I did not have the pox," Kit said, closing her eyes and turning away.

"Looked like you did. That red hair too… It may as well have already been on fire, burnt to a cinder." She giggled with the words. The innocent laugh sounded so odd against the cruelty that Kit opened her eyes again, slowly turning her gaze to the young woman with a glower. "A foundling. Took him ages to decide on your name. Did you know that?"

"No." Kit had not heard much of the time when she had first been found, nothing beyond the story of when she had pulled on Walsingham's cloak in the street, asking for money. "How do you know? You were not yet in this world."

"My mother told me, years later," Lady Sidney said, picking up some bread and eagerly eating. "She compared you to a redcap," she giggled. "One of those awful impish things that mop up the dead's blood with their hats. Your hair was that red, she was convinced you were something born of the devil."

"Thank goodness your father has some sense." Kit sighed, fighting the temptation to lift a hand and trail it through the short red locks.

"Scarlett… Kit Scarlett…" Lady Sidney toyed with the name in clear disgust. "My mother said he should call you Kit Redcap, but he preferred Scarlett." She looked up from her plate with a smile.

"I know not what you are trying to accomplish, Lady Sidney. Perhaps you mean to make me run from the room out of fear of hearing more of your ramblings, but I am staying put. I will not be moved." Kit's sharp words made Lady Sidney scrape the knife along the bottom of her pewter plate.

"Go back to the sitting room," Lady Sidney ordered, scraping the plate a second time for good measure.

"I will wait here for your father, and nowhere else." Kit was adamant, turning and looking to the door.

"Oh, so God mend me, just do as I…" Lady Sidney trailed off as the door creaked open. Kit kept her eyes on it, watching as the carved oak swung forward, revealing the very man she had been waiting for.

"Kit?" Sir Francis Walsingham's surprised voice was coupled with widening eyes and a spine that went rigid. His long face was still gaunt and as pale as ever, and he had one hand clutched to his lower back as he stepped forward. "Why are you here?"

Kit stood straight at the words and glanced to Lady Sidney; seeing the way she busied herself with her food told Kit all she needed to know.

"You were not aware I arrived last night?" she asked, looking back to Walsingham.

"No, I was not." He glanced toward his daughter as he walked into the room. The one hand Kit could see clearly was marked with the burns he'd suffered in the fire at Seething Lane back in the summer when Kit and Iomhar had pulled him free of the flames. "Why are you here?" he asked again.

"Father, you promised not today," Lady Sidney pleaded, looking up from her pewter plate.

"I know," he assured her with a nod and a gentle smile before turning back to Kit. "Not today, Kit. Come see me at Seething Lane tomorrow." He went to join his daughter at the table, but Kit knew deep down that Iomhar was right. Walsingham needed to be told what they had discovered sooner than that.

"We must speak now. Iomhar is here too. We caught the priest last night and —"

"I said not now, Kit," Walsingham spoke with a sharp tone as he sank down into a chair, wincing in pain. It was the same wherever he went, this pain followed him round, until he popped those opium pills into his mouth that were hidden in almost every drawer of his house. Kit had seen him take them often enough to know how much he relied on them.

Kit said nothing, though she reached into her doublet and pulled out the half-written letter she had taken off Father Montague. As Walsingham tried to place a cob of seeded bread on his pewter plate, Kit dropped the parchment in the way, making Walsingham hover the cob in the air. He veered forward in his seat, staring down at the parchment with squinted eyes.

"Where did you find this?" he asked, his voice cracking in the middle.

"The priest you wanted was writing it." Kit stood close beside Walsingham, refusing to back down. "This cannot wait until tomorrow."

"You are right, it cannot." Walsingham stood to his feet and snatched the parchment off his plate, letting the cob roll away across the veneered oak dining table.

"Father!" Lady Sidney called after him with insistence.

"I'll be back later, Franny," he said coolly.

Kit glanced over her shoulder to see Lady Sidney turning red in the face, the gilt-edged cutlery in her hands gripped so tight that her knuckles turned white. Kit offered a small smile that made Lady Sidney throw the cutlery down on the table.

# CHAPTER 6

"He made a mess of your face." Walsingham looked up from the parchment to where Iomhar stood.

"Thank ye for the reminder," Iomhar said drily, earning a smile from Kit.

The two of them were standing side by side in front of the desk in Walsingham's study. Unlike the room at Seething Lane that was full of papers and books, this room was sparse with barely anything of any use at all in it.

The walls were panelled on one side with mahogany, lined in embossed squares, whilst the others were plastered white with exposed brown timber beams running through the centre in periodic straight lines. In front of these walls were sideboards of ornaments, placed there by Walsingham's wife, including a black vase engraved with mother-of-pearl teardrop shapes and copper candlesticks moulded into angels with their wings stretching around the candlewicks to keep the flames safe.

"This should not be possible," Walsingham muttered, looking back down to the paper in his hand and throwing it on the thin desk he sat behind. "Gregorio Luca? Here?" He stood up and walked a little distance away from the desk before pausing by the leaden latticed window and clutching his back in sudden pain.

"You should sit down," Kit said, stepping forward away from Iomhar and moving to Walsingham's side.

"Stop fussing, Kit, I am perfectly well."

"Aye, ye look it." Iomhar's words earned him a warning glare from Kit that simply made him smile all the more. "Ye know who he is? Luca?"

"Yes, yes!" Walsingham turned and flapped a hand in Iomhar's direction impatiently. "How could I not know of him? My men in Rome and the Empire write to me frequently of his exploits. We cannot have this now. Not *now*. Of all the weeks for him to come!"

"What does that mean?" Kit asked. Walsingham froze, looking between the two of them sharply with his nose wrinkling. She recognised the action of old. He was trying to decide whether to tell her something. "Something has happened, has it not?"

Walsingham said nothing, but, returning to his desk, he reached into a drawer and pulled out a scrap of parchment before thrusting it in Kit's direction. Walsingham's movements were so frantic that she struggled to take it without dropping it.

"What is this?" she asked.

"Privy council papers. Look again."

Kit felt Iomhar move to her shoulder, peering down at the papers too. It didn't take long to figure out what they were. It was instructions for Scorpio's movements.

"I thought papers like this never left your office?" Kit wondered aloud.

"Your presumption would be correct." Walsingham marched back toward the leaden window. "I'd like to know how a privy council paper ended up in a priest's pocket."

"Whose pocket?" Iomhar asked.

"One of the priests you two arrested last week. He gave this up under interrogation. It was hidden within the lining of his belt."

Kit dropped the papers back down to the desk. "You mean … the only way a priest could be in possession of these papers, is if someone on the privy council gave them to him?"

"It means someone on the privy council is not who we think they are," Walsingham said, his voice growing louder as he marched back across the room, returning to the desk and flinging open drawers.

Kit flinched at the action. She had been passed information before that there was someone on the privy council who could not be trusted, but Kit had kept that information for Iomhar's ears only. The fact that Walsingham was on the council himself meant he could be who she had spoken of. At least, Iomhar believed he could be. Kit thought it a foolish idea, though for some reason, she still couldn't find the courage to tell Walsingham what she had learned. She supposed a seed of doubt had been sewn.

Walsingham grew more and more animated, hurriedly opening and closing drawers haphazardly.

"What are ye looking for?" Iomhar asked.

Walsingham carried on searching. "I cannot find them."

"Let me look," Kit spoke up, stepping forward and taking Walsingham's shoulder, slowly moving him out of the way. He made no objection and sat in the chair heavily, wincing in more pain.

"Hurry."

She did as he asked and searched through the drawers, aware Iomhar was watching her all the time.

"This is beyond the pale. Everything I thought I knew, everything I was certain of, it has all melted away," Walsingham murmured gravely, staring down at the parchment on the desk. "There is a man I trust, who cannot be trusted at all."

Kit found the bottle of 'Stones of Immortality' and presented it to Walsingham. He eagerly took it from her and tipped the contents of the glass bottle into his palm, yet only one tiny bead of black opium and citrus juice fell out. No matter how many times he shook the bottle, nothing else would come.

"You need some more," Kit whispered gently, trying to take the glass bottle back from him.

He looked up at her accusingly, as though she were the one who had emptied the bottle. For a minute, he clung to the empty bottle with a kind of desperation.

"It is empty." Her sombre voice shook him out of a sort of spell, and he released the bottle at last.

"This is not good." Walsingham tipped his palm up toward his lips, passing the opium into his mouth before smacking his dried lips together.

"What? The fact we have a betrayer in the privy council, that Gregorio Luca is on his way to England, or that ye are out of pills?" Iomhar asked.

"Iomhar," Kit stressed his name warningly, but Iomhar seemed unperturbed.

"It was a genuine question, aye." He held her gaze.

"The privy council and Luca!" Walsingham snapped. "Something has to be done. At once." He jolted forward and reached for the drawers again, making Kit jump backwards out of the way.

"What are you looking for now?" she asked.

He snatched fresh parchment out of a drawer and an ink bottle too before scribbling notes in a trimmed quill across the thick leaf. "We will set up an investigation. Each man in the council will be watched thoroughly, including Lord Burghley. Every man, even their secretaries, those men will be watched too," Walsingham spoke with vigour, his hand moving so fast across the parchment that his writing appeared to Kit more like squashed spiders than words.

"Who do you wish us to watch?" Kit began, leaning over the parchment to read it better, then Walsingham slid it away from her gaze along the desk, looking up to her with his dark eyes. She backed away, walking around the desk to show she had no intention of reading it after all.

"What did you ask?" he said distractedly.

"Our last commission is finished. Assign us a member of the council to watch." She gestured toward Iomhar along with herself.

"What? No, no." The exuberance with which he spoke made Iomhar step forward as Kit froze.

"Why not?" Iomhar asked.

"Because after the letter you found, we cannot risk it. Luca must be found."

"Who *is* Luca?" Kit implored to know more. "Why does the man's mere name seem to make everyone shudder with fear?" She looked to Iomhar who turned his gaze away. When she looked back to Walsingham, she found him sitting forward in the chair, clutching Father Montague's letter.

"Gregorio Luca is a Jesuit priest."

"That is hardly uncommon," Kit said, frowning still.

"Nay, Kit, it is worse than that." Iomhar spoke slowly.

"Indeed, much worse." Walsingham hung his head forward, though he kept his eyes on her at all times. "Gregorio Luca is an assassin."

"An assassin?" Kit asked, reaching for the letter. Her eyes tarried on the words, but there was little information there, nothing more than the fact Luca was to arrive. "You know of this man?" she asked, lifting her eyes to Iomhar.

"A wee bit," Iomhar said, crossing his arms. "Not much of a priest about the man from what I hear. Religious, aye, but the man is more of a weapon himself than someone devoted to religious zeal."

"My information says much the same thing," Walsingham agreed with a solemn nod. "I have heard many tales about him. Assassinations in France. In fact, murders that stretch across the continent, in particular with our Dutch allies. The Protestants are hit hardest."

"So, is he an intelligencer or an assassin?" Kit asked, but she didn't get an answer. She looked between Walsingham and Iomhar.

Eventually, Walsingham shrugged and shifted in his seat. "Who can be certain? What we do know is this man brings death in his wake," Walsingham said gravely. "I want you to find him. As soon as he sets foot on our soil, I want him arrested and questioned as to why he is here."

"Do ye think he is here to help Mary Stuart?" Iomhar's voice was quiet, almost apprehensive.

"It is possible, but not certain. There could be others he is sent here to support."

At the words, Iomhar stepped back, his manner sharp and jerky. Kit's eyes followed him, watching as he moved to a window, eagerly looking out as though he would find Gregorio Luca waiting there on the lawn.

"You have your orders. Both of you. Find this spy, Gregorio Luca, and bring him to a prison. There you will find out why he is on our shores. I do not expect him to leave England again."

Kit flinched at the words and turned her eyes to Walsingham. "You intend to kill him?" she stuttered. "That is murder."

"What has he done to hundreds of others?" Walsingham stood to his feet hurriedly. "No, I do not intend to kill him, Kit. I intend for him to face a trial for his crimes."

She nodded wordlessly, though she found herself still staring at Walsingham. For a minute she thought he had meant cold-blooded murder, with no trial at all.

"He is a murderer, Kit. A Catholic killer who will have been sent here to advance their cause, maybe even the death of our queen. Is that what you want to see? Her Majesty murdered, shot with a crossbow or a pistol, maybe run through with a rapier —"

"Yes, I understand." She cut him off and turned away from Walsingham's penetrating gaze and the frantic gesturing of his hands. "How are we supposed to find him?"

"Give me a few days," Walsingham muttered, reaching for parchment and a quill. "I have a man on the continent, well placed. If he asks the right questions, he might be able to find out more." He sat down and pulled forward the parchment, dipping his quill in an inkwell before he lifted his hand and waved the two of them away. "You may go."

Kit did not miss the way the muscles around Iomhar's new burn mark twitched at the words, but he said nothing as he walked toward the door.

"What is it?" Kit whispered to him as she followed.

"I do not take kindly to being dismissed like a dog."

"We work for him. That is all."

"Is that all?" Iomhar scoffed.

"Before you go," Walsingham called to them both, making them hesitate in the doorway and look back to him. "Go see a man called Knepp below stairs. He has something for you both. Something that could be useful, especially if you are going to hunt a man like Luca."

Kit nodded and led the way out of the door into the hallway. The door closed hard behind them, leaving Kit in a silent corridor with her footsteps the only sound. Realising Iomhar was not walking with her, she paused and stared back at Iomhar to see him hovering by the closed door with his brows knitted together. She opened her palms in his direction, silently asking what he was doing.

"Do ye not think that odd?" he queried, walking away from the door to reach her side.

"What was odd?"

"He kens someone in the privy council may be a supporter of Scorpio, yet he isn't keeping us here to help find who it is?"

Kit stepped back, startled by the words. "Iomhar, you have just said what a dangerous man Gregorio Luca is. Do you not think it worth our time to find him?"

"Of course, but there is something else here." Iomhar looked to the closed door. "I am certain of it."

"You think he is keeping a secret?"

"That's the problem with a spymaster, is it not? He always likes to know more than his spies."

# CHAPTER 7

"Shoes off."

"I beg your pardon?"

"Shoes. Off." The old man gestured down to their feet.

Kit glanced at her boots, frowning before turning her eyes up to the elderly man.

"Is that necessary?" Iomhar asked as he and Kit stepped off the stone spiral staircase into the cellars of Barn Elms.

"You want a spark? You want to send this house up with it? No? Then shoes off!" The old man — Knepp — gestured madly down at their feet again and the metal buckles with the nails that were fastened into the soles. "No spark down here. I will not risk it."

He turned on his heel and marched away across the darkened cellar, lit by just three windows that were no bigger than a man's face, peering down at them from near the ceiling. Kit watched as Knepp hobbled across the stone floor, his aging legs emphasising the slap of the felt slippers on the stones.

"Is it really so great a risk?" Kit muttered to Iomhar as she pulled off her buckskin boots. Iomhar did the same, but he didn't have time to answer.

"I may be old, but my hearing is that of a young man," Knepp called from the other side of the room. "Too much gunpowder here to risk a spark. So you can set those blades of yours down there too." He pointed to a table beside where they stood, the wood raising in ridges from the knots in the tree the wood had once been a part of.

Kit shrugged and pulled out her daggers, laying them across the table as Iomhar did the same with his rapier, so that it clinked with her daggers.

"Eh!" Knepp snapped.

"Nay spark," Iomhar said calmly, holding his hands up as if he were soothing a wild creature. "All is safe."

"Hmm…" Knepp muttered something under his breath and marched through the shadows of the cellars. Kit and Iomhar glanced at one another and then followed the old man. "Now, Iomhar. Walsingham said you would be needing this."

Kit and Iomhar walked across the cellar, circling barrels and crates of unknown goods with lids firmly fastened down. When they reached the far side, Kit grew interested in a wall of wool cloth, suspended by hooks from the ceiling, peeking beyond it to see just why Knepp was so nervous.

"That is a lot of barrels."

"Best stay away from them then." Knepp walked in front of her and drew the wool across further, hiding the gunpowder barrels from view. "You," he said, indicating Iomhar, "this way." Knepp urged Iomhar to follow him to the far side of the cellar. Kit followed behind them, though she kept glancing back at the gunpowder, wondering why Walsingham needed access to so much of it.

"These things aren't accurate," Iomhar scoffed. The words made Kit look round to see Knepp had opened a crate and pulled out something that he passed into Iomhar's hands. He raised the object a little higher, forcing Kit to squint through the gloom in the cellar to see what it was.

"A pistol?" she said in surprise. In the dim light, she saw a slim weapon made of darkened cherry wood, every inch of it inlaid with ivory that swirled into tulips and vine leaves. The base of the handle was made of brass, matching the mechanism of the trigger.

"This one you'll find is a little more accurate, though not as much as I'd like it to be," Knepp bemoaned, before stepping around Iomhar. Beyond another sheet of wool draped from floor to ceiling, a rack on the wall was covered in an array of weapons, rapiers and other types of swords, including the deadliest of pikes and halberds, mounted on mahogany spears with iron angled into such sharp points that they glinted even in the dim light. Here, they were so far away from the gunpowder that presumably the risk of sparks no longer bothered Knepp.

Iomhar added the gun to his belt as Knepp passed him wadding and a powder flask, rimmed with brass and etched in the middle with a woman's form.

Kit stepped forward and held her hand out for her own pistol, yet Knepp did not pass her a weapon. He scrunched his dark eyebrows together, much darker than his white hair, and looked at her with confusion.

"What?" she asked. "Am I not permitted one?"

"No."

"No?"

"No," Knepp said again and turned away. "Walsingham's orders."

Kit was about to argue, placing her hands on her hips, when she saw Iomhar's expression. He seemed mightily pleased with the situation. "You do not need to look so happy."

"Have ye ever fired a pistol, Kit?"

"No," she answered slowly, "but I could learn."

"As the one going with ye to find this Luca, I am glad ye do not have a pistol. With how much ye like to jump into things, ye'd be too eager on the trigger. Ye might shoot and end up getting me in my rear."

"I am not that bad."

"How do ye know if ye have never fired a pistol?"

"We could find out." She gestured toward him for the pistol, but he turned a little from her, still smirking as he placed the powder flask in his belt.

"Not today, thank ye."

"I'm good enough with a crossbow, am I not?" To her question, Iomhar clearly had to agree, nodding slowly. "Knepp, why will Walsingham not give me a pistol?" Kit said, deciding to change tact.

"His orders. That's all I know."

Kit folded her arms, ready to argue the point further, when Iomhar lifted the powder flask, a grin appearing on his face.

"Time to try it out, methinks."

# CHAPTER 8

"That one was a little close for comfort."

"It was far away from ye."

"I could feel it brush me like the wind!"

"It was still far away from ye."

Kit bristled at Iomhar's words as she sat in the garden off his house, looking out over the river where he had taught her to swim. He was practicing with the pistol gifted to him, with his cloak discarded over a leafless branch of a tree nearby and the crossbow slung beside it.

"Why would Walsingham not give me a pistol?" For two days the question had been burning within Kit. She breathed on her chilly hands, trying to ward off some of the cold of the wintry air.

"How many more times are ye going to ask me that?" Iomhar asked as he refilled the pistol with powder.

"Until I hear a convincing answer."

"Kit, I do not know why," he said with a sigh. Kit shifted where she was sat on a log, feeling the discomfort grow all the more.

"Do you think it is because I am..." She trailed off, uncertain about saying the words.

"Ye are what?" Iomhar looked at her, discerning her meaning without her having to utter the words. "Not because ye're a lass, of that I am convinced."

"What makes you so sure?"

"Because he trusts ye more than he trusts any of us." Iomhar turned away and lifted the barrel, pointing it at the trunk of a tree nearby. "Certainly more than he trusts me."

"He does?" Kit asked, sitting a little taller on her log.

"Is that a surprise to ye?" Iomhar didn't look back to her as he fired the pistol. Kit no longer jumped when he fired it, she merely blinked, feeling the shot so near that it was her body's defence against it.

"Very much."

"Ye trust him. Though I think that trust is misplaced, why should it not be the other way around too?"

"Walsingham is a man that can be trusted. I can assure you of that."

"Then tell me this." Iomhar reloaded the pistol. "Why have ye not told him what was said to you about an informer being on the privy council?"

Kit said nothing in answer. She looked away, staring down at the river nearby.

"Aye, that is the only answer I need."

"I did not say anything."

"Exactly."

Kit stood to her feet, ready to argue with Iomhar, but he was busy picking up his crossbow from the branch. Lifting it high in his arms, he fired the bow, with the bolt landing perfectly in the centre of the trunk.

"Until a pistol is as accurate as this, nay, I do not see much use for the thing."

"It is still deadly," Kit said, moving to the pistol Iomhar had laid down on the log and running her fingers over the weapon. The brass elements were cold to the touch, but the cherry wood was warm. With Iomhar focused on the crossbow, she lifted the pistol in her hands and turned to the trunk he had been firing at, peering down the barrel to practice her own aim.

"Ye want to try?" Iomhar asked, moving to her side.

She slowly nodded. She didn't care what Walsingham thought; she was confident she could handle the weapon as well as Iomhar could.

Iomhar took the pistol from her fingers and began to reload it with powder and wadding before he placed it into her palms. "Take your shot. Be careful, mind ye. It has a strong recoil."

"I will be fine," she declared confidently, tilting her chin higher as she looked at the trunk of the tree, aware of how close Iomhar stood beside her, watching her. It took only a few seconds for her to be confident in her shot, yet when she pulled the trigger, the power that erupted from the pistol sent her backwards. She recoiled away, stumbling on her feet as her arms bent, before something caught her.

"Aye, ye nearly fell over." Iomhar smiled at her, his hand on the base of her back, stopping her from going any further. She jumped away from his hand as he nodded his head forward at the tree. "See?"

"See what?"

"Ye didn't even hit the tree. These things…" He took the gun out of her grasp. "Deadly they may be, but it will take a lucky shot to kill a man. I prefer a crossbow."

Kit let him take the pistol as she thought of the events from only two nights before, with the gaoler injured by a crossbow.

"What of the gaoler? From the other night?" Kit asked, keeping her eyes on the bolt that was in the centre of the tree trunk. "Did he survive?"

Iomhar looked down, fiddling with the pistol as he made it safe. The silence stretched between them uncomfortably, making Kit impatient for an answer.

"Iomhar?" She nudged him.

"I received a message this morning. He didn't live."

Kit planted her feet firmly in the earth, feeling the horror wash over her.

"Ye all right?"

"I'm fine," she answered hurriedly. She turned, breathing deeply and trying her best to think of something else, just as a figure appeared on the far side of the garden, hurrying out of the house with a letter being waved madly in her hand.

"Elspeth?" Iomhar called to the portly woman, who usually cooked in his house. "Ye well?"

"This has just arrived, Sir," she said breathlessly, clutching her chest as she reached their side. "Young lad, he was. Said it was of the utmost importance that Miss Scarlett read it immediately." She pressed the letter into Kit's hands, distracting her from her thoughts.

Kit broke the red wax seal and pulled open the parchment, revealing the familiar scrawl of Walsingham.

*Kit,*

*I have received word from one of my intelligencers on the continent. GL is to arrive this next week as we first thought, yet he is not to land on our southern shores, but much nearer the border. Northumberland is the chosen landing place, where patrols of waters are slim, and the coast has many landing points.*

*You and Iomhar must go to the borders at once. My man will meet you at Hadrian's Wall, near Housesteads Fort. His name is Oswyn Ingleby, and he is prepared for your arrival.*

*Kit, I cannot tell you of the importance of this commission. If GL is here, then it is to spill blood, and the blood of an important man or woman. No other man would be sent for such a job.*

*You must stop him. Who knows whose life in the country now hovers on a precipice?*

*I wish you the best of luck in your endeavour. Write back soon and do not return from Northumberland until the task is done.*
*Taurus.*

"Iomhar?" Kit closed the letter up, folding it tightly. "We have our orders."

"Where are we heading?"

"Northumberland."

# CHAPTER 9

"Wait a minute more."

"Another minute? There is so much mist I cannot see anything, nothing more than the grass beneath my horse's hooves," Kit said tiredly as she adjusted in the saddle. The leather made her rear sore and her legs ache after so long a journey. They had changed horses multiple times in order to keep up the pace, but now she was as tired as the animal beneath her, in danger of falling asleep in the saddle after riding through the night. She stretched out her back and looked over her shoulder to see Iomhar sat astride his horse, somehow looking much more comfortable than her.

Iomhar was dressed in his usual dark green jerkin, with his black woollen cloak belted around his waist to ward off the cold Northumbrian wind. Through the mist, the wind bristled, ruffling his dark hair against the blanket of grey that surrounded them.

"Aye, I have never known anyone as impatient as ye. Look forward again. Ye shall see the wall at any moment."

"These are the borders? I wonder why men have fought over this land for so long. There is nothing but grass and mist. Is this the whole of Northumberland?" she asked, huffing and turning back round again.

"Some days, aye, it feels like it," he chuckled. "Wait … there it is."

Kit looked up from where she was patting the large chestnut's neck, soothing it beyond the reins, to see the mist was lifting a little in the early morning sun. The light was sharp, shining through the low cloud in beams across the landscape, revealing a world that was far from flat. The earth undulated in hills and knots, sometimes green and lush with grass, other times purple with gauze and dark brown bracken. There were a few trees around the bases of the hills, along the edges of farming walls too, bearing no more autumnal leaves, only their twiggy branches were outstretched like arms shrivelled and withered by cold.

As the mist began to lift from the hills, peeling the cloud off the earth, a jagged wall appeared following the tops of knots, half fallen down in places with stones crumbling to the earth. It was as though a giant man had walked across these hills, kicking stones off the wall for entertainment, sending some of them flying a good distance and leaving others behind in small, mounded cairns.

"What is this place?" Kit said, shielding her eyes against the brightness of the sun as she set her man's cap further back on her head.

"Hadrian's Wall. Built by the Romans, they say, many years ago." Iomhar steered his horse beside her own. They came to a stop, looking at the wall and hills through the mist as they stretched far into the distance, disappearing into the winter clouds. "He should be here."

Kit reached into her pocket, pulling out the small timepiece she had once been given by Walsingham. The pocket watch set within the dial of a compass ticked softly in the palm of her hand, the brass metal colder up here in the north than it had been in London.

"We are early," she explained, pocketing the item and inching her horse forward, nearing the wall. Iomhar travelled alongside her, until they were level with the wall, walking beside it like some sentry Roman guards, watching over the low-lying boundary to the other side.

"It used to be the border with Scotland."

"This?" She waved at the wall that looked so feeble. "It would not keep out a hare, let alone a man."

"Back then it might have. Aye, the border is much further north now, though some say the border isn't right. Most Scots I know wish to let the matter be." Iomhar kept his eyes trained over the wall, not looking at Kit as he spoke.

"I did not realise we were so close to Scotland. Are we anywhere near your family?"

"Nay, they are a lot further away. In the Highlands." There was a darkness in Iomhar's tone as he flicked his eyes forward again.

"Well, we are still a lot closer than we were in London. Perhaps whilst we are here you should see them?"

"Nay."

"Why not?" she asked, darting her head toward him. He didn't answer straight away. He seemed to concentrate on moving the horse forward, listening to the hooves clomping softly into the grassy earthy beneath them. "Iomhar?" She prompted for his attention.

"I rarely go back," he confessed eventually, lifting his chin a little higher. As the mist lifted, his face was bathed in an increasingly amber-tinged light.

"Why?"

"Is this any affair of yours?"

"You ask about my affairs often enough. Always poking your nose in," she pointed out. "It's a wonder you still have your nose after all you have asked of me."

"Ha!" he laughed, shaking his head. "That's different."

"Why?"

"Your life is a little more interesting than my own."

"What? A foundling on the street? That's hardly interesting as so much dull. I know nothing of my life." Kit pulled on her horse's reins, letting the leather cut into the supple red suede of her gloves as she angled the chestnut toward Iomhar's horse. He looked to her, apparently startled she had come so close. "If I had family I knew of, I would see them."

"Of course ye would, but my life isn't as simple as that."

"Why not?"

"Ye are full of questions today, aren't ye?" he said tiredly, ruffling the back of his hair.

"Yes!" she declared with triumph. "As we have so much further to go, you can rest assured I will just keep asking you until you answer."

"For the wee man's sake, I hope we find this man of Walsingham's soon."

"You are changing the subject."

"I'm certainly attempting to."

"You will fail. Iomhar, why do you not want to go home?" Her question this time was not met with so much resistance, but silence. He ruffled the back of his hair again and looked forward, out across the Northumbrian hills. Kit followed his gaze, staring at the curves of the ground as they rose and fell, with the old Roman wall following its path.

"I go back rarely, Kit," Iomhar murmured eventually with a sigh. "It isn't the same since we lost my father."

Kit kept her eyes forward on the landscape as the sun lifted a little higher, turning the world a misty orange through the thick fog.

"Iomhar, he will always be gone. Is that a reason to not go back?"

"Until I know what really happened to him, aye, it will stop me from going back often." Iomhar's voice was strong. "Now that ye have poked your nose into my mind for the day, shall we move onto the matter at hand?"

"You mean tracking an Italian assassin."

"Aye, it is rather important. Wait ... there."

"What?"

"Kit," Iomhar called impatiently, reaching out and taking the reins of her horse. It was an ungainly action, with the two of them misaligned, but he managed to take hold of the harness and pull her to a stop, with the horse snuffling in objection. "Look ahead. Between the hills."

There was a figure standing atop of one of the hills, his feet astride a cobbled wall. He must have seen them at the same time for he lifted a hand and waved it slowly above his head.

"What was his name?" Iomhar asked.

"Oswyn Ingleby," Kit muttered, "Walsingham's man in Northumberland."

"Hmm..." Iomhar hummed with clear uncertainty.

"What does that mean?"

The wind rushed up the valley. It struck them both at once, making them shiver in their saddles. Iomhar pulled the top of his cloak further around his neck as Kit grabbed onto her hat, holding it in place out of fear of losing it.

"Let's just say, I look at Northumberland like this northern wind."

"Ah, and I feared you were going to be cryptic in your answer," Kit spoke drily as he looked across at her.

"Bracing and cold," he explained darkly. "Northumbrian men and the Scottish are not the closest of allies, Kit. Remember that."

"Surely all the battles are in the past now?" she said, frowning at him. "There hasn't been a skirmish here in the borders for years."

"Forty years, if we are counting." Iomhar shook his head. "Aye, Kit, that is still within living memory. I wouldn't trust a Northumbrian man. That is all."

"You have not met the man yet." Kit pulled her horse's reins out of his gloved grasp. "He may be the kindest man you have ever met."

"Ye want a wager on that?" he grunted as they steered their horses forward, crossing the next valley toward the man that awaited them.

# CHAPTER 10

"You must be in jest, pet," Oswyn Ingleby cried as he jumped down off the stone wall, striding through the tall grass that banked along the edge.

"Pet?" Kit repeated in surprise as she clambered off the horse.

"I think he's talking to ye," Iomhar said over the saddle of the horse with a humoured smile.

"Do I look like a pet?"

"It's what they say." Iomhar shrugged and stepped around the horses.

"Aye, my eyes must be deceiving me," Oswyn said, wiping his eyes with his hands, his Northumbrian accent strong. "Walsingham sent a *lass* on this commission?"

"A lass who knows what she's doing." Iomhar's voice was dark and restrained, making Kit snap her head toward him in surprise.

"Oh no, he sent me a Scot too? Pah! A lass and a Scot. Does he want us to find this man or not?"

"See what I mean?" Iomhar gestured to Oswyn and addressed Kit alone. "Nay Northumbrian man likes a Scot. I would have thought him more open to a lass though."

"Aye, I like many a lass." Oswyn offered Kit a wink as he stepped toward her.

Kit tilted her chin higher and crossed her arms over the dark red doublet, feeling the stiff material bend in the winter chill. "This woman is reserving judgement on whether she likes you yet." She kept her voice level, though she was already beginning to think that there may have been something in Iomhar's fears.

Oswyn Ingleby was not a tall man, rather short and scrawny, shorter than Kit, with a pointed face that reminded her of a thin water vole. Even the stubble on his face was long, more like whiskers, and his light brown hair was tied up in a lengthy untidy ponytail that swung down his back, fanning behind the fur cloak upon his shoulders.

"Ha! Maybe I can change your mind, pet," he said, stepping toward her again. "Never thought I'd see a lass dressed as a man. I rather like it."

Kit bristled at his words, glancing down at what she was wearing. She wore the same dark hose she often wore, with her boots reaching high up around her knees. The doublet was a deep red, though unusually it bore a white collar gathered round her neck for warmth, and was embellished with white embroidery, designed to look like birds taking flight. The sleeves were dappled with white flecks too, hatched like feathers. It was the warmest doublet she owned, something Iomhar had warned her she would need in Northumberland.

"Oswyn Ingleby?" Kit asked, stepping back from him to place distance between them, and choosing not to reply to his last words.

"Aye, I am he." He nodded. "I usually shake hands with Walsingham's men, but I do not know how to handle a lass, shall I kiss your hand instead?"

"Come anywhere near me with those lips and you will regret it," she uttered, deepening her voice and laying a hand on her belt where her dagger sat. Rather than bringing a look of fear to his face, he laughed, tipping his chin back.

"Aye, I can see why Walsingham likes you. You, though," Oswyn turned his attention to Iomhar. "I am not so sure about."

"Ye do not need to apologise for it, I think the same of ye," Iomhar spoke slowly and stepped toward Kit. She raised her eyebrows at the move, wondering what he was doing. "Enough blithering. Walsingham said ye could give us lodgings?"

"Alnwick. In the shadow of the Earl of Northumberland's home," Oswyn declared with drama as he stepped back and jumped up on the wall again. "It will be another half day's ride from here, far north. Even closer to the border. You will be staying with me."

"With you?" Kit asked, feeling Iomhar elbow her in the arm. She glanced his way, seeing him shake his head slightly. He clearly liked the idea no more than she did.

"It is all I can offer you that is safe." Oswyn turned back to face them. "There are daily raids at the moment between the graynes. Even some of our Scottish brethren coming down to reive our cattle and sheep." His eyes narrowed on Iomhar who gestured to his breast with wide eyes.

"Surely ye can see I am nay cattle thief."

"If you work for Walsingham, I see you cannot be. It does not mean I have to like you."

"The feeling is mutual."

"God have mercy," Kit implored, lifting her eyes up to the clouds where the mist was rising more and more. "I do not think this is going to go well if you two will insist on exchanging insults every few minutes."

"You expect me to work with a Scot and say nothing about it?" Oswyn questioned, clambering down off the wall. "Dirty savages —"

"Ye dare to say such a thing to me —" Iomhar strode forward, his hand reaching for the hilt of his sword.

Kit moved between them, pressing both hands to Iomhar's chest and shoving him back before he could pull the rapier free of its thin leather scabbard.

"Iomhar!" she snapped, trying to get his attention. "What good will come from you wounding a man sent here to help us?"

"Nay, I will not have my kin insulted in such a way, Kit."

"Then insult him back and be done with it."

"Under the lass's thumb, I see." Oswyn chuckled as he sat down on the wall, pulling up his booted foot and resting it on his other knee. "Are you two wed?"

"No!" Kit's word was so loud, it echoed back at them off the stone wall. Silence descended, one in which Oswyn was still smiling. When Kit heard the rustle of cloak material, she looked back to see Iomhar with his arms folded, his green eyes staring down at her, rather narrowed. "What?"

"Ye said that so loudly, it was clear the thought appalled ye."

"I was not that loud," she protested, holding up a finger in objection. His eyebrows quirked upward, and he smiled a little.

"So, the idea intrigues ye?"

"Iomhar, be quiet!" She tapped him round the arm and turned back to Oswyn. "Enough insults between Northumbrians and Scots. We are here for a purpose. Walsingham wants us to find the Jesuit assassin, are you going to help? Or will you continue to sit on that wall in this winter chill and laugh at us?"

Oswyn seemed to work hard to control his mirth, though the smile still rested on his face as he looked between the two of them. He scratched the whiskers on his face for a minute before giving them a nod. "Aye, I do not want a Jesuit assassin here anymore than the two of you. I'll swallow my pride for now, if the Scot is willing to do the same."

"Iomhar." Iomhar corrected sternly.

"What?"

"That is my name. Not Scot."

"How odd. Is it even a name?"

"What happened to nay more insults, Sassenach?" Iomhar said tartly.

"Sassenach!?" Oswyn stumbled to his feet so fast, he fell off the wall.

Amongst the angry words, Kit turned to Iomhar with an intrigued smile. "What does that mean?"

"Let's just say it is nay nice term for an Englishman," Iomhar said with a rather mischievous smirk.

"I should run you through where you stand, Scot." Oswyn reached for the blade at his own belt.

"This is maddening." Kit sighed with the words, tipping her eyes to the clouds again. "That is enough!" Her bark made the two men stop as they looked at each other. With such a small distance between them and their hands on the hilts of their blades, she couldn't even step between them to separate them. "Do you two want an Italian assassin running round Northumberland whilst you fight?"

Neither of them said anything for a minute, though they turned from glaring at one another to looking at her instead.

"I thought not. Iomhar, step back."

"Why me first?"

"Do not be as petty as a child. Move away." She pointed backwards in emphasis, and he did as she asked, reluctantly though, dragging his boots through the grass.

"Hmm…" Oswyn tutted, lifting his hand from his sword and folding his arms. "Aye, you two certainly behave like you are wed."

"We are not wed!" Kit objected loudly.

"Aye, aye, I heard you the first time. She is getting louder each time she says it." Oswyn laughed as he stepped away, holding up his hands. "Gather your horses. We'll make our way to Alnwick."

As Kit turned to her horse, she found Iomhar blocking her path.

"What?"

"Am I really so objectionable?" he teased, tilting his head to the side.

"I am not going to answer that." She walked around him toward the chestnut.

"Why not?"

"Because anything I say, you will twist my words to mean something else."

"If you two are done jabbering," Oswyn called from where he was walking down the wall, using the broken-up stones like steps to descend the hill, "we should move on. You think it's cold now? Wait until tonight. Winter is coming."

"Is it not winter yet?" Kit asked, swinging herself up into the saddle.

"This is not even cold for this land," Oswyn shouted back as he hastened down the wall. "Yet the sheep have grown thicker coats this autumn. Our winter will be a cold one, and the wise woman in Alnwick cracked her acorns to find them empty this morning. Aye, it will be a bitter one indeed."

"What does an acorn have to do with winter?" Kit asked Iomhar as he pulled himself up into his saddle.

"Sounds like a question for the wise woman. Or for a fool."

# CHAPTER 11

"She must have been a wise woman," Kit muttered as she took off her gloves and reached for the fireplace, making the floorboards creak beneath her boots as she hurried toward the only source of warmth in the room.

"Because it is freezing?" Iomhar asked, following her in and bending down below low-hanging timbers. More than once did he have to jerk his head to the side, his tall height nearly colliding with the heavy dark wood, the colour of mud.

"My fingers feel like they are coated in frost." She stood by the fireplace, rubbing her fingers together to find some warmth as she looked around the small lodgings.

Oswyn's house was tall and narrow, built of timber, and wattle and daub, with low beams in each room and doorways so small that she was herself in danger of bending down to walk through them. It was pressed between other crooked buildings in the centre of Alnwick town, so thin and tapered between slate rooftops that they had nearly missed it with the thick night smothering the streets. Oswyn had eventually pulled their horses to a stop in the street, signalling to the tiny building over people's heads as they wandered about their business.

Inside, there was barely any light, with so few candles lit and a fire that was only just beginning to take hold. With the early darkness swathing the land, even though dinner was still far off, the air that seeped through the windows was cold and the plaster around the windows was turning speckled white with frost.

"It seems we have a letter. Left with my maid," Oswyn declared loudly as he stepped through the doorway into the small sitting room where Kit was warming herself by the fire and Iomhar had taken a seat, pulling out the wheellock pistol from his belt to examine it. Oswyn hesitated as he saw the weapon, his eyes lingering on the surface. Kit did not miss the lines creasing his brow.

"A letter?" she repeated, clearing her throat to get his attention.

He walked toward her, still glancing back at the pistol, carrying a folded slip of parchment in one hand and a candle in the other. The meagre flame did not add much brightness to the room now that the fire was alight, bathing the floor in a red glow.

"For you," Oswyn said, passing the parchment into Kit's hands.

She took it from him and pulled off her hat, tossing it through the air to where Iomhar caught it and added it to his own that he had placed on the table beside him.

"I know this hand," she whispered as she turned to the fireplace, opening the letter in the red light.

"Is it Taurus?" Iomhar asked, using the codename that belonged to Walsingham.

"Yes," she answered quickly and unfurled the parchment to read the scribbled note: *Kit, a letter from my man in Rome. It holds the key to where you will find Luca.*

She found another letter encased inside, addressed to Taurus. She passed the first note to Iomhar and opened the second, finding the red wax seal of the spy's letter had already been broken by Walsingham.

"Code?" Iomhar asked as he folded the first letter.

"Yes." She sank down to her knees before the fireplace, sitting on the roe-deer rug, thick with fur.

"She will need parchment to decode it," Iomhar said, turning to face Oswyn.

"I am not your servant, Scot."

"Nay, but ye are the host, are you not?" Iomhar pointed out wryly. "Would ye like me to go searching your cupboards in search of parchment and ink?"

Oswyn said no more, but he walked off, clomping his boots so loudly on the boards that it was clear what he thought of Iomhar.

"You could be a little kinder," Kit warned in a murmur, lifting her eyes from the letter to Iomhar.

"Ye didn't say that to him."

"One of you has to start it," she said quickly as Oswyn returned, passing her the parchment and a small vial of ink that she balanced on the hearth of the fireplace. It was a stone hearth, damaged with years of use and blackened from burning wood that had been turned to ash. She rested the implements on the hearth and turned her attention to the letter.

The first word was the only thing initially distinguishable — Taurus. The rest was written in a cipher, where numbers were assigned to letters in the alphabet, though the number one hardly corresponded with 'A'.

"I thought Walsingham had his men Phelippes and Somers for this kind of thing," Oswyn queried as he walked across the small room, heading toward what appeared to be a tall wooden cupboard, lined with shelves. Kit flinched at the words, looking up to him, ready to make her thoughts plain.

Phelippes and Somers were well known as Walsingham's codebreakers, and the thought rankled her. They had not been trained since children to crack such things with Walsingham watching over their shoulders. She had spent days in that way, until ink was spread so far up her palms and wrists that the lines in her skin were blackened.

"*No cipher is unbreakable, Kit,*" Walsingham had said to her once as he walked through the old attic room at Seething Lane. "*If you cannot find the key, you are looking in the wrong place for the lock.*"

"Ye want a codebreaker whose name is not known, surely." Iomhar spoke up before Kit, leaning forward in his seat. "What good is an intelligencer whose name is nay secret at all?" Kit was startled by the words. "What?" he asked. "Surprised I could give ye a compliment?"

"A little."

"Ye should have more faith in me."

Kit chose not to answer and looked down at the letter again. She hadn't wanted to work with Iomhar in the first place back in the summer, but since they had been placed together by Walsingham, they had not worked apart. She rather liked it, though she wouldn't tell him that. Their complaints about working together were part of the way they were with each other these days.

She returned her focus to the code and searched out the more commonly appearing numbers, trying to match them with the most frequently found letters in the alphabet. It was hard work, noting out tiny letters and numbers on the spare sheet of parchment with the fire beginning to burn her face from sitting so close. One side of her body was cold due to the wind slipping through the gap in the window, while the other side was turning red from the heat of the fire.

Oswyn brought out pewter plates from his wooden cabinet, presenting them with small, rounded cakes, dappled with fruit.

"What is this?" Iomhar asked, peering at it like he was being offered a carbuncle to eat rather than anything edible.

"A singing hinny."

"A what?" Kit asked as she was presented with her own version.

"A cake cooked over the fire. My maid may not be the finest cleaner, but she bakes a good cake. You'll need it after your long ride." Oswyn pushed the plate toward her, urging her to eat. She took it and smiled at Iomhar, silently telling him that Oswyn was capable of kindness after all. Iomhar seemed to take the meaning, for he shook his head, ever so slightly, but dug into his cake, nevertheless. His was gone in two bites.

When the quill feathers in Kit's hand were beginning to singe, turning a burnt black from the fire, Kit finally found the way into the cipher. The corresponding letters and numbers had all been moved up by seven places. So 'A' was seven and 'Z' was six, showing the numbers looped back round once they reached twenty-six. She began to scribble out the new decoded letter, aware that as she worked on her knees, leaning toward the fire, Iomhar and Oswyn grew interested. They both stood to their feet and walked toward the hearth, leaning over her to see what she had written.

"There," she declared triumphantly and sat back on the rug. "See? No need of Phelippes and Somers."

"Aye, pet, you have hidden talents I see. Anything else you are hiding under that doublet of yours?" Oswyn winked at her with his words, making Iomhar snap his head to look at Oswyn.

"Say the word, Kit, and I'll make sure he does not say such things again," Iomhar muttered darkly, never letting his gaze leave Oswyn.

"I can handle myself." She shrugged off the matter, standing and straightening out the parchment to read it. "Look at this instead of him." Iomhar moved to her side, carefully setting himself between Kit and Oswyn before reading the letter.

*Taurus,*

*Luca is to reach shore on the sennight of our final month. When the sun rises, he will reach Dunstanburgh Castle at Craster.*

*My information says he will arrive alone, one man in a boat, carrying all that he needs on this shore. To discover this, I intercepted the letter addressed to the man that was to meet Luca at the castle on the beach; though the codename means I do not know the identity of the recipient, this man can no longer receive his message.*

*As this traitor intended to meet Luca will not be there, it is my hope your men will be there to receive him instead.*

*Though I have heard no more on what Luca's task is on our shores, one thing I know for certain, he is carrying weapons, and from the bloodstains they bear, he has made it clear he is intending to use them again.*

*This assassin must be stopped, for who knows who his target may be. It could be Aries, or it could be Gemini. If either death were to befall our Kingdoms, I do not doubt civil war would begin, and ravage our countries.*

*I task your men to be quick, for all our sakes, for Queen, Country, and those that farm our fields.*

At the bottom of the original coded letter was an illegible scrawl, making the name impossible to read.

"Gemini or Aries," Iomhar muttered, taking the letter from her hand.

Kit turned away, resting her hands over the hearth and pressing the cold stone to her fingers in realisation. Aries was their code for Queen Elizabeth and Gemini was for King James VI of Scotland.

"The letter writer is right," she whispered, glancing to Iomhar.

"Let me see it?" Oswyn asked, trying to take the letter out of Iomhar's hand, but he snatched it out of reach, not quite giving in.

"About?" Iomhar addressed Kit alone, clearly doing his best to ignore Oswyn's protests.

"If he is here to kill Aries or Gemini ... we would see a civil war. On one side of the border, if not both."

"Then we best be at Dunstanburgh tomorrow morning, on the sennight, so Gregorio Luca makes it nay further into our shores."

"We take him to the dungeon at Bamburgh," Kit spoke decisively as she lifted the pewter cup of mead that was pushed her way by Oswyn. The maid had served up their food and drink before she had been hustled speedily out of the room, with Oswyn pressing a finger to his lips until she was gone. He didn't even trust his own maid not to betray his secrets.

Kit lifted the mead to her lips, drinking eagerly to find her mouth ached from the sweetness and spices that smothered her tongue. She eyed up the marchpane, her favourite, which had been served with the food. "What is this?" she asked, lifting the cup to her lips again.

"Mead from Holy Island," Oswyn explained. "Famous for it, they are, and their oysters, nought you'll find in my house."

"Holy Island?"

"Aye, you not heard of it? They also call it Lindisfarne. They used to have a priory there before King Henry's time. You can see it from Dunstanburgh."

"Can we return to our plan?" Iomhar asked impatiently. "If Gregorio Luca is half the man I have heard of in tales, he will not go easily, Kit." His voice took on a deepness. He leaned across the small mahogany table in the kitchen space of the house, as the fire in the grate behind them still spat noisily, boiling water in a cauldron above it that splattered angrily at the sides of the brass bowl.

"What tales have you heard?" she asked, aware that Iomhar reached for the serving platters of smoked kippers, chicken and cabbage, one at a time, before passing them toward her plate and serving her first, before himself.

"An assassin that prefers to kill a man with his hands than with a weapon, invoking the name of God with his actions." He held her gaze with the words. "A Catholic Jesuit through and through, *ad majorem dei gloriam*, he would say."

"A Scot that speaks Latin!" Oswyn said, laughing with the words. "Whatever next? Not so savage after all."

Kit kept her eyes on Iomhar, watching his reaction as a muscle in his jaw ticked. She had seen his own home more than a dozen times now. She had seen well enough how he was descended from money, with paintings of his family on the walls, by the court painter George Gower. He had the education to go with the wealth.

"It means for the greater glory of God." Iomhar said evenly, evidently choosing not to rise to Oswyn's jibe. "Luca is a man that will go further than ye think, if he believes God wills it."

"Who did you hear these tales from?"

"A man I haven't seen in years," Iomhar said, as that muscle in his jaw ticked again. Kit paused with her drink as he served up her plate, adding more smoked fish to the pewter. "Let us leave it at that."

Any other time, she would have pressed him on keeping his secrets to himself, but not with Oswyn watching them.

"Tomorrow, we will have to be careful with our plan." Iomhar's voice was firm. "I do not want Luca slipping through our fingers like an otter in water. He will jump on any sign of weakness, ye can be sure of that." He added one last piece of cabbage to her plate before turning to his own.

"Then as you say, we will have to plan carefully," she murmured softly, feeling herself sitting taller in her seat with the challenge laid ahead.

As Iomhar had said many times on their journey up to Northumberland, it did seem as though Walsingham had been hiding something from them back in Barn Elms. Perhaps he was indeed trying to keep them away from the privy council, for some reason. Whatever the cause of such an action, Kit would not neglect her duty. She was here for a reason — a purpose ordered by Walsingham, and she would carry through with it.

Gregorio Luca would not achieve whatever death he had come here to claim.

"Aye, man, you say you two are not wed," Oswyn's voice was loud as he leaned forward and gestured between the two of them.

"Aye, that's what we said." Iomhar didn't look up from his plate as he served his food.

"Then, why do you serve her food, Scot?"

Kit and Iomhar looked at each other, before glancing down at the plates.

"It's called kindness," Kit spluttered hurriedly.

"She does not eat enough if I don't watch what she eats."

"Oi, you are taking that much notice, are you?" Kit looked to him in surprise.

He smiled a little, clearly humoured by her response. "I've known ye for a fair few months now, Kit. Ye do not take the best care of yourself."

"I look after myself well enough."

"Hmm," he hummed with that noise again that spoke volumes.

"Aye, well," Oswyn said, chuckling away. "If you aren't wed yet, you two must surely be on the road to it."

"We are not!" Kit snapped, only to see Iomhar sitting back in his chair, looking at her. "What? We aren't."

"Ye do not have to say it with so much horror."

"I did not sound horrified." Yet as she spoke, there was something in Iomhar's expression she couldn't understand. "Let us talk of something else."

"Why? There's nowt more entertaining than watching you squirm in that doublet of yours."

Oswyn's words were met with Kit throwing her spoon at him, watching as the brass implement landed in his fish with a splat.

# CHAPTER 12

*Kit's hands were reaching toward the surface of the water once again as the figure bent down toward her. She couldn't breathe. No matter how many times she tried to cough the water clear from her body, it stayed in her throat, as though she were being smothered by wool stuffed into her mouth. A hand pierced through the surface above her, turning paler in the light that glistened on the white skin. It was bony, the fingers gnarled...*

"Kit?" the accented voice called through the doorway, accompanied by a tap on the door.

Kit stirred in the straw bed, sitting up to find all was still dark around her, with no light seeping through the window, and the room so dull that she could barely see the end of the bed.

"Kit?" the voice called, more insistent this time.

"I know. I'm coming, Iomhar," she called back, aware of Iomhar waiting on the other side of the door.

"Ye ready? We only have a short time."

"I said I'm coming," she called back with irritation as she clambered off the bed. She hadn't bothered to change, with so few hours of sleep it seemed pointless. With the frost hanging in the air and around the timber beams above the bed, it hardly made sense to wear less clothes for sleeping. She tightened the dark red doublet around her body and adjusted the collar under her neck before moving off the bed and flinging back the border tartan blanket, reaching for her boots that she had kicked away under the bed.

"Take your time, it is not like it is someone important we are to meet this morning."

"Anymore dry wit and I'll take longer about pulling my boots on," she said to the door, able to picture his expression perfectly, with the slightly shaken head.

She paused as she reached for the belt, setting it around her waist with the daggers in place, thinking back to her sleep. The dream had been there again, the same one that she had most nights of late, slipping under the water, but still, she hadn't been able to make out the face of either the person that walked away, leaving her under the water, nor the one who had been reaching down toward her.

"Kit!"

"Impatient man," she mumbled as she walked to the door, fastening the belt in place. As she stepped out of the door, finding Iomhar waiting for her with a candle in his hands, she thought of what Oswyn had said the night before over dinner, when Iomhar had helped her to her food.

Iomhar quirked his eyebrows together, clearly reading something in her own expression through the dim orange light. "Something on your mind?"

"Just a Jesuit assassin," she said hurriedly, closing the chamber door behind her.

"Hmm."

"There's that sound again. Hmm what?"

"I would wager a good deal something else was on your mind." His words made her look back to him, seeing the corner of his lips were turning up in humour.

"Like what?" she asked, feigning innocence.

"Ye have not stopped looking at me with that same expression since dinner last night."

"What expression?"

"That expression that says ye cannot figure something out."

"Those are just my eyes. You will have to grow accustomed to that look."

"Oh, aye, do ye permanently look confused?"

"Iomhar, enough," she pleaded, making a move to walk past him along the corridor.

He turned and followed her, making that 'hmm' sound again as he went. Kit tried not to think too much about it and brushed the mussed red locks back from her forehead that had become tangled when sleeping. She had an ivory comb somewhere in her bag for sorting out such knots, but now she had more important matters to attend to.

She spied Oswyn in the corner of the room, lifting up the sheet of wool that was covering the glass window and peering out.

"The sun will be up soon," Oswyn muttered, turning away from the glass. "We must go." He moved toward the door and snuffed out a candle. Kit hurried behind him, aware that Iomhar followed her, his eyes still on her.

Every step she took, she thought of the dream and that bony hand reaching through the water. Was it real? Some kind of memory? Or had she imagined it all?

"I hope you're ready for Dunstanburgh," Oswyn called as they stepped outside the house into darkness. "You think this is cold, wait until you are on the coast. Aye, any man on the coast can have his breath taken from him by the wind there!"

"It's not my own breath I'm worried about," Iomhar muttered from behind Kit, earning her gaze another time, but his expression disappeared into the darkness of the night and all she could see was his outline. "I'm more worried about who this Jesuit spy comes to seek on our shores."

"It hardly looks like a castle to me," Kit mumbled to herself as she walked alongside a wall of the ruins. The three of them had split up within the castle walls, looking out to the waves that crashed beneath the headland, waiting for the boat that was to bring Gregorio Luca to the shore.

Atop the yellowish grey walls, what had once been a full castle was now in ruins. Where full walls should have been, wispy clouds tinged purple and orange by the early morning sun were now framed by jagged stones. Half of a tower still remained, but the windows were full of nesting wigeons, with their white bellies poking out of the wall, and one wall gone, crumpled to the earth.

As the waves crashed below on the headland rocks, the North Sea wind whistled in, howling in Kit's ears and making her pull the white collar of her doublet higher. She was rather glad she hadn't bothered to comb out her hair, for it was tangled in knots, and her hat was stuffed tightly into her pocket. Had she left it on, it would have been lost in the ocean by now, along with the winkles and the bladderwrack seaweed that kept washing up onto the rocks.

A sound like a hissing wave made Kit look around and peer over the low-lying wall beside her, but it was no wave. Iomhar was trying to get her attention. Standing by a wall on the far side of the ruins some distance away, where they met an open stretch of grass grazed by cattle, he was pointing out to the ocean beyond, before he dived down to hide.

Kit followed where his gesture had been, looking out to the waves. For a minute, she saw nothing, only the rise and swell of the angry sea, rather like the boiling pot of water on the fire the night before, with white foam sizzling along the dark grey rocks. There wasn't much sand on this beach, only a small slip between the dunes on the rocks. One of the waves flattened, the crescendo of white foam crashing, revealing behind it a black dot on the dark blue sea.

"He's here," Kit murmured, stepping forward and squinting her eyes, looking out to the boat. At this distance, she could hardly discern a face, but the silhouette was plain to see. There was one man in the small wooden boat, rowing as fast as he could with his wooden oars, fighting the angry tide with each move he made. He had to be strong to fight such a swell all alone. Her eyes flitted up to the horizon, seeing a much larger ship that had clearly deposited the boat in the waters. The sails were turned away and unfurled as they sailed back out toward the continent, then grey mist swam forward, enveloping the ship and giving the illusion of it vanishing.

As fast as the sunlight glinted on the figure, it began to disappear. Kit hurried forward, trailing her hand along the edge of the wall as she realised what was happening. A sea mist was growing. All at once, as if a demon built of cloud was growing out of the sea itself summoned by Poseidon, everything she could see was disappearing behind the silvery cloud.

Thick like curdled whey, it stretched out from the waves toward the castle. Kit stepped back, peering over the walls again in search of Iomhar, but she lost sight of him. He was masked in the cloud, as fast as the tower was too, where Oswyn had hidden himself.

"This cannot work now," Kit muttered and strode forward, to her end of the headland. Their plan had been based on being able to find each other, and see where the boat landed, so the first person could advance toward it with two people in reserve; ready to catch Luca if he tried to escape.

Such a plan could not work. Soon, she could barely see a few feet in front of her, and had to tiptoe carefully forward, in case she stepped off the earth and out into the ocean. When she reached the end of the grass, her boots met rocks. She clambered onto them, taking one step at a time, ready to jump back if the ocean veered too high.

With this better vantage point, she tried to peer through the mist and see the boat again, but it was lost in the mist, and she had little chance of discovering if a wave had taken it to its depths, or if it had managed to reach land.

A cry pierced the air, far to her right. It lacked the depth of Iomhar's voice, but it could well have been Oswyn's. She hovered where she was for a minute, before deciding that if Oswyn were hurt, surely the most likely person to have done it was Luca, having finally reached shore.

She scrambled back off the rocks and onto the grassland, reaching out and finding the wall she had used to navigate before. She sprinted, running her hands along the lichen and moss-covered surface, aware of the coldness through her gloves as she ran. The closer she moved to the centre of the castle, the more the tower came into view, murky through the grey mist, with not a glimmer of sunlight.

Kit found a gap in the wall and stepped through, only she slipped on something, and nearly collided with the wall ahead of her. She reached out with her hands, stopping herself from falling as she looked down to find a pool of blood beneath her boots. She tried to scrape it off on a nearby tuft of moss, before a second cry pierced the air, this one much closer than the last.

She ran toward it, crossing the open end of the tower, hardly caring if she left blood-stained footprints in her wake. A cobbled-stone floor gave way to more grass, just as someone appeared in the mist.

"Oswyn?" she called out. He was on the ground, clutching his arm.

"That way. Follow him."

"Who is it?" she asked, grabbing his good arm and heaving him to his feet.

"Not Luca, another man. Kit — we are not the only ones waiting here for this Jesuit." Oswyn's words settled in her mind.

It meant that whoever had sent that coded letter to Walsingham was wrong. Either it was a trap, and men were waiting there for them, or other letters had been sent to those supposed to receive Luca.

"Aye, I am fine, Kit. Well, I will be. Go." Oswyn pushed her forward, in the direction that his attacker had run. She left Oswyn behind to tie up his wound that had cut through his fur cloak.

She was running blind, with nothing but the mist coming up to greet her. More than once did she stumble on the earth, with nooks of hidden stones and slabs hiding behind the greenery tripping her up. She held her arms out in front of her, feeling her way.

The sound of footsteps ahead was the first sign she was getting close. She reached for one of the daggers in her belt, pulling it out and cradling it in the palm of her hand.

As a figure emerged through the mist, unrecognisable with its lanky form and long hair, she was ready, only to find someone else reached him before her. The familiar shape of Iomhar jumped through the mist, draped in his belted cloak, with the pistol raised in his hand as he pointed it directly at the lanky figure's head.

"Do not move," Iomhar ordered as the stranger jerked straight, not moving another inch. "Kit?" he called through the mist.

"I'm here," she said, approaching behind him. The brief touch to his arm made him flinch and turn his head to the side, startled to find her so close.

"Down to the sea. The boat — it's arriving now," he said. "Go."

She didn't need telling twice. She turned, glancing back just long enough to see Iomhar strike the figure with the back of his gun. Hurrying across the ground, she felt it begin to slip away beneath her. Grass became dunes, with seagrass reaching up to her hips. Her boots clomped through the sand, getting closer to the rocks where the ocean crashed ahead.

The first sign she had of the boat coming nearer was the sea spray hitting her face. She stepped back, nearly slipping on the water-coated rocks, as a boat slapped on a final wave and clattered onto the rocks. Through the mist, a figure threw the oars off the boat then swung himself over the bow, with his leather-sandaled feet landing in the water and the white foam reaching up to his thighs, soaking his black robes.

Kit lifted the dagger as she approached, creeping forward this time, with the sounds of her boots in the shallows muffled by the loud waves.

The figure draped in black kicked the boat out to the ocean, not bothering trying to pull it fully onto shore, as a clue that some stranger had landed in England. He picked up one oar and threw it in after the boat, but as he reached for the second, he held the oar above his head, falling still as his head twitched to the side.

Kit's next step in the water was heard, for the oar swung toward her, the wooden plank heading for her face. Kit dived away, marginally missing the hit as she heard the wood swish through the wind. She jumped, lifting the dagger as she moved toward him, taking hold of the loose black cowl robe around his chest and using it to drag him forward. She pulled him off balance, forcing him to drop the oar as she placed the dagger at the tip of his throat.

"Gregorio Luca?" she asked, holding him in place as a wave splashed around their knees.

His face appeared as the sun began to glimmer through the mist. He was younger than she had expected, a man not dissimilar to her own age, but his skin was haggard and tanned from time in the sun. The dark eyes were almost black, and the head was shaved, revealing ears that stuck out the side of his head like breaded cobs. His pale lips curled back across blackened teeth.

"You were expecting me?" he asked, his Italian accent making the words sharp.

The sound of a wave came nearer. Kit flicked her eyes toward it, the fear of the water palpable. With the foam crashing toward them above her head height, she stumbled back, trying to drag Luca with her. She felt his fingers grab the sleeve of her doublet, trying to take the dagger from her hand.

Kit gritted her teeth, turning the dagger toward him, not afraid to injure him to stop the assassin from taking her weapon. She managed to nick the blade against his skin, but he backed her up further as the wave came toward them. She reached out, grabbing his robe around his neck, to try and stay standing, but one final shove to her chest sent her backward, falling to the stones with her head hitting a rock.

Stars filled her vision as something came away in her hand, something cold and wet to the touch, then the wave crashed, swaddling her in the dark green ocean.

## CHAPTER 13

Kit's arms were bound to her side from the sheer strength of the water. The insipid green filled her vision, tinged at the edge with white foam, making the misty sky seem a long distance off.

Her head was struck under the water — she rolled over, trying to cower away from the pain, but the wave merely rolled her further, pushing her like a toy spindle along the bottom of the ocean floor, along the stones and shingle. When she reached out, trying to grab for the surface and claw herself free, she no longer saw her red-gloved hand reaching upwards; she saw a tubby little hand instead, the fingers no longer than a baby's.

Kit tried to push the image away. She didn't need the memory to plague her now, but there was something about the cold water that made the image feel real, recalling what it was like the first time she had been plunged in water.

She kicked out, remembering everything Iomhar had taught her about how to swim, but the tide was too great. As fast as she pumped her arms forward, one after the other, trying to swim back to the shore or to the surface, whichever was the nearest, she was pulled backward again. The ocean had its liquid fingers in her clothes and was dragging her back, away from the stones.

The faster she pumped her arms, the more tired she grew, but she didn't give up. She kept swimming, heaving her body forward, clamping her mouth shut in the effort not to breathe in any of the salted water. When she squinted up, trying to see how close she was to the surface, she didn't see the mist or the castle on the land, she saw a figure above her.

It was the same one from her dream, the one that was bending down toward her. This time, when its hand pierced the surface of the water, reaching for her, she saw more of the fingers. They was gnarled, suggesting a little age. The nails were manicured, but they were short, and the thickness of the fingers suggested it was a man's hand.

Her tiny body had given up fighting, abandoned trying to swim, as the man's hand clasped over her little wrist, and she was wrenched forward, toward the surface.

The image vanished as Kit kicked harder, this time managing to make contact with the stones beneath her and use them to propel herself upward. She broke through the surface of the ocean, breathing deeply, treading water as she flicked her head back and forth. The mist was still thick, making the castle but a shadow. Along its embankment of what was once battlements and was now just earth and sand dunes, she could see shadows moving, many of them.

They were not alone. She saw a shadow she thought was Iomhar's, tall with the usual cloak belted around the waist. Suddenly he was struck to the side, knocked off a wall.

Kit tried to swim forward, her eyes set on the point where Iomhar had fallen. With the hiss of a wave behind her, this time she was thrust forward, and she used that momentum to kick harder, until she was washed up on the stones, her hands clinging to a great grey rock that sat amongst the others, sharp and sticking out like a giant's tooth thrown onto the shingle.

The wave faded back from her, loosening its watery fingers from her clothes, leaving her drenched and panting as she clung onto the rock, embracing it. She lifted one hand, finding there was something clutched between her fingers. Made of wood and tiny glass beads, the long string had ended up wound round her hand in the waves.

When she had tried to grab Gregorio Luca, taking hold of the smock around his neck and dragging him forward, she had unwittingly grabbed hold of his rosary beads, and in their scuffle had torn it from his neck. She didn't have long to peer at the beads, or the cross made of amber for the waves were hissing behind her again.

She scrambled forward, barely escaping the next wave as she crawled across the stones, reaching the dunes as quickly as she could. Once her hands were buried within the long grasses, feeling each strand as if they were feathers between her fingers, she looked up, searching for the shadows that had been chasing one another through the mist.

A bundle of shadows were moving away, across the castle, further into the mist. Two shadows were walking toward Kit. The tell-tale silhouette of Iomhar was one of them, whilst the other was holding onto his own arm, stumbling forward.

"Iomhar?" Kit called as she tried to stand amongst the dunes.

Iomhar ran forward, leaving behind the other person, running faster when Kit could eventually make out his face.

"What happened — och! God's blood, ye seem to have a habit of ending up in water, do ye not?" he cried, reaching for her. Kit held up the rosary, about to show him what she had in her grasp when she felt his hands close over her arms, dragging her even further away from the dunes.

"I am well, Iomhar," but as she said the words, she coughed, spluttering up more water. He clapped her on the back, freeing her lungs from the water that lingered at the edges, making her wince with pain. "Ah! You could do that a bit lighter!"

"Ye want to choke on water, do ye?" He quipped as he turned her round again. "What happened?"

"Gregorio Luca," she said, thrusting the rosary forward for him to focus on instead of her. "Let us say he was eager not to be caught. I took this off him."

"Aye, the man we are looking for then." He glanced down at the rosary, though not for long before he looked back up to Kit. "There were too many of them."

"How many?" she asked.

"Six at least!" Oswyn's voice called. Kit spun round to see Oswyn staggering the last few steps toward the two of them, still holding his bleeding arm. "If you ask me, pet, I think they were waiting for us."

"Aye, I think ye are right," Iomhar said, walking past Kit and pulling the belt free of his waist. He slapped the leather around Oswyn's arm, making the man stumble forward, his eyes going wide.

"Off with you, man!" Oswyn tried to pull his arm free.

"Ye want the bleeding to stop? Be still, ye tadger."

"What does that mean?" Kit asked.

"Do not ask," Iomhar said, with a smirk that only she saw. Oswyn looked ready to argue again, but Iomhar tightened the belt around his arm, latching over the cut that had been left there by one of the men who had attacked. "There, that should do until we get ye some stitches."

Oswyn turned purple at the words and angled his head away.

"Six of them," Kit muttered as she stumbled down the last of the dune bank, walking into the mist. "Are they gone?"

"Aye," Iomhar called, following her.

"They were waiting for us. They were ready."

"The letter Walsingham's man intercepted, the one telling the man who was supposed to meet Luca where to go. It cannot have been the only letter. He had a welcome party waiting for him, and if I am not wrong…" Iomhar paused, urging Kit to look back to him. "I think they were waiting for us too."

"A trap?"

"Not necessarily a trap," he faltered, shaking his head. "Yet they knew we were coming. They were hiding, waiting for that mist to fall before they came out."

"What do we do now?" Oswyn asked, his face pale as he hastened after them. "Dunstanburgh was all we had."

"Then pick up your feet and we will go after them." Kit urged him on, striding forward to cross the castle and reach the other side.

"Oh, aye, you expect to be able to track a man through these hills?" Oswyn scoffed, shaking his head as he examined Iomhar's work with the belt on his arm.

"Every man leaves tracks, nay matter how hard they try to cover them up." Iomhar pushed Oswyn forward, gentler than Kit had seen him do before, urging him to follow.

"It is not so easy out here. The wind changes, then the earth and grass change direction with it. You want to track them like you're hunting a stag? You are a greater fool than I thought."

Kit opened her mouth, ready to object when she reached the other side of the castle, striding out onto the track road, with a muddied path and the earth cambering at the side. The mist was beginning to lift, and she could see the empty fence posts where they had tied their horses.

"God's blood," she muttered.

"What is it?"

"Well, I have to agree with Oswyn. For one thing, tracking a man on horseback is very difficult when you do not have a horse yourself." She gestured to the empty spot in the road where their horses had been before, wrapping her arms around her as the wind whistled off the ocean and buffeted her still dripping hair.

"I was right," Iomhar accepted with a sigh, moving to the place where they had left their horses and bending down to the earth to examine the tracks.

"About what?" she asked.

"When I told Walsingham this is not the task he thinks it is." He looked up to her, finding her gaze with his. "Gregorio Luca is here for a reason. They are prepared, they're organised, and it will not be as easy to find him as Walsingham thinks."

Kit looked at the rosary beads in her hand, twizzling the beads between her wet fingers as more salted water ran off her palms. She had a feeling Iomhar could be right.

## CHAPTER 14

"Feeling better?" Iomhar asked as Kit stepped out of her chamber door. She was so startled to find him close in the corridor that she jumped and promptly dropped the candle she had been carrying.

They had returned to Oswyn's house in Alnwick, where she'd had to bathe and change following her dip in the water earlier that day. With the early nights pulling in, it would still be a while before she retired for the night, forcing her back into the warmest doublet she could find in her saddlebags.

"Can you not announce yourself or something?" Kit asked as she bent down in the darkness and scrambled to pick up the brass holder.

"Made ye jump?"

"No, I just felt like dropping the candle for the amusement of it. I rather like grappling around in the darkness," she said wryly as she searched the floorboards. She found the brass holder and reached for the candle, finding the warm tallow stick beneath her fingers, only another hand touched it at the same time, and Kit reared back, jumping again.

"Aye, ye are as jumpy as a new-born deer. It's only me." Iomhar picked up the candle and stood to his feet, his footsteps on the floorboards the only indication that he was walking away from her, down the corridor. Kit followed, using her hands on the walls either side of her to track her path in the darkness.

In the distance in the sitting room, she watched as he struck a flint in a tinder box, the spark jumping to life like a shooting star as it was lifted to the wick of the tallow candle, casting dark orange flames across Iomhar's features. He placed the candle in a new brass holder beside him and turned to face Kit, his eyes narrowing when he found her.

"Ye sure ye're all right? Ye have not looked the same since ye've been in the water."

"I am fine," she said, her voice coming out slightly sharper than she had intended it to.

"Kit ... ye do not have to pretend ye are not afraid of it —"

"Can we stop talking about this?" She turned away from him and circled the room, feeling the floorboards creak beneath her feet as she reached for Gregorio Luca's rosary that she had placed on the mantelpiece above the fire. "Where is Oswyn?"

"I left him with a physician, squealing like a sow as they put the sutures in his arm."

Kit pressed the boards beneath her feet, listening to them creak.

"What are ye doing? Dancing?"

She didn't answer at first, she was too busy repeating the movement.

"Where do Jesuits go when they know they are at risk of being discovered?" She turned on the spot and pressed the boards again, making clear her meaning. Iomhar nodded slowly.

"Well, we pulled out that priest beneath the floor of Farleigh Hungerford Castle. The wee man above only knows how he bore being pressed in that darkness for so long."

"Exactly. A priest hole." She stopped creaking the floor. "Gregorio Luca will be looking for somewhere to hide."

"I'm not done asking if ye are all right, and ye are already moving back to the task at hand?"

"Yes!" she argued firmly, looking away and winding the rosary beads around her wrist. She heard Iomhar sigh, though she didn't ask why. "It is what we are here for, Iomhar, is it not?"

"Hmm." It was the only answer he gave as she continued to twist and play with the rosary, admiring how some of them were made of coloured glass and others of wood, painted in different hues.

"We need to know what Catholic families there are round here, what castles and manor houses where Luca is likely to find someone to take him in." Kit's voice was full of purpose as she turned away from the fireplace, lifting the rosary and placing it around her neck.

"Ye intend to wear that thing?"

"I am not going to leave it here, am I? What if someone thinks Oswyn is a secret Catholic?" She tucked the rosary beneath the collar of her doublet. This one was the colour of sand, made of light tan leather that was soft, yet adorned with black embroidery across the torso and back, shaped to look like kestrels with their beady eyes staring out from the leather.

Iomhar looked up from the rosary at her neck and ran a hand through his hair, huffing about something, though before she could ask what was upsetting him, he spoke again.

"I know someone in this area. Someone who is good at asking questions. If I can get a message to them, aye, maybe they can tell us which families and houses we should be looking at to find a priest hole." He moved to the edge of the room, reaching for a cabinet where Oswyn had placed some parchment with quills and inkwells.

"Who is it?" Kit asked, her eyes following him across the room.

He smiled a little and looked up in response. "Allow me a few secrets, Kit."

"You have many ... bampot," she added the last playful insult with a smile, seeing the way it made his smile greater.

"I think ye rather like that Scottish insult."

"Well, it is useful at times."

He wrote his letter hurriedly, finishing it with a scrawl that did not resemble his name, but was more like his initials, I. B., for Iomhar Blackwood.

"I'll go now. Before Oswyn comes back."

"You still do not trust Oswyn, do you?" Kit asked, following him as he hurried out of the door. "He works for Walsingham, remember?"

"As I don't trust Walsingham as much as ye do, allow me some doubts. Even if they prove to be unfounded."

She followed him out of the house and into the darkened streets of Alnwick town. At this time of the evening, people were still up, using the light of the moon and torches that were burning in the streets to guide their way.

"Will you tell me where we are going?" Kit asked.

"I'm going. Ye are following." Iomhar turned down another street, away from the main track road where people were wandering to candlelit taverns for refreshments. They walked all the way to the edge of town, where the tall narrow buildings faded away into small, cobbled cottages with thatched roofs that sat along the bank of the River Aln.

Iomhar held up a hand, silently asking Kit to wait a minute. They crept back through the darkness under the cover of a copse of oak trees, for there were no torches in these parts, only a handful of tallow candles that were placed in cottage windows and in the open doorway of a stable to a coaching inn. Kit waited, her eyes dancing across the darkened river beneath the bridge that connected them to the hills beyond the town. Resembling treacle, the river's surface was blackened by the night sky.

"Wait for it," Iomhar whispered, earning her gaze and nodding his head toward the stable. She peered past him, watching as two elderly men exited the stable, laughing about something as they stumbled together down the track road.

"I thought you wanted someone to deliver your message? They are leaving."

"Aye, but they are old, look rather drunk, and are likely to let their tongues run away with them if they are given enough ale for the task. They are not the messengers I want." He turned his head back to the stable as a young lad stepped forward. Somewhere in his adolescent years, the lad was humming to himself, lazily scratching at the spots on his chin as he finished tidying up the stable for the night. "That is the one I want. Wait here."

"Why?" she asked, stepping out to follow him.

"Because I want the lad focusing on this," he said, holding up the letter in his hand. "Not asking why a bonnie lass is dressed like a man. I'm tired of people asking me that question."

"Oi!" she said, but before she could reprimand him anymore, he had left her side and walked to the stable.

Kit skulked in the shadows, watching as Iomhar moved toward the boy, proffering the letter in one hand and some coins in the other. The lad nodded eagerly, reaching to tack up a horse as fast as he could with a fresh saddle and reins. As he pulled away from the stable and galloped across the bridge, off into the night, Kit stepped out of the shadows, toward where Iomhar was lit by the moon.

"What did you say to him?" she asked.

"I told him the letter was in the service of this country, and he mustn't breathe a word of it to anyone. Fortunately, he believed me. That's the thing about young men over old men, they still have hope."

"You are a cynic."

"Grow a little older first, Kit. See more of the world, ye can tell me I'm a cynic then."

## CHAPTER 15

"It's been two days, and that is all they send in reply?" Kit asked, taking the parchment out of Iomhar's hand and waving it in the air in amazement. "Two numbers and two letters?" She looked at the yellowed note once again, seeing the simply scrawled handwriting that read *1. 2. B. B.*

"I thought ye were supposed to be a codebreaker," Iomhar said, snatching the parchment back out of her hand. He folded it up and slipped it through his jerkin, into a hidden pocket. "Ye want to find out what it means?"

"No, I prefer the unknown," she answered drily, folding her arms.

"Then fetch your horse," Iomhar said with a smile, hearing her hidden meaning.

They were standing outside Oswyn's townhouse. It was a bright day, with the sun lifting over Alnwick Castle on the far side of town and casting the narrow timber buildings in a deep amber light. As Iomhar walked off, Kit glanced up to where Oswyn was still in the upper rooms

"Should we not take Oswyn?"

"Nay, definitely not," Iomhar called from down the road, prompting Kit to spin on her heel in the dirt and hurry to catch up with him, diving around the early-morning risers of the town who had all risen to face the dawning sun.

"You don't think he will wonder where we have gone?"

"I told him we had an errand to run for Walsingham, a message ye had to deliver to a man north of the border. When I said it was to do with border patrols, he appeared thoroughly bored and muttered something about being nay better than a donkey in Walsingham's stable."

"You mean you tried to make it sound dull."

"It worked," Iomhar declared happily as they reached the end of the road and the coaching inn where they had purchased fresh horses after their last ones had been taken. "Now, we do not have long. If we're going to make it there and back before Oswyn asks too many questions, we need to go now."

"Would it matter so much if Oswyn knew where we were going? You are going to have to start trusting him someday." Kit walked into the stable first, reaching for the tall grey she had purchased. The mare leaned toward her, nuzzling her nose against Kit's shoulder in greeting. "He is not as bad as you think."

"Ye are merely saying that because he gave ye marchpane last night at supper. I have never seen ye smile so much."

"It's marchpane! Who doesn't smile at that?"

Her words were met with laughter as they busied themselves preparing the horses. Within minutes, they were ready to go, with their boots in the stirrups and their horses' noses turned toward the bridge over the River Aln. "Still no clues as to where we are going?" Kit asked as they reached the stone bridge.

"Aye, I'm beginning to reappraise my view of ye as a skilled codebreaker. Nay clues, Kit. Figure it out alone."

She scrunched up her nose and reached for a pebble, no bigger than a bumble bee, that she found balanced on the top of the stone wall of the bridge, bending away from the saddle to pick it up, then she threw it in Iomhar's direction. He chuckled and barely managed to dodge it in time.

"One. Two." Kit recalled the numbers she had read on the parchment, chewing her lip as she realised what it had meant. "Midday."

"Aye! Ye have half the note now."

Kit steered her horse to follow Iomhar's as it rained. Starting out as small drops, it was soon coming down in sheets, practically raining sideways and battering Kit's face, much to her grey mare's complaint who snorted and hung her nose a little lower toward the ground.

"I hope whoever we are meeting is worth riding through this!" she called to be heard above the rain. They had long since left Alnwick town far behind and were riding through tall hills. They had passed through a forest that had sheltered them from the first drips of the rain, but now the sky was darkening, and the rain fell like long needles. They were far away from any shelter, crossing over bare green hills with only a few wayward trees and stones covered in dappled moss around them.

"Aye, I hope so too," Iomhar said, gritting his teeth and angling the horse forward.

"Who is it we are meeting?"

"Ye'll have to wait to see that."

Kit huffed another time and pulled her hat out from in her doublet, hooking the tanned leather cap over her forehead to try to cover her hair from the rain, though it did a miserable job. Within minutes, she was sodden, the rain chilling her bones through the tanned leather doublet and her black hose, right down to the boots where water was running off the pointed toe caps. She was soon shivering, burying her fingers deeper within the red leather gloves.

"Is it colder in the Scottish Highlands than it is here?"

"Aye," Iomhar called back to her, glancing at her over his shoulder as he angled their horses up another hill, walking parallel to an old farming wall that appeared disused and falling down. "Ye've been to Edinburgh."

"That was the summer."

"Are ye cold?"

"Let's just say remind me never to go to Scotland in the winter."

Iomhar laughed and turned back. "We are nearly there now."

"Where is 'there'?" she asked, but she didn't get an answer. The rain came down harder, cloaking the hills in a misty carpet of grey and the sound muffled their voices.

The closer they moved to the top of the hill Kit saw something appearing in the distance. Crouched down between two hills was an old farmhouse, different to any other she had seen, blackened as though by fire, with the land empty around it and part of the roof missing.

"What is that?" She practically had to shout to Iomhar to be heard.

"A bastle," Iomhar called. "Fortified farm. Your animals are on the ground floor at night, and your farmer sleeps above."

"It looks disused."

"That will be from the reiving." Iomhar paused, seeing her frown of confusion. "Consider it like a raid. Northumberland is not a peaceful place, nay more so than the furthest reaches of Scotland. Aye, as the clans raid each other, so do the graynes of Northumberland. Barrowburn has not fared well with the reiving. Those that lived here moved out years ago, tired of every day being a battle."

"Barrowburn ... B. B. Those were the initials in the letter you were given." Kit wrinkled her nose and moved her horse alongside Iomhar's, feeling a darkness had descended on the land as she looked to the cloud-clad horizon. "Dangerous place?" she asked.

"Aye, not a man whose lived in these parts who would not agree."

"Then how do you know of this place?" Her question made Iomhar look toward her with a small smile. "Another secret?"

"Aye, another secret." He nodded then pointed ahead. "Ye'll be rather pleased though, Kit. One of my secrets is about to be unearthed."

Kit followed his gesture and looked further up the hill. At the very top, there was a figure, though they were not standing on the ground waiting for them. They had climbed one lonely tree at the top of the hill and were sat on the bare branch that shivered in the winter breeze, with their hand over their eyes, clearly shielding their gaze from the rain.

"Iomhar!" the figure called, betraying a deep voice as his other arm lifted from the branch and waved.

Iomhar urged his horse forward sharply, galloping up the last stretch of the hill. Kit had to scramble to chase, following a few steps behind on her mare. As they reached the very top, the stranger sat on the branch jumped down.

"Well, ye didn't mention ye were bringing someone with ye," a Scottish voice said, making Kit dart her head to the side in surprise.

By the time she reached Iomhar's horse, he had already clambered down from the saddle and walked toward the figure they were meeting. He was almost as tall as Iomhar, with longer hair the colour of cinnamon, tied loosely at the nape of his neck. The two of them clasped hands, then they embraced.

As Kit went to climb down from her horse, the sight of seeing Iomhar embrace the man made her fall, landing awkwardly on her ankle and letting out a little yelp of surprise.

"That didn't sound like a man," the stranger said, pulling a laugh from Iomhar.

"That would be because she is nay man. Kit?" Iomhar called to her.

She walked round the horses and stepped toward the two men; seeing them standing side by side felt a little odd. In many ways, they were different. Different hair, different features in the face, but their figures were the same and the eyes were a similar shade of piercing green.

"Kit, this is Niall." Iomhar gestured to the man who bowed in greeting to her.

"Niall?" Kit repeated, remembering where she had heard the name before. Iomhar had mentioned it once when they were standing by a painting in Iomhar's house, looking at the portrait of his family. "Your brother?" she asked, crossing the last distance toward them.

"I'm honoured he mentioned me at all," Niall said, extending his hand toward Kit. As the rain began to ease, she took his hand to shake, aware of the way Niall had narrowed his eyes on her. "Is this the lass ye mentioned in your letters to our mother?"

"Aye, it is," Iomhar confirmed, not lifting his eyes to Kit.

"You mentioned me?" Kit raised her eyebrows, unable to keep the smile from her face.

"I see ye every day. It would be hard not to mention ye." He shrugged off the matter, though Kit did not miss the way Niall clapped Iomhar's shoulder.

"Aye, that must be the reason," Niall declared, smiling. "It's not very often ye come this far north these days, brother. Why are ye here?"

"A commission," Iomhar answered simply. "We are looking for someone. I hope ye can help us with that."

"Well, I came all the way down from the border, so I'm hoping I can too. First, let's get out of this rain. Ye've seen the bastle?" Niall asked, pointing to the decrepit fortified farmhouse that was falling apart.

"Aye."

"It's empty, apart from a fire and some old wood we can throw on it to keep warm. Let's head there, I do not fancy my bones turning to icicles out in this weather."

"What happened here? A fire?" Kit asked, stepping through a door that was hanging off its hingers into the lower floor of the bastle. The stone walls had but one window set high in the corner that let a feeble amount of grey light into the room, revealing the walls were blackened and the staircase was barely still intact, burnt to a carcass of what it must have once been.

"Aye," Niall said, following her into the bastle and shaking the water off his clothes the way a dog shuddered coming out of the rain. "The latest woes between the graynes in these parts. The place was burnt to a cinder, and the family retreated."

Kit felt something pressed against her back, she flinched away, realising Iomhar was encouraging her to the side as he reached for a brass bucket in the corner of the room that was blackened by ash. Niall raised his eyebrows at her, making her look quickly away.

"They kept their animals here?" she asked, pointing to the mess of burnt straw and where empty troughs sat at the side of the room.

"Ye could not leave the animals out in the wilderness. They'd be rustled." Niall moved toward the old staircase. "I'd say we would be more comfortable up the stairs, but aye, getting up there does not sound particularly easy."

Kit walked toward the staircase, looking up to the gap in the floorboards above. Some of them had been burnt away, vanished from one side of the building, revealing a somewhat cavernous ceiling, but the other side was intact.

"Get that fire going, Iomhar, before I freeze!" Niall rubbed his hands together and crossed the floor toward his brother.

"I should be the one ordering ye around, little brother," Iomhar said with a smile and started making up the fire regardless.

"All right, keep your dirk straight. I'm helping." Niall bent down beside him and started to help with the firewood.

"What's a dirk?" Kit asked distractedly, her eyes still on the staircase, wondering how to get to the top floor. When a laugh came from the other side of the room, she looked to the men, seeing Niall sniggering.

"It means a dagger, Kit," Iomhar answered, his face perfectly plain. She shook her head, realising the innuendo of the humour and reached for the wall. "What are ye doing?"

"Climbing," she replied simply. Avoiding the staircase completely, in case it fell beneath her, she began to scale the wall, clambering up the cobbled structure and reaching to the gap in the ceiling.

"She climbs like a cat!"

"I know. She broke into Edinburgh Castle that way once."

"By scaling that tall wall? Ye must be jesting."

"I would have said so too, had I not seen her escape the same way."

Kit ignored the rest of the conversation, taking hold of the floorboards above and heaving herself up onto the surface. Once settled, she looked around the room, finding it sparse and fire damaged on one side. Near to where she crouched there were the remnants of where a family had lived with beds that were used, harvest jugs on their side, cracked and broken, and chamber pots rusting.

Kit slowly stood to her feet and walked across the boards, wandering the room and examining each thing in detail.

"Be careful up there," Iomhar called to her.

"I am not a child, Iomhar."

"Do ye want to fall through the floorboards? They're already missing on one side."

"Ye two always argue like this?" Niall's voice from far below made Kit freeze in her wanderings.

"Aye." Iomhar sighed. "She will not listen to reason. Or good sense."

"I heard that."

"Ye were meant to. She has a habit of jumping in without thinking."

"I heard that too!"

"Any tables and chairs up there? I don't fancy sitting on the straw," Niall asked.

"That's because not all of it is straw." Iomhar kicked away something blackened around him, perhaps something left behind from when the animals were brought into the lower floor.

"Some." Kit set to work, carefully retrieving three small stools and a tiny table to pass through the gap, with Niall taking each one and handing it to Iomhar to set up in the corner furthest away from the fire damage.

With the last stool passed down, Kit hesitated as something caught her eye. Slowly, she straightened up and moved to where a window should have been, but a hole just existed, half covered with grey woollen tartan. Placed within a crevice in the wall was a cross, plain dark brown wood, with no ornament. It felt Protestant in structure, had it not been for the gem placed into the back, a gleaming bright silver. She lifted the cross and held it high in the air, examining the spindly stem in the light that filtered through the woollen tartan.

"Are there many Catholics in these parts?" Kit called.

"Nay. Why?" Iomhar asked, his face appearing in one of the gaps in the floorboards.

"When was the fire?"

"Last winter. I know," Niall called with a hiss. "I know the family that were forced out."

"Someone has been here since then." Kit walked toward the gap, showing Iomhar what she had found.

"A jewelled cross?" He held the glimmer of a smile. "Aye, only a Catholic would have that." His words seemed to change things as Niall appeared sharply in the gap beside his brother, his eyes narrowed.

"Catholics sneaking around Northumbria? Nay, that cannot be good."

"That's what we're here to talk about," Iomhar said, still looking up at Kit.

"Nay, Iomhar. We're supposed to have a handle on this area. It is my position to."

"What do you mean your position? What do you do?" Kit asked.

"I'm a Captain in the Scottish army," Niall revealed, standing a little taller. "I patrol the border between England and Scotland."

Kit dropped down to the lower floor, jumping back when she found herself face to face with Iomhar, and he was standing surprisingly close.

Iomhar turned away, taking one of the stools they had pulled down and sitting. "Niall, we need to talk about what ye know of the area."

"Catholics, aye, ask your questions," Niall said, taking the stool opposite him. Kit sat too, between them on one side of the table, taking off her tan-leather cap and squeezing out the dregs of water until it dribbled on the burnt straw floor.

"We are looking for someone. A Jesuit arrived this week on Northumbrian shores."

"Well known?" Niall asked.

"Aye, Gregorio Luca." The name seemed to mean nothing to Niall who shook his head.

"If ye think I may know where he is, I'm afraid I have to disappoint ye."

"Nay, that would have been too much to hope for." Iomhar leaned forward, resting his elbows on the table. "As ye said, it's your position to know who the Catholics in this land are. The big names, the wealthy families, who are they?"

"We are looking for someone who can offer him shelter." Kit took up the thread of conversation, attempting to place her tanned cap back on her head before realising it was a pointless endeavour and dropping it onto the table, squeezing the water out of her short locks instead. "A priest hole, perhaps."

"There I can help ye," Niall said. He leaned forward, resting his elbows on the table in much the same way Iomhar did. The similarity made Kit dart her gaze between them. "There are many families in these parts. Aye, it's been twelve years since the last Earl of Northumberland was beheaded for plotting against Queen Bess. A staunch Catholic, he was. He sought to put Mary Stuart on the throne. He was offered to be saved from execution if he renounced his faith, but he refused."

"He's long dead though," Iomhar muttered, shifting in his seat. "We're looking for people alive now, Niall."

"The Drakes, aye, they are thought to be Catholic, but though they have their reputation, they do not have the wealth nor the wherewithal to house a Jesuit priest at the moment." Niall was thinking aloud, sitting back and looking up to the ceiling in thought. "There's Lord Waters, but he renounced Catholicism nearly twenty years ago."

"Did he mean it?" Kit asked.

"Well, we do not know for sure either way, but there is nay evidence to suggest he went back." Niall paused, with his eyes flicking to Iomhar, his face abruptly set into sharper lines.

"What is it?" Iomhar asked. "Ye have had a thought."

"Can ye always read my mind? He's always been that way, even since we were bairns," Niall said, turning to Kit.

"What was he like as a child, or a 'bairn' as you say?" Kit asked, leaning forward.

"Ha! She's looking for stories about ye."

"Now is really not the time." Iomhar leant forward in the same manner Kit had done, though his voice was firmer. "Tell me the thought, Niall, before she wheedles a tale out of ye."

"Aye, very well." Niall held up his hands in surrender. "There is one family that comes to mind, they claim they are Protestant these days, though they have always been something of a mystery, and we know for certain their recent forefathers were Catholic, much favoured by Queen Bess's older Catholic sister."

"Who?" Iomhar asked, clearly growing impatient.

"I speak of the younger brother of the first man I mentioned. The Earl of Northumberland, Lord Henry Percy. He has been in and out of the Tower of London these last ten years on suspicion of being complicit with Mary Stuart's aims. I believe he is at Petworth now, but his son, another Henry, is in the castle whose shadow ye are currently residing in. Alnwick Castle."

Kit shifted in her seat, looking to Iomhar.

"Ye believe they are Catholic?" Iomhar asked.

"I certainly believe it, despite what they say. The current earl has been to the Tower too many times for me to disbelieve it, each time because he has looked on Mary Stuart favourably. It is my opinion that it will not be long before he is back in the Tower, maybe this time facing the executioner."

"Do ye have any evidence the rest of the family residing at the castle are practising Catholics now?" Iomhar asked.

"Nay, but I did hear of something the other week relating to them which will interest ye. Of their encounter with a man ye and I always like to keep an eye on."

Kit was aware of the mood around the table shifting. Iomhar sat back in his seat and rested his hands over his weapon's belt, with one palm resting on the wheellock pistol and one on the hilt of his rapier.

"Go on," Iomhar prompted him.

"Lord Ruskin passed into the Northumbrian border not three weeks ago." Niall's voice became much more solemn than Kit had yet heard it. She knew Lord Ruskin was the man believed to have killed Iomhar's father. "He was not here long before he crossed back into Scotland, retreating before any soldier could find him and ask him about his wife's recent exploits in London. Yet I spoke to one man who claimed he saw Lord Ruskin going into Alnwick Castle."

"You are certain of this?" Kit asked.

"Nay," Niall muttered quietly, "but it is possible the man was telling the truth."

Iomhar muttered a curse and stood to his feet, so sharply that the stool fell backward and collided with the floor, sending burnt straw everywhere.

"Iomhar, it could be a coincidence —" Niall's voice was rather desperate as he stood, leaning over the table, but Iomhar's sharp about turn with a wayward hand silenced him. The movement being perfectly clear in asking for quiet.

"Aye, what are the chances that a Catholic man like Lord Ruskin, a known figure to plot against the queen, would be in the same county but three weeks before a Jesuit priest arrives?"

"An assassin at that," Kit mumbled, much more inclined to agree with Iomhar.

"An assassin?" Niall repeated, his body going stiff. "Ye mean ... this Gregorio Luca isn't just a priest?"

"He's a priest that worships blood as much as he does God, Niall," Iomhar said as he paced up and down, rubbing his face in his stress. "Nay, I cannot believe that is a coincidence. If Lord Ruskin came here, then it must be connected."

"There is nay point jumping to conclusions. It is a suspicion only. Search Alnwick Castle. If ye find the Jesuit, then ye know it is connected, but ye cannot be certain until then." Niall was still pleading with his brother, but Iomhar didn't seem to take notice. His mind was made up and the expression was darkened. "Kit, ye help me to persuade him not to run away with the idea."

"Why?" Kit asked.

"Something tells me ye have more power over him than I do."

"You are his brother, so that is unlikely," she said, standing to her feet as well. "I also agree with him. Under three weeks? That does seem like too much of a coincidence."

"Then we are agreed?" Iomhar asked. "We will search Alnwick Castle, but if we find this Jesuit there, lord help Lord Ruskin when I get my hands on him."

"After what he did to our father, if he faces any of us again, he'll end up in the same sorry state." Niall's words made Kit back away from the table, looking between the two brothers' faces that were set in stone.

# CHAPTER 16

"Time to go." Iomhar strode out of the bastle first, leaving Kit to follow with her arms folded and her eyes set on his back, thinking of the darkness that had been in his features when speaking of Lord Ruskin. Niall followed alongside him, clapping him on the shoulder to try and offer some comfort, but it clearly did little use, especially when the mere mention of Lord Ruskin's name seemed to make Niall as angry as it did Iomhar.

Kit followed them out beyond the old farm wall to where their horses were tacked up with their reins looped over loose stones. Kit turned to her horse first, about to place her foot in the stirrup, when she heard Niall speak again.

"Write to our mother and brother more often. Duncan may be turning into a grouch in his old age, but being Earl of Ross is not a task to make the happiest of men."

"What —?" Kit whipped her head round as she threaded her foot into the stirrup, but in her alarm, she had pushed down on the horse, spooking it enough to jump forward a couple of steps, sending Kit flying onto her back with her foot caught in the stirrup. She came to a stop a second later, with her head flat on the grass, staring up at the grey sky that had at last stopped raining with her hands bundled in the earth and one foot still high above her, connected to the horse.

"Now, before I laugh, did ye hurt yourself?" Iomhar appeared above her. He was standing directly over her head, bending with his hands on his knees, looking at her upside down.

"No," she said, huffing from being winded.

"Good." Iomhar cracked a smile as laughter guffawed from nearby. Kit didn't need to look around to know it was Niall, for his laughter was deep, not dissimilar to Iomhar's own. "Care to tell me what surprised ye so?" Iomhar asked, walking to release her foot from the stirrup. As he took hold of her boot, she snapped it out of his hold and hurried to her knees, jumping up as he reached to help her up.

"An earl! That's what he said. Your older brother is an earl?"

"Ah ... ye hadn't told her that part?" Niall asked, earning both of their gazes.

"What? Was her reaction so subtle that ye need me to answer that question?" Iomhar asked, still smiling.

"True." Niall laughed and turned back to his horse. "Perhaps I should leave ye two to your argument."

"We're not arguing." Kit flicked her head back to Iomhar. "Not yet anyway. You never said your brother was an earl!"

"It's not exactly easy to slip into conversation."

"I asked you once if your family had money, and your rough answer was something along the lines of 'a little'."

"A little?" Niall scoffed as he pulled himself up onto the saddle over his chestnut horse. "Our mother would roll her eyes if she were here."

"Does that mean you have a title?" Kit asked.

"Nay title." Iomhar shook his head.

"Seeing him in a new light, lass?" Niall asked.

"Have ye not caused enough trouble for one day?" Iomhar quipped in Niall's direction.

"And with that word, I'll bid ye both goodbye." Niall bowed his head toward the two of them before clicking his tongue and turning his horse around. "Kit, do us a favour and make sure Iomhar writes more often."

"I..." She couldn't quite answer, her mind was reeling too much from what she had heard.

Niall offered one last wave before tapping his heels into the horse's side and cantering away, down the slope of the hill. With him disappearing into the clouds, Kit turned her head back to Iomhar, bearing folded arms and a narrowed glare.

"What?" he asked.

"Why did you never tell me that?"

"I do not tell anyone that, Kit."

"You and your secrets!" Kit was about to snap when she felt Iomhar take her arm and steer her toward the horse. "What are you doing?"

"Ye are about to start an argument. We might as well have it on the way back to Alnwick. It gets dark early and by the time we are back, at this rate, it will be night. So, we can argue on the way."

"You are so infuriating — ah!" she yelped in surprise as he took her waist and helped her up onto the saddle of the horse. "I am perfectly capable of getting onto the horse by myself."

"Aye, I know ye are, but ye did just end up crumpled on the earth at your first attempt. I think ye are a little distracted."

"Kit, I think ye are overreacting a little here."

"It's as good as lying."

"Nay, it isn't. It is omitting."

"It is the same thing!"

"Nay, it very much is not."

Kit grumbled under her breath and turned the horse round. It was barely mid-afternoon, and the sun had already slipped down beyond the horizon, casting the sky into dark shades of purple as the last light of the day mingled with the growing night sky. The heavy cloud from the rain was lifting at last, revealing a gradually clearing sky with a few stars winking down at them.

"Why are ye stopping?" Iomhar called, having to halt his horse ahead as they reached the edge of Alnwick. Kit stopped on the far end of the bridge over the river and jumped down from her horse.

"I just want a few minutes alone."

"Why?"

Kit towed the horse to the end of the bridge, tying the reins around a post and stepping to the side to look out over the river.

"Call it time to myself," she said and strode away from him.

"Kit!" he called after her, but she did not turn around.

"Go back to the lodgings, Iomhar, I'll be there soon."

Iomhar must have accepted her request as she heard the sound of horse's hooves on the track road, moving away, and she continued down a sloping camber toward the river.

In the chill of the growing night, she wrapped the doublet collar tighter around her neck, trying to ward off the gnawing wind that scratched at her cheeks. She was uncertain how long she stood there, beside the bridge overlooking the river with her eyes watching the occasional rings appearing in the water from fish bobbing beneath the surface. Her mind felt like the tangled reeds at the side of the water, uncertain where one thought ended and another began.

She crouched down eventually, hiding herself amongst the reeds, trying to understand why it had upset her that Iomhar hadn't told her he was the son of an earl. She didn't have an answer. Instead, her mind returned to Walsingham, thinking of the way he had ushered her out of the door, with Lady Sidney smiling in the doorway, thrilled at Kit's exit.

She stood to her feet again, realising why the two thoughts were connected. They both made her feel as if she did not quite belong. She had been ousted from Walsingham's house, and she was not trusted with Iomhar's secret.

"Go back, Kit," she whispered to herself, hearing the words on the wind. "No good comes from being out here."

She had a task to do, find Gregorio Luca. Wallowing in self-pity was hardly going to help her accomplish that.

She turned away from the river, about to scramble up the slope back toward her horse when she saw a shadowy figure skulking toward her, hurrying down the bank in her direction. "Iomhar?" she called, hoping it was him, but this figure did not bear his silhouette, nor his tall height.

The stranger stepped down off the cambered slope, reaching her level on the riverbank. Wearing trousers and a loose fur jerkin, he was dressed like a labourer or farm worker.

"Who are you?" Kit asked, holding her ground. When he didn't answer, she made a move to walk around him and clamber up the slope toward the horse, when he jerked his hand. He pulled something out of his belt and in the moonlight, it glinted.

It was a long billhook that he raised in her direction.

"What do you want?" Kit demanded as she stepped back, away from the billhook. The weapon was curved at the very end, an implement that Kit had seen many times already in Northumberland, used in the fields for farming.

He advanced toward her, his grip around the wooden handle of the billhook tightening.

"I said, what do you want?" Kit asked again, this time raising her voice.

He launched himself toward her, the move so sudden that though Kit went for the dagger in her belt, she couldn't reach it in time, and ended up with her arm sandwiched between the two of them, trapped.

With the man's face pressed close to hers, in the moonlight she finally saw his features. He had to be at least fifteen years older than her, his face beginning to be haggard with age, and the brown whiskers around his chin were turning grey.

"I bring a message," he said, the Scottish accent now so familiar to Kit's ears that she froze.

"From whom?"

"A man ye have never met. He says, this is for justice."

With eyes flitting downward, Kit caught sight of something black and inked above the high collar of his fur jerkin. She had seen it before, that same tattoo with what appeared to be the horse's head risen toward the sky, and the unicorn horn atop its temple.

"Justice?" Kit repeated, watching as the billhook rose in the air, coming toward her face.

She stamped down hard on his foot, making him cry out, and elbowed his stomach, dislodging his hold on her. Kit did not fancy sticking round for the fight. He was bigger than her, stockier, and in the darkness, it could be hard to see any of the fight. She tried to run around him, flee for her horse, but she felt a hand take hold of the back of her doublet. She was wrenched backward, stumbling away until her feet splashed into the river.

With one harsh blow to his elbow, she managed to break free from his grasp, but he tackled her, forcing her down into the water.

Kit barely had time to take a breath before she fell back with the man above her. She was under the water for only a few seconds before she drove her elbow upward, into his nose, dislodging him enough for her to push her head above the water and take another breath. Yet he was stronger and reached for her another time. As he brought the billhook down, she reached out, placing one of her hands firmly over his grasp on the curved blade.

Kit was pushed down under the water again and she held her breath, barely in time. It was ice cold, but with the moonlight growing strong, she could see the billhook above her, with her hand over her attacker's trying to prise the weapon out of his grasp. As it angled down, the curved blade tipped perilously toward her nose in the water.

She shifted on the earth, digging one foot into the riverbed and lifting the other to strike between the man's legs. It was a mishit, but close enough to strike him in a painful area; he released a roar of pain and loosened his grasp on the billhook.

She snatched the billhook from his hands, using her nails for good measure to tear it free from his fingers, and pushed him off her. Rearing above the water, she stumbled on her feet, taking another deep breath as she found him coming for her again. When he reached for the billhook, she veered her arm backward to push it out of his reach, but the wet blade slipped through her fingers, disappearing somewhere in the watery depths.

"Ye wee gowk," the man spat, reaching forward for her.

Kit couldn't wade through the water in time to escape and went for the blades in her belt as his hands found her doublet, pushing her down another time. She took another deep breath before he pushed her under the water.

This time, he had full control. With her legs pinned beneath one of his knees, she couldn't wriggle free. One of his hands had her palm, keeping it away from the daggers in her belt, and his other had her neck, pushing her into the earth.

She was under the water for too long. Unable to take a single breath, she could feel her body beginning to tire. She closed her eyes, looking for any last strength she could muster as she shoved against his chest.

In that darkness, she thought back to the dream that plagued her, with the image of the man's hand coming down to pull her free of the surface. The shock of the cold water reminded her of the moment. She saw it all so clearly this time, as though the water wasn't even murky anymore, but as clear as glass. When the man took hold of her wrist and pulled her small body out of the water, she saw for the first time who was above her.

She could recall coughing, struggling to breathe with a man patting her on the back, pleading with her to breathe through her nose.

"*Breathe, little one, breathe.*" His English accent was plain to hear as his face came into focus.

It was Walsingham.

Kit's eyes shot open, not understanding where the memory had come from, or even if it was her imagination that could have filled in the gaps. She had escaped the water before, many times. She knew that beyond doubt now. Surely, now, she could escape again.

Pushing past the fear of the depths above her head, she reached out with her one free hand and went straight for her attacker's face. He jerked back, trying to escape her wayward hand, but he wasn't fast enough. He cried out in pain as she clawed at his eyes before tearing off her completely, giving her the moment she needed.

She grabbed the dagger from her belt and leapt to her feet, coughing and clearing her lungs as she stumbled through the water. Through her coughing, she tried to shout for help, only the word 'help' was not the one that passed her lips.

"Iomhar!" she screeched the word as loudly as she could, aware that her attacker was coming for her again with one hand over his eye.

She whipped round and turned the dagger toward him.

"Take another step..." she said through wheezing breaths, the threat clear.

They stared at one another through the moonlight, their eyes flicking down to the blade of the dagger.

"Kit!" Iomhar bellowed her name, but she didn't look round.

Her attacker seemed to think the better of it, facing a fight with two people he couldn't win. He began to retreat across the river. Kit took a step forward, prepared to go after him, when the riverbank slipped beneath her feet. Feeling the fear ripple up through her body, going from her toes to her heart, she scrambled back again. With enough distance between her and the stranger, she turned and tried to swim toward the riverbank, but each time she lifted her feet off the earth, she felt that same fear, and she put her feet back down again, wading instead of swimming.

"Kit?" Iomhar called, much closer this time.

Looking up as she reached the bank, she saw Iomhar jumping down the slope toward her.

"What happened — what was..." He trailed off, his eyes slipping toward the other side of the river as he clearly caught sight of her attacker.

"He had a billhook," Kit said, clambering onto the bank, but her body was shaking too much to accomplish it. She felt Iomhar's hands take hold of her arms, easily pulling her out of the water and up onto dry land.

"Why?" Iomhar barked, his eyes flitting back toward the attacker's position. Kit looked too, seeing he was now on the other side of the river, fleeing as fast as his feet would carry him, far away.

"Why do you think?" Kit cried and looked away from the river, remembering the way he had held her down under the water. "I dropped the billhook. Then ... he tried to drown me."

"Stay here," Iomhar said, about to release her. It was clear he intended to go after the man, but Kit couldn't let go of Iomhar, she clung onto his arms, not doing as he asked. "Kit, ye think I am going to let him escape?"

She said nothing, she just kept holding onto his arms as her body shook. Seconds later, the sound of a horse's hooves made Kit's head dart round, seeing the stranger was escaping on a horse on the opposite riverbank. Iomhar gave up any attempt to leave her after that.

"Well, I will hardly catch up with him now," he muttered in clear anger, though he clung just as hard onto Kit's arms as she did his. "Kit, are ye hurt?"

"No." She struggled to say the word as she shook her head.

"Was he a thief?" he asked.

"No," she said again, her voice weaker than before. That tattoo on his neck had been too plain to see. She had seen it before, back in the summer, and the sight of it again had made her body numb. "What does a gowk mean?" she asked, recalling what the man had called her.

"Clumsy, or an idiot."

She nodded, remembering the anger in her attacker when she had dropped the billhook. "I-I'm cold," she muttered, stammering as the realisation struck her. The bitterness of the wind coupled with the sodden clothes was making her shiver.

"We need to get ye back to the lodgings." Iomhar lifted his hand to the belt around his cloak. "Kit, ye are going to have to release me for this to work."

She shakily did as he asked, feeling as if she could fall over at any second. She was still consumed with the feeling of being pressed under the water, so certain that death was on the horizon. Iomhar pulled his cloak free and wrapped it around her shoulders, using it to tug her closer.

"Ye can hold on again now."

She did as he said, letting him help her up the slope toward where the horses waited.

"Ye are going to have to keep walking to stay warm. I'll come back for the horses."

She reached out for the horse with hope but felt Iomhar steer her past the mare into town.

"F-faster," she said, stammering through her shivering.

"Nay, it will not be faster, Kit. The horses are too tired from our journey to gallop into town."

When she slipped on the stones in the road, struggling to stand at all, Iomhar wrapped both arms around her waist, heaving her back to her feet and practically dragging her.

"I'll carry ye if it comes to it, but ye have to keep moving to stay warm. Aye, Kit?"

"Aye," she said, mimicking his Scottish accent.

"I'm in nay mood to laugh, Kit."

"I'd like a reason to laugh right now," she whispered. The more they moved along the track road closer to Alnwick's streets, the more torches she saw had been lit by the townspeople, to brighten the early night. She hurried toward the light, preferring it to the darkness down by the riverbank.

"I do not understand," Iomhar muttered, as they moved toward their lodgings. "Ye said he was not a thief. Then what? Tell me he wasn't…" He stopped.

"Was not what?" she asked. He watched as his eyes flicked further down her body, telling her his meaning. "No! That is not what he wanted."

"Thank the wee man for that." Iomhar dragged her forward. "Then why did he attack ye?"

"He wanted me dead, Iomhar." She chose not to look at his face as she said the words. She kept her eyes on the road instead, focusing on nothing more than putting one foot in front of the other. "He had the tattoo."

"What tattoo?" Iomhar asked. "Ye feel like ice." He clearly couldn't concentrate. He was busy urging her to walk faster, attempting to keep her warm.

"The unicorn," she said, breathlessly as she felt Iomhar tow her forward, increasing their speed. "The one adopted by Mary Queen of Scots' most loyal followers."

# CHAPTER 17

Bruises were developing across Kit's neck. As she peered into the mottled mirror, the one candle that lit the darkness revealed the paleness of her face that stared into the very centre. As she angled her chin upward, the bruises from where the attacker had held her neck came into view.

Each line of where his fingers had been pressed was beginning to grow purple and blue, the marks faint in places and bold in others, so that they rather resembled a butterfly's wings fluttering and blooming beneath the skin. She lifted her hair, the better to see the marks, for they stretched all the way around her neck and so high that they nearly touched her chin.

"Kit?" Iomhar's voice called through the door. "Are ye in there?"

"Yes," she spoke calmly as she sighed, letting the short locks of her hair drop down again, wishing they were a little longer, so that she could hide the bruises.

"Will ye let me in?"

She turned to the door and unbolted the latch, giving him entry. He pushed open the door, his silhouette basked in the lonely candlelight. When he caught sight of the bruises, he took a sharp intake of breath, the strange hissing sound filling the air.

"It's fine."

"Och. That is not fine, Kit."

She turned away from him, grabbing the doublet she had thrown off before, and pulled it on, ignoring its wetness and shrugging it tightly over her shoulders and the loose-fitting white shirt. With the high collar, she quickly hid the bruises from view, buttoning it tight. When she turned back to Iomhar, she found his body restless, and he was breathing heavily.

"What is wrong?"

"What is wrong?" he repeated. "Do ye not understand what has happened here tonight?" he asked, stepping forward, his voice so irate that the sinews of his face around the two scars on his cheek were pulled taut. "Someone tried to kill ye."

Kit flinched at the words and turned away.

"Well, they did not succeed, did they?"

"That is all ye can say? Not why were they trying to kill ye?"

"It could have been a random attack," Kit insisted, though she didn't believe it. She just wished she could.

"What of that tattoo?"

"I do not know." She turned back to face him, keeping her voice strangely calm. She was exhausted, her body still spent from the fight. She did not have the energy to rant and panic about what had happened.

"Let's try this another way." Iomhar paused for a minute, folding his arms as he fixed his gaze on her. "The night the gaoler was shot with the crossbow."

"What of it?"

"Do ye remember what I said? How in that darkness with three figures dressed in similar clothing, it would be hard for the shooter to know who he was firing at?" His words left Kit cold. She stepped away, finding the wall with her back and pressing her body against it. "Think, Kit. He shot the gaoler first, then where was his second shot fired?"

She looked down, remembering how the bag containing the gown and corset had saved her life, slowing down the bolt with only the arrowhead peeking through.

"You think he was there for me." Kit's words didn't need an answer. Iomhar stepped forward again, bending his head down a little to her height, clearly trying to gain her gaze.

"We have to consider it an option. That tattoo… It is too much of a coincidence."

"Iomhar, it doesn't make sense." She shook her head. "The tattoo, we think it links supporters of Mary Stuart, yes?"

"Aye."

"So why would they spend time coming after me?" she asked, placing both hands to her chest. "In fact, how would they even know where to find me? Walsingham is the only other man who knows we are in Northumberland."

Iomhar turned away, running his hands through his dark hair and pulling on the locks in frustration.

"When you think of it plainly, it cannot make sense."

"Aye, so ye think it was a random attack from a man who happened to be bearing that tattoo, hmm?" Iomhar questioned with evident disdain as he looked back to her. "That makes even less sense."

Kit opened her lips to argue, but she had no words.

"Nothing ye can say will persuade me otherwise, Kit. That man was here for ye. Nay doubt in it."

"And in London? What of the man who killed the gaoler?"

"Aye, same height, similar build…" Iomhar lifted a hand showing how similar she was in height to the man that had been shot. "I think ye are being targeted, Kit."

"Aye, some success this is turning out to be." Oswyn's voice was despondent as he sat back in his chair, pulling at the bandage around his arm.

"Stop fidgeting with it," Iomhar warned as he walked past Oswyn, heading for where Kit was sitting on the far side of the room, with her gaze trained out of the window. "Ye'll undo the doctor's stitching."

"Good. He was too rough with the needle." Oswyn lowered his hand, despite his words. "So, two injured intelligencers and only one unharmed, we do not have much strength left between us to find Luca now, do we?"

Kit didn't answer him, she kept her eyes out of the window, looking toward Alnwick Castle. They hadn't told Oswyn about her attacker bearing the tattoo, or the possibility she could be targeted. As far as he knew, it was a thief chancing his luck. As Kit had tried to tell him the truth, Iomhar had shaken his head, not trusting Oswyn with the secret.

Iomhar reached her side, sitting down with something in his hands. More than once did she lift her hands to her neck, trying to loosen the collar around her doublet, hoping it would ease the pressure on her bruising.

"Kit, eat this."

"What is it?" she asked, taking it from him without much thought.

"Stottie. Ye need to keep your strength up."

She bit into the stottie but struggled to swallow it. Hanging her head forward, she forced the stottie down, with a hand at her throat.

"Still sore?" Iomhar asked.

"A little." It seemed the pressure her attacker had placed on her throat had left her with a pain to remember the moment.

"Ye can say a lot."

Kit didn't add anymore, but turned her eyes up to Alnwick Castle, thinking on what Niall had revealed to the two of them the day before.

"When do we go to the castle?"

"Soon," Iomhar said, standing to his feet again. "There is something I am waiting for first."

"Go to a castle? Which castle?" Oswyn asked, looking up from the bandage on his arm.

"Kit, eat up." Iomhar's words were gentle, urging Kit to look down to the stottie again. He ignored Oswyn's questions.

"I'm fine without it."

"Aye, running on an empty stomach. Sounds wise, does it not?"

Kit shot him a knowing look. She was well aware what he was doing, staying at her side constantly.

"I do not need watching over, Iomhar."

"I did not say ye needed watching over." Iomhar turned away. For a minute, Kit let her eyes follow him, wondering what he meant though he added no more. It wasn't long before she returned her eyes to the window, looking out to Alnwick Castle. At this distance, she could see jackdaws circling the turrets, some landing on the battlements and others hovering in the air.

"Are the jackdaws back?" Oswyn asked from across the room.

"Yes," Kit said, turning her eyes on him.

"The wise woman in town. She says they are an omen of death."

Kit felt Iomhar's sharp gaze upon her, but she didn't return the stare.

"I hope your wise woman is sometimes wrong," Iomhar muttered.

There was a tap at the door before anyone could answer him and Iomhar moved toward it, opening the door to reveal Oswyn's maid on the other side who proffered forward a slip of parchment. Iomhar thanked her before closing the door again and tearing open the seal.

"What is it?" Kit asked, turning away from the castle.

"What I was waiting to hear." Iomhar walked back to her side, leaning over the back of the settle bench to pass her the letter. She angled it in the light of the window to see it was a letter from Niall.

*Iomhar,*

*It seems some of my men were watching more of Lord Ruskin's progress than they first revealed. A few choice questions last night to the right soldiers revealed it is known exactly where Lord Ruskin went in Northumberland. He did indeed go to Alnwick Castle.*

*I'd say ye have your evidence to search the castle. If your Jesuit priest is found within those walls, then it is certain. His purpose must align with Lord Ruskin's. He is here to help put Mary Stuart on the throne.*

*God be with ye, brother,*
*Niall*

Kit folded up the letter and passed it back to Iomhar. Oswyn opened his hand to be passed the letter too, but Iomhar refused, placing it back in his doublet.

"Lord Ruskin, a known supporter of Mary Stuart, was seen going into Alnwick Castle three weeks ago." Iomhar pointed out of the window.

Oswyn jerked forward in his chair. "That is not possible."

"Nay?" Iomhar asked. "Because I'm beginning to wonder how ye can have Catholic dissenters not five streets from ye, and yet do not know about them."

"I was not even here three weeks ago." Oswyn jumped to his feet, striding toward Iomhar with purpose, yet Iomhar did not back down. He merely stepped forward, looking down at

Oswyn to show his superior height. "I was in Newcastle, at Taurus's orders."

"Yet ye have nay one here that could tell ye Lord Ruskin went to that castle? Ye can see the castle from this very window!" Iomhar jabbed a finger at the glass.

Kit tried to speak up, to quell the argument, but her voice was quickly drowned out by Oswyn.

"It's a castle. It has fortifications and high walls. Aye, man, you expect me to be able to see through those walls, do you?"

"I expect ye to be keeping a better eye on the very town ye live in."

"Bloody Scot, telling me how to go on."

"Sassenach, useless, aye? Hardly surprising."

Kit whistled loudly, placing her fingers in her mouth to make the sound high pitched and piercing. Both men looked to her at once, jerking their heads so sharply in her direction that she thought it a wonder they didn't crick their necks.

"Whilst you two are arguing, a Jesuit priest could be running around the corridors of that castle, plotting how to kill his next victim. Gemini or Aries." Kit slowly stood to her feet, feeling the pain in her throat as she moved. "Argue as you wish to, but at least do it whilst you are walking."

She moved past them, heading for the door, aware that Iomhar and Oswyn followed behind her, no longer arguing. As Kit hovered by the door, pulling on her cap and dark red leather gloves, she saw Iomhar's hand come up over the door, holding it closed in the frame for a minute.

"Is there a reason you are blocking the path?" Kit asked.

"Aye, I do not wish to see ye nearly drowned in a river again." The bluntness of his words made her sharply look away from his hand on the door, finding his gaze. Those green eyes were piercing, unblinking as they stared at her.

"My heart is still beating, and I am still breathing. I don't look dead yet."

"I wish to keep it that way." Iomhar refused to lower his hand from the door.

"What are you trying to say, Iomhar?"

He shifted awkwardly between his feet for a minute, glancing back at Oswyn.

"Perhaps Oswyn and I should search the castle."

"Placing your faith in me, Scot?"

"Placing her life above yours, aye," Iomhar concluded simply, smirking as he looked back at Oswyn.

"Aye, fair enough."

"Iomhar." Kit pulled on the door handle, forcing his hand to lower from the door. "I am not staying here."

"Not even if it means keeping ye safe from another attack?"

"What would Walsingham say to that?" she asked wildly, feeling anger build by the minute. "That I was a craven for hiding here when I could have been finding this killer."

"I do not care what Walsingham would say on the matter." Iomhar held her gaze as he spoke, making her anger rise like bile in her throat all the more.

"I'm coming with you, Iomhar. Try to leave me behind, and I would simply climb out of the window to follow you." She smiled with triumph as he sighed, shaking his head and breaking the eye contact.

"As I know ye would do just that, I see nay point in arguing with ye anymore."

"Good!" Kit flung open the door and stepped outside, aware as she walked down the corridor that Iomhar and Oswyn walked behind her, staying alongside each other.

"She doesn't listen to reason much, does she?" Oswyn whispered, not so quietly that Kit couldn't hear him.

"Nay. She likes to do things without much thinking."

Kit chose not to respond and hurried out of the house, pausing only when she was in the street, and she could see Alnwick Castle in the distance. The mottled yellow stone walls stood on the far edge of town, protected by an embankment. In the very centre was a tower, made up of smaller turrets with the top of the castle crenelations stretched around the tower, marking the high vantage point within the walls.

"It's vast," Kit murmured as Iomhar reached her side. The walls along the embankments stretched far and wide. "It could take us hours to search."

"Then we best start searching." Iomhar moved forward, urging Kit and Oswyn to hurry to keep up with him. "Oswyn, ye know the Justice of the Peace in town?"

"Aye."

"Then we best see him first. We are going to need some help to search that castle."

## CHAPTER 18

Kit stood back on the driveway of Alnwick Castle, looking between the pursuivant soldiers that had been gathered for their task and the gateway up ahead. Beyond the long-pebbled driveway, a portcullis was lowered, with the iron-black gate stark against the yellow and brown stone, standing as an omen. Above the gate, the jackdaws continued to circle, cawing every now and then before they settled on the crenelations at the very top of the two towers that made up the gatehouse.

"They know we're here," Iomhar whispered for Kit's ears only.

She turned away from where Oswyn was talking to the pursuivants, giving them their orders. "How do you know that?"

"Look." Iomhar nodded his head at one of the windows, beyond which there was a shadow moving, calmly shifting back and forth, whereas behind it, there were numerous shadows that were all infinitely more active and animated, darting about in the sunlight that streamed through the windows. "If Luca's here, they'll be hiding him now."

Kit moved forward, determined not to give them too much time. When they reached the portcullis, she addressed the guard standing on the other side. "Tell your master the Justice of the Peace has ordered a search of this castle."

Her words were met by a young face that contorted into worry. "A search?" he asked, his Northumbrian accent strong. "I must speak to my master first."

"Ye will open the portcullis first," Iomhar said, his dark tone brooking no refusal. "Then ye will see your master." The lad appeared wrongfooted, looking behind him to where a pike was resting against a stone well, apparently debating using it. "Do not be a fool, boy. Ye think one lonely pike will defeat so many pursuivants?"

The boy didn't answer, but he went to reach for the pike regardless. Kit was in no mood for a fight, not with her neck still burning in pain. She reached for Iomhar beside her, with her hand taking hold of the pistol looped through his belt and pulling it free from its confines. She pointed it directly through the iron bars of the portcullis, straight at the boy's chest. She kept her finger away from the trigger, knowing she would not truly shoot it.

"Open the portcullis. Now." Kit kept her voice calm, but the threat was enough. The boy dropped the pike and sent orders for the portcullis to be lifted high above, shouting and calling to guards in the gate room. As the portcullis was raised, slipping somewhere into the rafters, Kit passed the pistol back to Iomhar as he leaned toward her, whispering in her ear.

"Ye do know it isn't loaded, do ye not?" he asked quietly.

"I did, but he did not." She smiled as she stepped forward, pulling a soft chuckle from him.

They stepped into the castle with Iomhar shouting orders, making it clear Oswyn and the pursuivants were to begin the search. Kit followed the guard through the castle corridors, with Iomhar hurrying behind her, determined to find the master of the house.

The corridors were vast and wide, covered with a stone arch ceiling and bathed in sunlight that streamed through stained-glass windows on either side. The courtyard within the castle was on one side of the corridor, revealing the sheer breadth of ground that the castle covered.

"Seen any signs of a priest hole yet?" Iomhar whispered to Kit as they followed the guard.

"No." Though her eyes darted around, looking for any odd imprints within the stonework that could indicate a secret door or a thick wall within which a small chamber could be hidden.

As they walked, she reached round the neck of her doublet, pulling at the collar to loosen it from her bruises, before her fingers found the rosary beads that she had taken off Gregorio Luca. The beads were cold to the touch, but she played with them between her fingers for a minute, thinking on the man they were there to find.

"He was slim, and not too tall. He could hide almost anywhere."

"Reassuring," Iomhar said wryly as they reached the end of the corridor and followed the guard up a staircase. The spiral stairs looped tightly around themselves, scarcely leaving enough room for a lady that wished to walk through with a farthingale hanging at her ankles. Kit took the steps two at a time, impatiently following the guard.

When they stepped through a wooden doorway into a large room, she pushed the rosary beads back down beneath the collar of her doublet, hiding them from view.

"What is the meaning of this?" a loud Northumbrian voice called.

Blinded by the sunlight streaming through the stained-glass windows for a minute, Kit had to blink a few times for her eyes to adjust.

Before her, an opulent dining room stretched out, with a long oak table in the centre, dressed with plates of food. Some silver platters held chicken, others held pork, each plate adorned with ornamentation, spices and winter berries, displaying wealth. It looked more like a meal prepared for a guest rather than a family meal. To Kit's mind, those sat at the table seemed to make an appearance of eating, trying to look interested in their food.

"Who are you?" the same voice said again, urging Kit to look to the end of the table. At the head, a man was on his feet. With a high hairline and such a long nose that his face looked stretched on the rack, he was a noticeable figure. His cheeks were alabaster white, suggesting he had barely spent a day beyond his castle walls, and the eyebrows were dark, appearing painted on his pale forehead. The face was young, even younger than Kit.

"We are here by the order of the Justice of the Peace," Iomhar spoke plainly, striding forward until he reached the other end of the table, meeting the gaze of the master. "We have come to search your castle."

"Whatever for?" the young man stepped out from his chair, urging the two younger boys sat at the table to raise their heads.

"Catholics."

"I am Henry Percy, the lord of this house whilst my father is away, and I will not have us tainted by suspicion of my father."

"Then an innocent man would not object to us searching his castle, would he?" Kit asked.

Henry Percy turned his eyes on her, those orbs going wide when he found her face. "Is that a lass or a lad?"

"Object to our search and it will not only be passed onto the Justice of the Peace, but Francis Walsingham too." Kit's threat appeared to work, for Henry Percy turned panicked eyes toward the older woman at the table. Kit followed his gaze, realising quickly that this had to be Henry Percy's mother. She gave an almost imperceptible nod, never once lifting her eyes from the ornate pewter plate before her. "Are you an innocent man, sir?" Kit asked, still waiting on his answer.

Henry Percy looked back to her, his manner fidgeting as he clutched the back of one of the younger boy's chairs. The boys began to whisper together, talking animatedly, until Henry Percy knocked them around the ears, one after another.

"This is our father's house, remember that," he muttered to them. "That is right, is it not?" he asked, looking back to Kit and Iomhar. "Anyone housed here is at the discretion of my father, not of me."

"Ye have just claimed to be the lord of the house, have ye not?" Iomhar asked, making Henry Percy stand taller and fidget with his doublet. "Ye can discuss the matter of a charge with the Justice of the Peace, if we find something."

Iomhar turned to leave, about to begin the search.

"Wait!" Henry Percy called, jerking forward. "I have not said you can search yet."

"Will you object?" Kit asked again. "Remember how an innocent man would sound, sir." Her reminder was enough.

"A-aye," he stammered. "We have nothing to hide."

"That remains to be seen," Kit murmured with a small smile and turned away, joining Iomhar back on the staircase as they descended the floors of the castle.

"What do ye think?" Iomhar called back to her as they hurried down.

"He's here," she said. "The mother did not once look up from her plate. That was the act of a woman who was not lost or confused. Any woman startled by our entrance, baffled by it, would have been questioning what was happening. I'd say it is beyond doubt. Gregorio Luca is either here, or that family knows exactly where he is."

"Nothing."

"Nothing?" Kit said. "You mean nothing *yet*, Oswyn."

"Aye, very well, nothing *yet*."

Kit turned away from him, standing at the top of a vast staircase and looking down to the main hall of Alnwick Castle. Every now and then she saw a pursuivant walk past, murmuring to another before they hurried off in a different direction. Oswyn was standing by Kit's side, reporting on their failing, whilst Iomhar sat at the top of the stairs, deep in thought.

They had been searching for what felt like hours into the dead of night, but the castle was such a rabbit warren of different corridors, that they could be there for hours more yet. What worried Kit so was the thickness of the walls. She had seen many priest holes that were hidden within deep walls that had been hollowed out. If they had to check every inch of wall in this place, they could be there until the new year.

"Iomhar? Any thoughts?" Kit called to him.

He didn't answer right away but sat a little straighter on the stairs. Kit walked down a few steps before leaning on the carved wooden banister, with each curve in the wood shaped to look like a face, rather like gargoyles in a church.

Iomhar met her gaze, still barely moving. "Ye and I have seen enough priest holes to know they never make them easy to find."

"It is true."

"Still, I can imagine in a place like this, it will be easy for even the man who made the priest hole to lose track of it."

"No man is so foolish," Oswyn muttered, sitting beside Iomhar on the stairs.

"A man who owns a house like this might be," Iomhar said slowly. "One wall is much like another, one set of stairs the same as another. Aye, men can become lost in their own castles. How difficult can it be to find something that is not supposed to be found?"

"You had much experience of a lord's castle, have you, Scot?" Oswyn scoffed. "I find that rather hard to believe."

Kit shifted against the banister, watching the way Iomhar bristled at the words. Kit hadn't asked Iomhar what kind of house he had grown up in being the son of an earl, but she could imagine well enough it would be a grand place indeed, perhaps something as fine and illustrious as the castle they stood in now.

"This castle. It is owned by an earl, is it not?" Kit asked, keeping her gaze on Iomhar.

He turned to her with a small smile, evidently reading her thoughts. "It is. Not all earls live in castles, Kit." It was the only answer she was clearly going to hear with Oswyn sat so close. "This place, it is too vast and confusing for a priest hole to be remembered easily. Nay, mark my words. There must be something that signposts where this priest hole is. There often is. People need something to tell their Catholic guests where to hide when pursuivants come calling."

"That is wishful thinking, I am sure of it." Oswyn sighed and sat down on the stairs. "Where have we not searched yet?"

"The bedchambers," Iomhar said slowly. "The chapel has been done, the lower floors too."

"What of the kitchens?" Oswyn asked.

"Not yet."

"Then I'll start there. I'll leave you two to do the bedrooms." He wandered off, chuckling.

"Why is he laughing?" Kit asked, but Iomhar merely shook his head, apparently none the wiser. He stood to his feet and walked across the landing, heading in the direction of the bedchambers. Kit hurried to follow, lifting a candle high in her hands to light their path.

They began to search the rooms in silence. In the first chamber, they performed all the tricks they usually did, knocking on walls to see if there were hollow sections between the panels of wood and blocks of stone. They searched basic hiding places too, such as under the bed and in the wardrobe, then they looked for secret nooks, perhaps a wall that would open out, or lifting rugs to search for loose floorboards, but in the first room, there was nothing.

By the time they reached the second room, they were both growing agitated. Their movements were much more erratic and frantic, with the two of them repeating searches that the other one had already done.

"I've searched that already," Iomhar said as she tried to knock out the back of a wardrobe to seek for a secret space.

"No harm in being thorough."

"Then ye will not object to me doing this." Iomhar went around the room knocking on panels in the walls where she had already searched.

"Yes, I see your argument."

They both sighed when the second chamber proved fruitless and went onto the third. This room was bigger than the other two, leading Kit to hover in the middle of the room for a minute longer, gazing upon the opulence. The ceiling was moulded into geometric lines, each one interspersed with a diamond, within which there was an ornamental painting of a tale from the bible. Beneath this canopy of artwork, the room held some of the finest furnishings she had seen in the entire building with lustrous red coverings upon the bed and a thick rug before the fireplace surrounded by dark wooden settle benches.

"Odd," Kit murmured as she walked toward the hearth, tapping the grey stone where the fire should have sat. "No fire."

"What do ye mean?" Iomhar's voice was muffled thanks to his head being beneath the bed as he looked for loose floorboards.

"Well, the other chambers had fires, and this one should certainly be occupied. It is too fine to leave empty."

"Perhaps it is Lord Percy's. He is not here at the moment, so it would make sense for the room to be empty."

Kit didn't comment. She was too busy with her wandering gaze as she walked away from the hearth, searching the vanity table nearby that was scattered with men's toiletries and a washbasin with a jug beside it. She placed a finger to the bottom of the washbasin, finding it still wet.

"No, this room is being used." She crossed back to the hearth, looking at the mantelpiece with interest. The stone hearth was deep, testament to how grand the room was and the large flames that would be needed to heat it. Beneath the mantelpiece, there were carvings in the solid stone of three distinct effigies. The first was of the ark that Noah built to survive the flood, the second of Moses parting the sea, but the third stood out to Kit the most. She ran her fingers across the scene, marking the way Adam and Eve were hiding between the trees.

"They are hiding," she whispered. It did not make sense to her. Amongst scenes that celebrated the power of God and people's success, why was there one that showed Adam and Eve in all their shame?

"Ye found anything?"

"Maybe." Kit stepped closer into the fireplace, bending her head down to peer within the darkness. "You said some priest holes have signposts, clues for where to find them."

"Aye, some of them."

"I need more light."

Iomhar appeared at her side, striking another flame from a tinderbox flint and passing her the lit candle. She held it aloft within the chimney, turning her eyes downwards to see if there was any crack in the stone floor. She kicked the spent wood and ash to the side, watching as the dark powder sat within the crevices of stones. A few stomps to the stones showed they would not be moved.

"Hold this." Kit passed the candle into Iomhar's hand, pushing his arm a little so that he held it high in the chimney.

"What are ye going to do?" he asked.

"I'll give you a guess," she murmured with a small smile as she stepped forward inside the chimney and took hold of the stones.

"Do ye have to climb every surface ye find?"

"It's not every surface," she argued in defence, but Iomhar was clearly not in the mood for bickering. As she climbed, she could feel his keen gaze upon her, watching her carefully. She made slow progress at first. In the dim light from the candle, it was difficult to make out just where she was putting her hands and feet in the crevices. Once she was climbing above Iomhar's head height, disappearing inside the chimney, she had to move using touch alone, with the candlelight barely reaching her.

"Ye need a light?"

"Yes." She paused and held a hand down toward him. It was difficult, with him having to strain and stand on a ledge to reach her, but he passed her a candle that was not lit and she pressed it into a pocket. Next, she felt him hand her a tinderbox that she tucked into the open neck of her doublet. Once safely in place, she climbed higher.

"What do I do if ye climb out on the roof?" Iomhar called up to her, his voice beginning to echo through the vastness of the chimney.

"Pray I do not fall off," Kit said wryly as she continued to climb. The stone was grainy beneath her fingers, suggesting the fire had indeed been lit at some point, as the ash filled the lines of her hands and made it slippery beneath the toes of her boots.

When she found complete darkness, she reached up, finding there was a gap in the wall. Feeling around blindly for a second, she managed to figure out a mental image of a space within the chimney wall. She thrust herself through the gap, clambering up until she found her body crawling onto a wooden floorboard, with a ceiling so low that she couldn't stand for fear of hitting her head. Sitting back on her haunches, she took the candle and the tinderbox, then struck it alight. It took a few attempts, but when the sparks eventually jumped to life and the flame took hold of the candlewick, a soft orange orb filled the space.

Before her was a wooden alcove built into the chimney stack with the furthest corners difficult to see beyond the glow of the candle. The wooden floor and ceiling was made of dark oak, creating such a small space that no more than four people could sit down comfortably within it. To Kit's side, there was a loop of rope that had been wrapped around a metal hook, suggesting that this was how someone climbed in and out of the priest hole.

Something moved in the corner of the alcove, something within folds of a cloak-like material, then a face appeared, gaunt and white.

## CHAPTER 19

"God's wounds!" Kit veered back in shock toward the chimney opening as the face came into focus. Then, as the man crawled out from his hiding space in the very corner, she said, "Good evening, Luca."

"*Donna.*" He spat the word in her direction as he lunged forward, his hands stretching out toward her.

Kit dropped the candle as she reached for the dagger in her belt. The light was instantly snuffed out, casting them into darkness, as a pair of hands closed over Kit's neck. She fell backwards onto the wooden floor with a heavy thud, so loud that far below her Iomhar began to call out to her.

"Kit? Kit! What has happened?"

She couldn't shout back for the pressure on her throat was too strong, pressing on the existing bruises. She acted instead, taking advantage of the darkness. Unable to reach her dagger, she brought her hands hard down on Luca's wrists, forcing them to crumple and fall away from her, then she hitched up her knees. She brought them into her chest so she could kick Luca hard in his abdomen, pushing him up so high that his back collided with the low ceiling, winding him. He fell down on her, wheezing with his body weakened.

Kit rolled him off her, feeling madly around in the darkness. When she found the rope that was looped round the metal hook on one end, she pulled the other end free and used it to tie Luca's wrists, bringing his arms so far up behind his back at odd angles to one another that he began to yell against the wood.

"Kit! Are ye alive?"

"Yes, of course I'm alive!" Kit snapped back. "You think I could die that easily by climbing into a chimney?"

"Nothing would surprise me," Iomhar called back to her. "What's that noise? Ye found him?"

Kit shoved hard down into Luca's back as he tried to wriggle free, making him yell out in pain.

"That was Luca saying good evening." Her call down the chimney was met with approving laughter.

"Good. How are ye going to get him down?"

"That is a good question."

Once she was certain Luca was too winded to fight against the restraints against his arms, she sat in the middle of his back, keeping him pinned to the floor and reached for the spent candle. It took some fumbling around in the darkness, but she eventually caught the wax stick, mere inches away from rolling out of the gap and down the chimney. Using the tinderbox, she struck a light, lifting the candle low down to Luca's face.

With a cheek pressed to the wooden floor, he was peering up at her with one eye. The white of the eye appeared bloodshot, probably from being sat too long in the darkness. The sinews down his cheek and through his neck were taut as he tried to struggle against her, but with his body flattened in such a way and his arms held back at an angle so bent they almost looked broken, there was nothing he could do.

"Remember me?" she whispered, holding the candle closer toward him.

"*Donna insanguinata. Dio porterà l'inferno sulla terra per punirti per questo.*"

"I do not speak Italian."

"Consider it a curse upon your name, *donna*." His voice was dark and barely above a whisper. As Kit lifted the candle higher, debating how she was going to get him down, a drip of wax trickled down the shaft of the candle, landing on his cheek. He growled at the pain from the burn.

"My apologies. If you did not try so much to escape that would not have happened." Kit smiled when he began to curse her name all the more.

She placed the candle at the edge of the alcove and lifted the rope. Seeing there was much more to the length, it was enough to lower him down to the bottom of the chimney.

"Time to flee your hole, Luca," she said, clambering off him and pushing him in the direction of the gap.

"You think I will go because you tell me to?" he asked, practically spitting the words as he tried to kick out in her direction, pushing her away.

"I think you will go because I'm making you." She smiled triumphantly as she pulled on the other end of the rope and pushed him out into the open space. He roared in fear, but as Kit dug her feet into the wooden floorboards and the walls around her, using her whole weight to lever on the other side of the rope, he stayed suspended in the air, his eyes dancing back and forth across her.

"You will not hold me for long."

"Very true," she agreed with him. "Iomhar? Look out for something falling above you," she called, watching as Luca's eyes widened in realisation. When she began to lower the rope, she was not strong enough to lower him slowly. It unravelled rather quicker than she had intended, leaving Luca to cry out as he barrelled toward Iomhar at the bottom of the chimney.

A heavy thud at the bottom of the chimney made her grimace and peer over the edge of the gap in the wall to see below her that Iomhar had half caught Luca, leaving the assassin somewhat crumpled against the wall and Iomhar's legs.

"I could have done with more of a warning, Kit," Iomhar said, looking up toward her through the darkness.

"No need to complain, we have found him, haven't we?" she asked with triumph and blew out the candle before climbing back down the wall. It was difficult work, with her feet slipping more than once on the ash-covered walls.

When she reached the bottom, she found Iomhar had dragged Luca out of the chimney place and tossed him into a seat nearby. Luca was struggling, wriggling like a worm afraid of being eaten by a blackbird, in desperation to get the ropes off his hands. His cheek was covered in soot from the fireplace, and he was leaving stains on the chair from his blackened clothes.

"Here." Iomhar stepped to Kit's side and proffered a handkerchief.

"What's this for?"

"Your face."

Kit took the cloth and tried to wipe the soot free from her cheeks as Iomhar turned toward Luca, bending down in front of him until he had his gaze. Luca began reeling off more Italian, words Kit had no chance of understanding, though she could guess easily enough that he was pouring curses upon both Iomhar's and her own head. When he was done, Iomhar stood straight.

"Call for God's help all ye wish, Luca. Maybe He has forsaken ye, for He has sent ye into our hands now, hasn't He?" Iomhar's words made the Italian snap his head upwards, looking greatly afeared at the idea.

"Where now?" Kit murmured, done cleaning her face.

"To a dungeon. Taurus will have some questions that we need answering."

Kit pulled on the chains around Luca's wrists, dragging him out of the gaol cart and pulling him into a cobbled square. The sun was beginning to fall, casting the castle before them into a dark red light.

"It is the lights of hell. Come to take us all," Luca whispered.

Kit pulled him forward again, glancing briefly at Iomhar who winced at Luca's words.

"It is Bamburgh Castle. Not hell," Iomhar said over his shoulder as he led their path up to the castle.

"Is it safe to hold him here?" Kit asked quietly, glancing back at the pursuivants who stood at the far end of the driveway by the horses, all murmuring amongst themselves. As they clambered up the steep drive, heading to the castle atop the mound that overlooked the ocean, Kit felt a strange disquieting.

"Ye think Catholics could break him free from here?"

"One castle was hiding him. Who is to say there isn't someone here who will help him?"

"Bamburgh's dungeons are impenetrable." Another voice joined them. Oswyn appeared at Kit's side. Despite his smile, there appeared to be something different in his manner, something that Kit had not seen before. "Aye, pet, you can trust this place. He will not break free of here."

Kit nodded slowly, looking back to Luca as he trailed behind her. He didn't even pull tightly on his chains, as if he had already resigned himself to his fate.

With the sky beginning to darken, they were led by the dungeons' guards around the castle wall, following a stony path that soon meandered down into the recesses of the castle, beneath a cobbled archway and a metal grate. What had been basked in the red sunset before became swathed in a darkness that was as black as night, until torches lit and fastened against the wall appeared in the distance.

Not large enough for two people to walk astride, Kit led Luca down the corridor, with Iomhar following closely behind the two of them. When they reached a cell, a barred door was pushed open to reveal a room that was not only clad with thick irons to prevent escape and no windows, but all manner of evil-looking instruments. Kit froze when she laid eyes on them.

"Walsingham has not authorised torture. Has he?" she asked, looking back at Iomhar and Oswyn.

"Nay," Iomhar agreed, taking the chains out of her hands and moving to fasten Luca to the wall with fresh chains.

"It will only be a matter of time." Oswyn's words made Kit shift and step further back in the dungeon, moving away from the instruments. There was one that was made of nothing but sharpened sticks, in such a way that she wasn't even sure how a body was supposed to be flung across it. Beside it, there was a table, complete with thumbkins and other small devices designed to be applied to the body.

Behind Luca, the dungeon was made mostly of hollowed out stone, with wooden boards across the ceiling, so low that they nearly touched Iomhar's head. The floor was scattered with loose straw, stinking of excrement that the previous prisoner hadn't quite managed to get into a bucket. Beside the chains, there was a settle bench, but this seat was not intended for comfort. There were three looped ropes fastened to the backrest of the bench, designed to thread round the prisoner's neck and wrists.

Kit had to look away from the sight, feeling her mouth turn dry as she reminded herself that Luca was a known murderer. There was a reason he was being brought to such a place, with the scent of sweat and excrement that made her want to gag.

"It is done," Iomhar said as he stepped back from the chains.

"Done? You think because you have me here, that our work is *finito*?" Gregorio Luca's voice was sharp. After so long spent in silence, his voice made Kit jump. She turned and took one of the lanterns that the guards had been carrying, lifting it further into the cell and holding it near Luca's face. He reared back, as if frightened the flames hidden behind the glass could truly burn him.

In the orange light, the lines of his face were more visible, each one making his face appear surprisingly haggard for one so young. He appeared old beyond his years and his skin bore scars that shone in this light, marked by fighting.

"Who were you here for?" she asked calmly.

This was what she had to do now. She had Gregorio Luca, as Walsingham had asked, but it was not enough. She needed to know who he was here to kill.

"You have what you want, pet," Oswyn called to her. "Let us leave."

"No," she announced resoundingly and stepped forward, bringing the lantern light closer to Luca's cheeks. The light bounced off the whites of his eyes, revealing the red veins that ran like spiderwebs. "Another could simply take his place and do his task. We must know why he came. Luca, who were you here for?"

He smiled. It was a chilling smile, one that made the tops of his cheeks hollow out as he tipped his chin backwards. He evidently had no intention of speaking to her.

"Then it will have to be torture." Oswyn's words made Kit raise the lantern even higher, refusing to look away from Luca.

"Torture is not as effective as you would like to think, Oswyn."

"No?" He laughed with the word. "It has a knack for making a man talk."

"And for making a man confess to crimes he hasn't done." Iomhar's words made Kit look back at him, startled to see he was in agreement with her. He nodded slowly, in silent encouragement for her to ask Luca again.

"Tell us why you are here," she said, turning back to Luca. "You know you cannot escape from such a place. Whoever's orders you are following, well, they matter little now."

"You wish me to speak, *donna*?" he asked, the Italian accent making every other word hiss. "You wish me to betray my kin? I have more loyalty than that."

"Loyalty hardly matters when your friends cannot help you." Kit was aware out of the corner of her eye of Oswyn moving to the side of the room where the torture instruments were laid out on the table. Iomhar followed him, before taking the thumbkins out of Oswyn's hands and laying them back down on the table once more.

"They will make him speak."

"And he will then tell us nothing but lies to make the pain stop. Ye must think of another way to make him talk."

"What of survival?" Kit offered. Her simple word seemed to resonate with Luca, for he lifted his chin higher. "Tell us who you came here for, and we can ensure the trial you face for your crimes is a fair one."

"I'm a killer, *donna*," he answered calmly, leaning toward her. "Any trial will send me to the gallows."

She stepped back, seeing she was making no progress. Her hand lifted automatically to her throat, thinking of the bruises round her neck when he mentioned the word 'killer'. She had nearly been the victim of such an attack. As she fiddled with the collar of her doublet, the rosary beads she had taken from

Luca slipped out. His eyes flicked toward them, lighting up before his body wrenched forward, straining at the irons.

"You took them, *donna malvagia*."

"What does that mean?" Oswyn asked.

"Evil woman," Iomhar answered.

"How do you know that, Scot?"

"Maybe my upbringing wasn't as savage as ye believe it to be," Iomhar said quietly. His hand touched Kit's arm, calling her to step back. She did, but only a little, aware of the way Luca fixed his eyes upon the rosary, his stare never leaving those beads.

"You took them. Return them to me."

"You dropped them in our scuffle in the ocean." Kit gritted her teeth with the lie. "Why do you want them so badly?"

"They are my link to God." He darkened his words as he pulled against his chains, with so much vigour that the sinews of his hands grew taut, fighting with the strength of the irons.

Kit chewed her lip. There was something odd here, she was convinced of it. She turned away from Luca, lowering her voice so only Iomhar could hear her as she continued turning the beads between the pads of her fingers.

"You once said religious zeal is his excuse for killing. Did you mean it?" she asked.

Iomhar nodded slowly, keeping his eyes on Luca. It was evident his suspicions were rising as much as her own were.

"Perhaps he is more devoted to his God than I thought," he said in the end.

"This is moving too slowly for my liking." Oswyn grabbed a basilard from the table and strode toward Luca. The assassin cowered back within his chains, planting his spine flat against the stone wall.

"Oswyn, stop!" Kit roared as he stood over Luca, holding the basilard to his throat.

"What are you here for?" Oswyn demanded. "Are you here to put Mary on the throne of England? Is that it?"

Luca smiled, the malicious curling of his lips spreading wider.

"*Qualcose bolle in pentola*," he whispered, then he grunted. It was low and quiet, with not much sound to it, but within the stone walls it echoed, sounding much louder. Oswyn thrust the basilard forward again, making the grunt cut off sharply.

"What does that mean?" Oswyn cried loudly.

"It means that something is brewing. In a way." Iomhar moved forward sharply, grabbing hold of Oswyn's hand and jerking the blade out of his grasp.

"Scot, you have no —"

"That is enough." Iomhar's sharp bark made Oswyn fall still. Silence descended between them as Kit rested her eyes on Luca, watching him closely. He still made no attempt to escape, and his eyes were only on one thing, the rosary beads.

"If you truly intend to put Mary on the throne, your Catholic queen, then you intend to see Queen Elizabeth murdered, do you not?" Kit asked, stepping forward. "Whether you are here to kill her or another, that must be part of your plan."

He didn't deny it. He merely stared forward.

"Is it God's will to kill a woman? How can any religious man justify that to themselves?" she scoffed and turned away. "We'll write to Walsingham," she said as she moved to the door of the cell. "Perhaps he will interrogate Luca himself."

Iomhar and Oswyn followed her, but before Kit could step out, Luca called out to her.

"You think a woman's death is always the wrong thing, *donna*?" His shout made her fall still with one hand on the bars as she looked back to him. "What if that woman is evil? What if she is responsible for another's death, what would you say then?"

There was something in those words that made her body turn numb.

"Kit, don't let his words creep into ye." Iomhar placed a hand to her back and steered her forward an inch, out of the cell. She went, but she never stopped looking back into the cell, not until the door was closed and Luca's face was split by iron bars. Even then she could see he was staring at her.

She took hold of the rosary beads around her neck and tucked them down beneath her collar.

"Ye all right?" Iomhar asked her as they walked away, heading down the dark corridor.

"I feel like I have just exchanged words with the devil."

# CHAPTER 20

"You two do not have the stomach for it. That is all." Oswyn's words burned within Kit. They'd heard nothing their entire ride back to Alnwick other than his complaints that they should have allowed him to hurt Luca.

Kit steered her horse between Oswyn's and Iomhar's, fixing her gaze on Iomhar alone. "What will happen to the Percys?" she asked.

"The Justice of the Peace will make that decision." He urged his horse toward their lodgings. Darkness had fallen and they were navigating by the light of the moon. "It depends largely on whether Henry Percy can persuade him that letting Luca into the house was his father's decision or not."

"Aye, I see I am being ignored from now on," Oswyn called, blowing air harshly out of his mouth.

"When you say foolish things, I think we are within reason," Kit answered honestly as they reached the house, jumping down from her horse.

"We wait for Walsingham's answer," Iomhar said hurriedly, warning Oswyn with a lifting of his finger not to speak again. "Any torture must be authorised by Her Majesty Queen Elizabeth, ye know that."

"I reckon she does not know half the things that happen in her kingdom."

Kit tacked up the horse to the nearest post and walked to the house, not wishing to continue the debate any longer.

Oswyn unlocked the door, allowing them all to step inside and move up the stairs to Oswyn's lodgings, where they lit candles. When they reached the sitting room, Kit felt her feet fall still beneath her.

"What is that?" she asked, pulling on Iomhar's arm. He turned the candle in the direction she was pointing. By the corridor that led to their chambers, there was something shadowy on the floor. She stepped forward, reaching toward it as Iomhar followed her with the candle.

"My maid must be growing worse at her job. Hardly tidy in here!" Oswyn laughed, moving around the sitting room as he lit more candles.

Gradually, the place flooded with light, allowing Kit to see what was on the floor. She kicked out at it, swiping up a loose cloak, then caught it from the air.

"Yours?" She proffered it to Iomhar. He shook his head, gesturing to the one on his shoulders.

"Too small for me. Oswyn?" he called back. Oswyn appeared, peering over Iomhar's shoulder as he stood on his toes.

"Not mine."

"Your maid's?" Iomhar asked.

"This is a man's cloak," Kit said, pushing it toward Iomhar to carry.

"From what I've seen, it does not mean a lass wouldn't wear it." He nodded his head in her direction, glancing down at the men's doublet and buckskin hose.

She didn't answer, she was too busy turning down the corridor and quickly pushing open each door at a time.

"That's my room!" Oswyn protested when she kicked open his door, peering inside. "Gently does it, now. That's not a thing for her, is it?"

"Nay," Iomhar said, following her down the corridor. "She'll do something fast and with vigour if it needs to be done."

"I don't see the point in waiting to see who has been in our lodgings, do you?" she asked snidely, kicking open Iomhar's door next. This room was just as empty and infinitely tidier than Kit kept her room. Iomhar's belongings were all folded together by his bag and on the table beside the small straw bed was a small golden chain that glinted in the candlelight.

"What's that?" Oswyn asked, pointing toward it.

"That is my matter." Iomhar closed the door again. "Nay one in there, Kit." She moved on, heading for her chamber, the last one off the tiny corridor. When she kicked this door open, she nearly fell into the room as the candlelight spilled over the space.

Her room may have been unkempt before, but it was now ransacked, with each item of clothing that had once been in her bag strewn across the floor and the furniture. The one lonely cupboard she had been using had the doors flung open. Her spare boots had fallen out and were lying on their side.

"What the —" Oswyn broke off behind her, following Kit and Iomhar as they stepped into the room. "Nowt good about this. You've been robbed, pet."

"Kit." Iomhar tapped her arm. "Has anything been taken?"

She moved forward, with her body abruptly animated as she searched the space. She took no care in her search, the room was already a mess, and there seemed hardly any point in trying to tidy it now. She searched her clothes, her bag and the cupboard, but there was nothing of hers that appeared to be missing.

"No, I do not think so." She was aware as she stood straight that Iomhar was passing the candle into her hand. "What are you —"

"Hold that for a wee moment." He turned around and grabbed Oswyn's doublet, holding it by the scruff of the collar and practically lifting him off the floor with the toes of his boots trailing on the wooden boards.

"Wait, Scot!" Oswyn scrambled to try and be free, pulling at Iomhar's hands. "Why are you taking hold of me!?"

"Was the door forced downstairs?" Iomhar asked, already knowing the answer.

"No."

"Then how did a thief get in?" Iomhar's words were harsh though not loud, stopping Oswyn from being able to argue.

"I ... I do not know."

"Does your maid have a key?" Each of Iomhar's questions came faster than the last. "Have ye ever given a key to anyone?"

"No. No!" Oswyn said, shaking his head back and forth. "Put me down, Scot, for our lord's sake."

Iomhar released Oswyn, so suddenly that Oswyn nearly fell over.

"Iomhar," Kit said as he looked back to her. "Was that necessary?"

"Kit, if they didn't break in and nay one else has a key, there is only one way someone else could have been in here. He let them in."

"Why would I do that? Eh?" Oswyn walked past Kit, trying to straighten his doublet as he moved to the window. "Did you shut this?" He pushed once on the glass, so that it swung open. Kit stared at it, baffled for a minute.

"I thought I did."

"Well, clearly you did not." Oswyn walked back through the room, straightening the collar of his doublet. "They must have climbed up through the window. Think again before you accuse me next time, Scot."

Oswyn strode out of the room, leaving Kit and Iomhar staring at one another. Kit was slowly shaking her head.

"Why would someone search my room then not take anything?"

"They were looking for something, Kit. Something in particular."

# CHAPTER 21

"A letter for you." Oswyn passed a letter into Kit's hands. She took it with a nod, looking between Oswyn and Iomhar as they ate their breakfast in complete silence. For two nights and days, neither one of them had spoken to each other. Kit kept glancing Iomhar's way, but it was clear he wasn't going to relax his suspicions. He kept glaring at Oswyn over their breakfast of kippers and oatbread.

Kit cleared her throat, trying to get Iomhar's attention. He flicked his eyes toward her and she raised her eyebrows, warning him to treat their host a little kinder, but it had no effect. He slyly shook his head and returned his stare to Oswyn. Giving up, Kit returned her focus to the letter in her hand, unfurling it to find Walsingham's familiar script laid out before her.

*Kit,*

*This is wonderful news! We must transport GL to the Tower to be interrogated, but it is imperative we do not waste time whilst we have him. I don't doubt the asset he is to our Catholic betrayers, and I believe them capable of any deception to try to recover him from the dungeons.*

*You must extract from him at once who his target was. It will not be easy, but I have authorisation from Her Majesty for you to use torture as needed to make the assassin talk. Once we know who he was targeting, we know where to send our intelligencers. I fear that once the Jesuits hear their assassin has been caught, they will send more to take his place and complete his task.*

*Do not waste time.*

*I will write in a few days once I have arranged for him to be transferred to the Tower. From there, he will face trial for the murders he has committed.*

*Taurus*

Kit let the letter sit in her hands for a minute, feeling nauseous at what had been approved.

"Is it Taurus?" Iomhar said, reaching forward for the letter. She passed it over to him, watching as the muscles in his chin grew taut when he read the same lines that bothered her so much.

"And?" Oswyn asked. "Has he approved torture?"

"It seems Her Majesty has authorised it," Iomhar admitted quietly, lowering the letter down to the table.

"Good, then why are we bothering with breakfast?" Oswyn asked as he stood to his feet, tossing the knife he had been eating with down on the table, so that it clattered against the pewter plate. He strode out of the room, heading straight for his chamber and closing the door loudly behind him.

"Something tells me he is still upset with you," Kit said as she reached for the letter again.

"Really? Aye, I think he likes me. A wee bit, anyway." Iomhar's jest brought a small smile to Kit's face, but it did not last long.

"I agree with you."

"Agree?" Iomhar sat straight, losing interest in his breakfast. "Ye agree with me on something? I might fall out of my chair."

"I agree with you. Sometimes," she added the latter part and pulled a wry smile from Iomhar.

"What do ye agree with me on?"

"If we torture Luca, it will not move us any closer to the truth." She put the letter within her pocket and folded her arms, sitting back from the table. "Luca ... he struck me as a man devoted to his cause. Would you agree?"

"Aye. Entirely." Iomhar turned in his chair and sat forward, lowering his voice as he glanced at the corridor down which Oswyn had disappeared. "Ye think whatever he would tell us under torture would be simply him trying to distract us. Putting our attention somewhere it does not belong."

"I do." Kit sat forward too, so they were both leaning out of their chairs toward each other. "No good can come of it."

"There's more to this though." He tilted his head to the side as he watched her.

"What do you mean?"

"It sickens ye, does it not?" he asked, nodding his head toward her. "The thought of it."

She looked down, fiddling with her hands for a minute. "Of course it does. I think any person would have lost their heart to think torture a good thing."

"Couldn't have said it better meself." Iomhar's words startled her into looking up from her hands.

"Now you are agreeing with me?"

"Aye, looks like we're starting a new path, one where we're not always arguing with each other," he said with a smile.

"We're not always arguing."

"Aye, we are."

"We're not."

"Isn't this an argument?"

"Yes, but you are very much doing this intentionally."

"I am not." He chuckled as he sat back.

"You two?" Oswyn's voice called to them, cutting through their laughter. "Once you've finished your wooing, shall we head to Bamburgh?" He walked to the door, slinging a cloak around his shoulders.

"That was not wooing," Kit objected hurriedly as she moved to her feet, discarding the last of her breakfast as she reached for her hat and gloves.

"Aye, you keep telling yourself that, pet."

Kit looked back to Iomhar, about to ask him to say as much himself, but he was too busy laughing.

"I am not convinced this will work."

"You have not thought of anything else on the ride, have you?" Kit asked as they climbed down from their horses. Iomhar came close to her, so she could whisper quietly without Oswyn overhearing the two of them. "What choice do we have? If Oswyn gets into that dungeon —"

"Aye, I know," he muttered, his voice hissing with frustration. "Aye, very well, we'll see if it works."

"It will work."

"What makes ye so confident?"

"Because he cannot resist an argument with you." Kit nodded in Oswyn's direction as he strode off up the path toward the dungeons. She hurried after him with Iomhar at her heels, tracing the route Oswyn took as they circled the castle, walking alongside the walls and across the cobbles until the entrance of the dungeons came into view, flanked by the guards.

"How long do ye need?" Iomhar asked her.

"Half an hour. Maybe more."

"Half an hour!" Iomhar repeated. "Ye think I can argue with him for all that time?"

"Oddly enough, I have no doubts on that matter."

"Sometimes I wonder how little ye really think of me."

"That was praise, Iomhar."

"Was it?"

"Now. Before he reaches the door." She took hold of Iomhar's arm and pulled him forward; he went at once, striding toward Oswyn.

"Oswyn?" he called. Oswyn hesitated just before he reached the guards, turning round to face Iomhar.

"What, Scot?"

"We need to change our lodgings."

"Change lodgings? Whatever for?"

"Are ye blind?" Iomhar scoffed. He grabbed Oswyn by the scruff of his doublet and dragged him away from the dungeon entrance, putting on a façade of fearing being overheard by the guards. "Someone broke into your house. Aye, they searched Kit's rooms and didn't bother to search our own, is that not odd to ye?"

"He did not take anything."

"That is even stranger." Iomhar shook his head, glancing once to Kit as she made her way toward the doorway to the dungeons. "What of the attack on Kit? Alnwick is not a safe place."

"You are overthinking things. That is all."

"It is ill jesting with edged tools. That's what I think."

"What on earth does that mean?"

Kit drowned out the argument as she nodded her head at the guards and moved past them, entering the dungeons. On the other side, one of the gaolers was waiting for her with a set of keys twirling in his hand.

"For Luca?"

"Yes," she said, pulling the bag she had brought with her tighter over her shoulder. It wasn't much, merely a small leather satchel, but it suited her purpose. The gaoler led her through the corridors, heading along the torchlit stone warren before reaching the cell in which Luca was locked up.

As Kit waited for the gaoler to unlock the door, she peered through the bars, finding Luca was stood on the other side, staring straight back at her with the whites of those eyes visible in the candlelight.

"How long do you need?" the goaler asked as he swung open the door.

"I'll call you when I'm done." Kit stepped in before turning round and lowering her voice for only the gaoler to hear. "Do not let anyone else in here. Understood?"

"Aye, ma'am." He nodded his head and closed the door behind him though he did not lock it.

Kit lowered the bag to the settle bench looped with ropes before turning her eyes on Luca. He was leaning against the wall, his shoulders hunched, and his legs outstretched to the side, keeping himself standing.

"Did you sleep?" Kit asked. Luca's head jerked to the side as his eyes narrowed.

"Do you care, *donna*?"

She smiled a little, showing the truth of the matter.

"From what I hear, you have killed many. No, I do not care if you slept ill." She sat on the settle bench beside the bag, letting silence fall between them as she stared at him. At first, Luca returned the stare, but after a minute of that uncomfortable peace stretching out, he shifted between his feet, making the chains fastened to his wrists rattle before he glanced to the barred door.

"Are the two men not joining us?"

"No," Kit answered quickly.

"I thought you would be using what sits on that table today." He motioned his head toward the side of the room where the torture instruments sat. Kit shifted as her eyes rested on the thumb screws and the set of spikes beside the table.

"I had something else in mind." Kit unlatched the satchel beside her and pulled out bundles of muslin cloth. Beneath the first cloth were chunks of cheese and in the second was a stottie cake. When the food was revealed, Luca's chains shifted again.

"You think I will be tortured by you eating before me?"

"No." Kit stood to her feet and passed the cheese into his hand first. "This is for you to eat."

Luca didn't move at first. His face froze in an impassive expression, staring at her. As she returned to the settle bench, he lifted the cheese to his lips. With the chains around his wrists, it was difficult, but he was eventually able to pass the cheese chunks into his mouth.

"Why are you feeding me, *donna*?" he asked with his mouth full of cheese, as the flash of yellowy white chunks appeared every now and then past his lips. "Keeping me alive for torture?"

"I am feeding a hungry man. As a man of God, I thought you would sympathise with such a thing." She sat back on the settle bench and pulled the rosary beads out from where they were hidden beneath the collar of her doublet, letting them hang down her chest. He reared forward at the sight, his eyes flicking down to the crucifix at the end of the beads.

"Give it to me," he pleaded, his voice turning deep.

"Why do you want it so badly?"

"*Dal corpo di Cristo.*" The Italian words were evidently a curse from the way he spat them out. "I am a priest, am I not?"

"You are an assassin first, from what I hear."

"Then why are you not using one of those devices on me, *donna*?" He jerked his head toward the torture instruments once again. "You know what I am. Why do you have any qualms about using such things?"

"You may not value human life, Luca, but we are not all the same." She pulled open the second muslin cloth and prised the stottie into two pieces, taking a bite for herself. "I cannot kill as you do, and I will not hurt as you so freely do either."

"What if I am not who you think I am?" he asked gently, a wicked smile curling his lips.

She laughed, but without humour. "When you landed on these shores, to escape me you pushed me into the ocean, prepared to see me drown. No, I know exactly what you are."

Luca didn't make any further objection, he merely nodded slowly. "Yet you will not hurt me in return?"

"A court will decide your punishment. Not I." She stood to her feet and proffered him the second piece of stottie.

He took it warily, curling his nose as he sniffed it. "What is it, *donna*?"

"A cake. Try it."

He did, with the suspicious curve of his lips lapsing the moment he tasted it. "Why are you giving me food?" he asked, looking down at what remained of the stottie in his hand rather than meeting her gaze.

Kit returned to the settle bench, eating her stottie as she stared at him. "I will not torture you for answers, but I can give you this. I can keep you alive, give you food, give you something of comfort whilst you are here. Is that not worthy of some information from you?" Her question made him pause with the food and look to her once again.

"You are cleverer than you appear, *donna*."

"I suppose that is a compliment." She nodded her head slowly. "So, will you tell me something?"

"I will not betray my kin, *donna malvagia*." He swallowed what was left of the stottie, maintaining her gaze. "Know this though, what you aim for is pointless. Those that hide in the shadows will come forth."

Kit fell still at the words. It was what she had feared, that even with Luca here there would be more to take his place and accomplish his mission. "Who?" she asked.

"*Angeli sulla terra.*"

"Angels?" she asked, trying her best to translate.

"Angels on earth, *donna*. Angels on earth." He tipped his eyes to the ceiling, as if able to look through those wooden boards and iron pins to see to heaven.

"What angels, Luca? Who are they?" she asked quietly, leaning forward on the settle bench.

"You have had all you will have from me." He lowered his gaze once more. "But ... you should know this, *donna*. Not every man will take your view of the world."

"What view?"

"That they can keep a man alive." He gestured to the muslin cloths where she had brought the food. "Do not spend your charity on the wrong person."

"Are you the wrong person?"

"I am entirely the wrong person," he said, his lips curving into a smile that slipped back off his teeth, revealing blackened teeth.

Kit was dissatisfied. This was not the progress she had hoped to make. Maybe it was too much to hope for, but she was not going to give up trying, not whilst there was a hope of avoiding those instruments sat on the other side of the dungeon. She sat forward on the bench one more time, pinning her gaze on Luca.

"Who are you here for, Luca? Who were you sent to kill?"

He smiled and looked to her, revealing that the smile was rather empty, for it did not reach his eyes.

"Is it Queen Elizabeth?" Kit asked. "Or is it the king of Scotland?"

"Both Protestants, aren't they?"

"Wait…" Kit stood slowly to her feet. "Are you here for them both?" The thought made her stomach turn over.

Beyond the cell, there was a clattering sound, of irons bars colliding with each other. What followed were such great shouts and cries that Kit was forced to turn away from Luca and hurry to the door, opening it and stepping out.

"You there?" she called to the nearest guard. "Lock him up again."

The guard nodded, bending his head so low that the slashed felt hat covered half of his face, blocking out his eyes. As the guard hastened to do his duty, Kit ran out of the corridor, heading toward the light at the end. She only just stepped outside when she was forced forward into the light of the courtyard, mobbed by a group of men that had escaped the dungeons, dressed in rags.

Kit placed herself flat against the wall as the men made their escape, pushing past her into the open courtyard. It was a riot, with each man trying his best to reach the exit. Some on route were not afraid to injure the guards, engaging in fights that were bare fists against weapons.

"Guards!" she cried. "Your prisoners are escaping!"

The guards turned to catch the prisoners, but it almost seemed too late. Already, some of the men were streaking ahead, reaching the far side of the courtyard. At the very end, Kit could see Iomhar standing alone, looking about himself in a confused way.

"Iomhar!" she called to him. "Where's Oswyn?"

"Good question." His shout back was muffled by the prisoners' cries.

# CHAPTER 22

"Luca." Kit whispered the assassin's name as the guards regained control of the courtyard. She hurried back toward the doorway to the dungeons, moving so quickly that she slipped on the cobbles more than once.

"Kit? Where is Oswyn?" Iomhar called, chasing after her into the corridor.

She glanced over her shoulder, looking at him in the torchlight. "Were you not watching him?"

"He strode off in the middle of our argument, saying he could not bear it anymore."

"Did he come this way?"

"Nay. He strode out of the castle walls and down the drive."

Kit hurried toward Luca's cell, where she found the barred door ajar. She froze, her feet skidding to a halt on the straw scattered across the stone floor.

"It's open," she whispered as Iomhar stopped at her side. He didn't waste time and flung open the door. Kit followed him, nearly colliding with his back as he came to a sharp halt.

"Kit. Where is he?"

Kit peered around his arm, finding the chains where Luca had been manacled minutes before were now empty, with the cuffs of each chain hanging down to the cobbled floor.

"That's not possible," she murmured. "He was just here."

"Well, he's not here now." He turned round, urging her back through the door. As they stepped out into the corridor, he pointed down at her throat. "Hide that."

"What?" She reached up, finding the rosary beads still exposed around her throat.

"Ye want anyone to see those? They'll think ye are a Catholic," he called as he ran down the corridor.

Kit stuffed the rosary beneath the collar of her doublet before running after him, hurrying past the torches. On the way, Iomhar stopped and looked in every cell.

"What are you doing?"

"Luca was not in that courtyard. We would have seen him," Iomhar spoke quickly as he searched the cells. "Either he's still here or he found another way out."

"None of these cells have windows." Kit followed him into each cell in turn, realising it was futile. Even as they searched, the guards were bringing back some of the prisoners, forcing them into each room. When the final door was locked, she and Iomhar gave up hope of finding Luca in the cells and hastened into the courtyard.

Some of the guards were injured, seeing to each other's wounds as a familiar face walked through the crowd.

"What happened?" Oswyn asked, walking toward Kit and Iomhar.

"An escape," Kit answered, turning her head frantically back and forth. She was looking for any sign of Luca, of a fleeting glimpse of his black clothes, but there was nothing, only the guards and the slashed felt halts atop their heads.

"Luca?" Oswyn asked.

"Gone."

"No. No!" Oswyn sprinted to the door. "I go to a privy and in the time that I'm gone, you let the man escape?" he asked wildly, turning back only long enough to thrust an accusing finger in Kit's direction.

"You think I let this happen?" Kit gestured to her own chest.

"Someone did. How else would he escape?" As Oswyn stepped down into the corridor, Kit turned away, finding Iomhar's gaze on her too.

In a way, she had to agree. Someone had to have helped, how else would Luca have fled?

"We need to search the castle. Now." Kit strode forward, with Iomhar at her heels. He didn't object or blame her, he merely gathered some of the guards and gave them orders, instructing a full search of not only Bamburgh Castle, but the town and the beach at the foot of the foundations.

Kit attended the search, but the longer she searched, the more her hands began to tremble. When she reached the beach, staring up and down the dark yellow sand, there were midges in the air, tiny flies that shot back and forth, landing on her cheeks and nose before worming their way under her hat and into her hair. She growled in frustration the further down the beach she searched, yanking the hat off her head and shaking out her hair in the effort to escape the midges.

"Kit? What is it?" Iomhar called to her from further down the beach. He was searching the sand dunes, with the wispy grasses like the beach's mop of hair coming up to his thighs.

"How could this happen?" she cried. "How could we let him escape?"

"Nay one let him escape, Kit." Iomhar shook his head, focusing on searching the dunes rather than looking back to her. "Ye cannot blame any of us for this."

"Can't I? I was the one in the cell with him. Why did I leave?"

"I am not having this conversation, Kit." He strode away, further through the grasses, heading to the far end of the beach where there were great boulders. He bent down between each pale grey rock, searching every crevice and possible hiding place for Luca.

"God's blood," she murmured, walking along the sealine, looking out to the ocean, seeking any sign of a boat that could have taken Luca away. "What will Walsingham say now?" Her question made Iomhar pause and look up from the boulders.

"That is not at the top of my worries." His words made her flinch and look away. "I am more worried that an assassin is loose on our shores." He strode out of the boulders, walking past her, sending the sand scattering around his boots. "Stop worrying what Walsingham always thinks, Kit," he muttered with clear anger, not even pausing as he passed her. "There are more important things to think of in this world."

She didn't answer him, she merely balled her fingers into fists as she watched him walk away, heading back toward the castle. She breathed deeply, staring out across the ocean.

"Walsingham will not forgive us for this," she whispered, before turning to follow Iomhar.

"Tell me again what happened," Oswyn ordered the guards. They were gathered in a semicircle within the courtyard, facing Oswyn and Iomhar as they questioned them. Some of the guards were still fussing with bruises that they had earned in the scuffle with the prisoners, others were leaning on pikes, and some were sat down on a nearby low-lying wall, staring in wonder back at the dungeons.

Kit was sat on such a wall with her own eyes trained on the door to the dungeons. It didn't make sense to her. It was clear there was only one way in and out of that dungeon, and she had been standing there the entire time. The only moment she hadn't been in the way was when she had stumbled into the courtyard, watching the scuffle between the guards and prisoners.

"He could have crept out behind me," she whispered to herself, yet dismissed the idea the next moment. She or Iomhar would have seen him.

"No, man? No one is going to speak up?" Oswyn barked, his voice growing irate. "How did the first prisoner escape?"

"We do not know, Sir." One of the guards stepped forward. "Craig was found unconscious at the side of a cell with his keys stolen. Someone must have crept up on him."

"In the name of the wee man," Iomhar cursed, rubbing his brow. "That is too much of a coincidence."

"What of the guard that came to lock Luca's cell?" Kit spoke up, looking away from the dungeons back at the guards.

"What guard?" Oswyn asked.

"When the prisoners broke out, I asked a guard to lock up Luca's cell." Kit stood to her feet and stepped up on the wall, the better to see all of the guards that were now looking her way. "Who was it?" Each guard started looking at the one beside him, murmuring amongst themselves. "No one wishes to declare themselves?"

"What did he look like?" Oswyn asked her.

"His hat was pulled low. I didn't have a good look at him." The moment the words were out of her mouth, she realised the implication. Iomhar appeared to realise the same, muttering a curse under his breath as he turned back to the guards.

"It was none of ye, was it?" he called loudly. "Someone crept in here, disguised as one of your own, and none of ye realised it?" The guards at least had the duty to look ashamed, but it was done. "Aye, safest place in all of Northumberland to hold a prisoner. That was what ye said, wasn't it, Oswyn?"

"Do not blame me for this, Scot."

"Who else should I blame?"

"How about the intelligencer that was watching him when he escaped?" Oswyn said loudly, pointing in Kit's direction. Kit sighed and jumped down off the wall. "Where are you going?"

"Shouting at each other will not make Luca reappear in that cell." She walked past them all, heading into the dungeons once more. Some of the guards followed her, taking their places outside each cell. Kit walked past all of the bolted doors, heading straight for Luca's cell at the far end.

She pushed open the barred door and stepped inside. The empty satchel bag she had brought with her was discarded on the settle bench along with the muslin cloths. Where Luca had once stood, the only sign he had been there at all was the way the straw on the floor was mussed around where his boots once stood.

Kit walked forward, turning and standing in the exact spot Luca had been in before picking up the manacles and looking at each one in turn. It was clear the locks hadn't been picked, for there were no scratch marks around the locks. They had been unlocked by a key.

As she let the manacles drop down at her side, she looked toward the settle bench, seeing something beneath it, pushed against the side. Squinting her eyes to see through the orange torchlight, she reached down to the object that lurked in the shadows, pulling it free from where it rested beside the bench. In her hand, there was a piece of black cloth. She stood straight and moved toward the torch, unfolding the cloth until she realised it was the black doublet that Luca had been wearing.

"Oh god," she whispered, folding the doublet back up again. "That was how he escaped."

She tucked the doublet under her arm and ran out of the cell, heading back along the corridor and up to the courtyard, where she found Oswyn and Iomhar still arguing.

"Enough." She stepped between them, thrusting the doublet high between their faces, forcing them to back off from each other.

"What is that?" Oswyn asked.

"Luca's doublet."

"Just so," Kit nodded her head in Iomhar's direction. "Think, why would he take this off?"

"It's too cold to shed clothes," Oswyn said, affecting a shiver.

"Because he had something else to put on," Kit answered her own question, watching as Iomhar muttered more curses.

"Am I missing something?" Oswyn asked, looking between the two of them.

"Who was going to pay attention to another man dressed like a guard, Oswyn?" She pushed the doublet into his grasp. "Whoever crept in here dressed as a guard gave Luca his clothes. We weren't watching the guards, were we? We only searched the prisoners' faces."

Iomhar reached forward and took the black doublet out of Oswyn's hands, holding it aloft in clear thought before he turned and hurried to the other side of the courtyard.

"Where are you going?" Oswyn called after him.

"To find out where he went."

Kit and Oswyn followed Iomhar as he ran all the way down the pathway, toward the stables at the far end.

"Ye there?" Iomhar called to a stable boy who jumped away from the horse he had been attending. At the sharp tone, the boy nearly fell backwards. "Have any guards come through here in the last hour? Any guard requested a horse?"

"Aye." The boy nodded, looking between the three of them. "He took a horse. Didn't ask for it, just took it."

"Did he say anything?" Kit asked, stepping forward.

"Aye." The boy pointed down the road. "He asked which road to take for Newcastle."

# CHAPTER 23

"Ye've not seen him? Nay one matching that description?" Iomhar asked the man standing beside the coaching inn.

"I said no the first time, didn't I, Scot?" At the name, Iomhar bristled, but behind him Oswyn sniggered.

Kit looked away, her focus much more on the sun that was now slipping out of the sky, streaking the clouds that were left behind in dark purple hues, showing night-time was not far away. As night crept in, a bitter coldness came with it, making her lift the collar of her doublet around her throat and chin, trying to mask herself from it.

"This is hopeless," Oswyn said as they walked away from the coaching inn together. "We must have asked every coaching inn on the way to Newcastle if they have seen Luca. There is still no sign of him."

"Then we keep looking," Kit muttered firmly.

"Aye, I agree." Iomhar walked out into the road beside her, staring down at the town as she did.

They were on the very outskirts of Newcastle, looking down at where the cobbled and timbered houses wound their way along the river. Each thatched roof was turning purple with the growing night.

"The bellmen will be out soon to signal evening curfew," Oswyn said, hurrying to catch up with the two of them. "I do not wish to spend a night in gaol, do you?"

"Then we stay here for the night," Iomhar said conclusively. "We need to change lodgings as it is."

"You are returning to this subject?"

"I never abandoned the idea."

Kit furrowed her brow and looked to Iomhar at her side. She had thought it was just an excuse to start an argument with Oswyn, but it was clear Iomhar would not be moved on the matter.

"What if we each take one of the coaching inns?" Kit asked, pointing down the hill toward the centre of town. "Oswyn, you said there are three more coaching inns."

"Aye, there are."

"Then we each take one, see if they have seen Luca arrive on his horse."

"Aye, as you wish. This is hopeless if you ask me though." Oswyn shook his head and pointed down a small lane he was intending to take. "I'll head for the Bell Inn. You two take the others. Meet at the Bell when you're done?" He didn't wait for a reply but hustled down the street, clearly not intending to be out for long.

"I hate to utter the words, but Oswyn might be right." Iomhar gritted his teeth as he spoke.

Kit followed him as they descended the main hill, heading into town. "What do you mean?"

"I do not expect to find Luca at a coaching inn. He's more likely to hide with someone he thinks he can trust."

"At this point, it's the only choice we have."

When they reached the river, they parted ways, with Kit and Iomhar heading in opposite directions toward the coaching inns Oswyn had described. When Kit found the inn that she was searching for, she watched the place for a minute or two, observing the comings and goings. It was clearly a place for travellers, with many a man and woman drinking beer in the alehouse. At the doorway, the innkeeper stood, watching those who came in and out.

"You had an Italian come here tonight?" Kit called to him as she reached the door.

"No Italians here, pet. They be Catholics, aren't they?"

"This one certainly is." She sighed and turned away. Even as she backed up, she tried again, offering a full description of Luca, but the innkeeper continued to shake his head.

"No man like that here. Best you run along before the bellmen find you, pet."

She smiled a little as she nodded her thanks and turned away. Even if the bellmen found her, she wouldn't stay long in a gaol.

She headed back to the Bell Inn, traipsing her way through the streets and heading up the hill away from the river. She had to dig the heels of her boots into the earth to find purchase to climb such a steep hill, watching as the narrowed houses either side of her began to fade away, disappearing into the growing darkness.

When the moon came out, she traversed the hill using the silvery light, yet it played tricks on her mind, with shadows moving up ahead. At one point, she thought a shadow was watching her.

"Who's there?" she called, with her feet falling still. Yet the shadow didn't move. Deciding it was nothing more than a shadow in a doorway, she moved on, though she kept glancing back, unnerved.

Despite the chill, her palms began to grow sweaty as she climbed faster and faster. When she looked back another time, she could have sworn the shadow had moved. It was no longer in the doorway of the house, but at the side of a building under the eaves. She froze, watching it for a second with her hand on the hilt of the dagger in her belt. The shadow didn't move.

A cloud came over the moon. The street turned from being basked in a silvery glow to such darkness that Kit couldn't see anything in front of her. She blinked madly, trying to adjust her eyes to the new darkness, but it was deep and as thick as trying to walk through the gravy of one of the pies found in the coaching inns.

The sound of boots on the cobbles was the first sign the shadow had moved. Kit turned, about to run up the hill, when she felt a hand latch onto the rear of her belt, jerking her backwards.

Kit tried to shout out, but a hand clamped over her mouth. The hand that had wrenched her belt came up around her body, pinning her arms to her sides. She tried to kick at the earth beneath her, in the hope she could make an escape, but the attacker was too strong, pulling her down the hill. With their weight tipped backwards, she would have fallen over, had he not been holding onto her.

"Ye escaped once. This ends now."

She recognised the voice instantly. It held the same raspy tone of the man that had attacked her at the river in Alnwick.

"You failed once." Her voice was muffled around the hand over her mouth. He released her, only momentarily to allow her to speak. "I will not die now." She was defiant in her tone.

His fingers latched over her lips again, preventing her from speaking another time. Despite her words, she couldn't reach the weapons in her belt. She kicked out in front of her instead, forcing him to step backward and nearly lose balance as he half carried her down the hill.

"It will be quick. He wanted ye to suffer. Said it was right. Yet that way I cannot be certain the task is done." He took a firmer hold of her jaw, trying to turn her head.

Kit knew what he was doing, that he was trying to immobilise her. She had been taught it once by one of Walsingham's intelligencers. He had been a brute of a man, standing under the timber beams of the attic in Seething Lane, teaching Kit how to defend herself. When he tried to encourage her to attack him, it never went well. She was too small to cause damage at the time, and he was too stocky. In the end, there was only one thing she could do, and she had to do it now.

Her teeth clamped down on her attacker's hand so harshly that he growled in pain behind her. The metallic taste of blood passed Kit's lips as she wrenched her head away from his grasp. With the element of surprise, she had the upper hand and turned within his grasp, lifting her knee sharply so that it crunched the area between his legs. He wailed in pain, releasing her and allowing her to stumble out of his hold.

She didn't wait to watch him fall to the ground, clutching his most private area. She grabbed the dagger from her belt, knowing she might need it yet and fled up the hill, running so fast that her lungs burned within seconds. Sprinting up such a steep incline made her legs tire faster, and her thighs began to tingle, as if being poked by a hundred needles every second.

She ran through the darkness at first, before a light appeared ahead. Lanterns fastened to houses began to bask her path in the dullest of amber glows. It was all she needed to make her escape.

Kit had not been running for long when she could hear the footsteps behind her. The man was gaining ground.

She could see the inn up ahead, with the sign bearing the words *The Bell Inn* swinging in the wintery breeze, only visible thanks to the lantern that was pinned outside of the building to the stone wall. It was her one chance of escaping him — find a public area.

The footsteps thumped behind her on the cobbled ground as she reached the corner that led to the inn. A yelp escaped her, loud and piercing as he tackled her. Her jaw landed against the cobbles, with warmth spilling out against her skin, drawing blood. She heard him take out a blade with the metal scraping against another weapon. She took a tighter hold of the dagger in her hand and dug her feet and elbows into the ground, using that hold to jerk her body upwards and throw him off her. It gave her enough room to roll over on the ground with the dagger outstretched.

In the lantern light, she could see a dagger coming down toward her in his grasp. It was inches from her face, about to pierce her when she lashed out with her own blade. She acted just as she was taught in Seething Lane, swiping upward and cutting through the side of her attacker, before bringing the tip down across his hand, slicing his wrist and forcing him to drop the blade.

The roar of pain he emitted was animalistic. He crumpled down over her, his body falling onto hers. She yelped at the weight of it before rolling him off her, tipping him over as she scrambled backwards across the cobbles and hurried to her feet. She turned round to face him, bearing the dagger forward in both hands in case he came for her again.

She wavered at the sight before her, for he was hurt badly.

The man slowly stood to his feet. His figure just about discernible in the lantern light. He was clutching the wound on his side, but the brief lifting of his hand revealed how deeply she had cut him.

"Ye will die," he muttered to her. The words made her step back, heading toward the inn. "He will still want ye dead, nay matter what happens to me."

"Who? Who is it that you speak of?" Kit demanded to know, feeling her voice shake with anger.

"He wants justice," the man muttered. "That is all ye need to know." He stepped toward her again, lifting his hands to his wound. The anger began to dissipate from Kit's body as the growing realisation struck her that this man was gravely injured, possibly fatally.

Kit stepped away in horror, looking down at the bloody dagger in her hands. The blood glistened as the moon crept out from behind the covering of cloud, as if it were an eye, peering at her, watching what she had done. She let out a whimper she could not control, nearly dropping the blade as she backed further away, stumbling in the direction of the Bell Inn.

"Kit? Is that ye? What's all this shouting?"

She knew that voice, yet she couldn't respond to Iomhar. She was too busy watching the man before her. He was crumpled forward, holding onto his side where she had cut him, groaning in pain. As he looked up, his face was basked in moonlight.

It was now unmistakeable. He was the same man that had attacked her in Alnwick. Even as he tilted his head to the clouds, as if pleading with the heavens for why he had been hurt, she could see the glint of the tattoo on his neck.

"It is you," she whispered.

He groaned and stepped toward her, keeping one hand on his side as the other reached for the belt around his waist. As he pulled out another dagger, Kit's shaking hands gripped her own blade tighter.

"Kit? Kit!" Iomhar was getting closer.

"Here," she managed to utter, calling over her shoulder.

Her attacker froze, looking toward the inn before he stumbled backward on his feet, replacing the dagger in his belt.

Kit couldn't take her eyes off the way the blood seeped through his fingers, the wound growing worse by the second as he hurried away. His movements became frantic as he spun on his heel and ran off through the night. The run didn't last long, it soon turned into a lope, with his body half crumpled forward. When he moved a distance down the street, he reached out and held onto the building beside him, using it to navigate his way.

He disappeared from Kit's view, practically falling into an alley as she felt a hand on her shoulder.

"No!" She jumped away, lifting the bloodstained dagger another time.

"It's me," Iomhar shouted, leaping back from her and holding up his hands.

Kit dropped the dagger from her fingers, letting it clatter to the cobbles beneath her. Iomhar's eyes flicked down to it, those orbs growing wide in the moonlight.

"Blood?" he asked. "Is it your own?" He lowered his hands and stepped toward her. She shook her head, erratically, glancing down the street as she did so, wary of the man coming again.

"It's another's?" he asked. His voice was panicked, growing deeper and more insistent. "Kit, speak! What has happened?" He took hold of her elbows and tried to pull her toward the inn. At first, she tried to stop him, until she stumbled over the dagger. She pulled away from him and picked up the dagger before thrusting it into his grasp.

"We need to get rid of the blood." She was trying to be practical, despite the trembling in her fingers.

"Whose blood is it, Kit?"

"The man. The one who attacked me in Alnwick, who tried to drown me in the river. He's here. He was following me. All the way up the street before he tried to..." She trailed off, not needing to say anymore. She looked down at the dagger again, seeing the blood gleam. The sight made her nauseous.

She gagged before delving a hand into her doublet and pulling out a handkerchief, trying to dry the dagger clean of the blood, yet it merely spread it, swathing the grey material in dark red splatters.

"God have mercy," she whispered, watching as the blood spread all the more.

"Kit, ye did what ye had to." Iomhar took the handkerchief and the dagger from her. He wrapped the blade in the cloth and stuffed it into a thin scabbard in his belt. "Did ye kill him?"

"I do not know." The thought made her shiver all the more, uncertain whether it was from the cold or the terror. "I am not a killer, Iomhar. I cannot have killed him."

"Was he still breathing when he walked away?"

"Very much."

"Then he's not dead yet." He glanced behind her, clearly watching for his return.

"What if he does die?" she asked, not looking to Iomhar as she asked the question. She was staring forward, not concentrating on anything. "I'll be a murderer then."

"It's not murder, Kit." He took her arm and tried to draw her forward, but she didn't move. Her body had frozen solid, and she had planted her feet in the ground. "Ye want to stay out here all night and discuss it?" She shook her head, but still struggled to move. He wrapped an arm around her waist and steered her forward.

"What are you —"

"Getting ye into that inn one way or another," he said quietly, pushing her up the couple of steps that led to the front door.

The moment they stepped through Kit had to blink against the sharp light of the candles. It didn't last long, for Iomhar stepped in front of her, offering her a clean handkerchief.

"Ye have blood on ye, Kit," he whispered harshly. "Your cheeks."

Horrified at the idea, she tried to wipe them clean, but she could feel it smearing higher across her cheekbones. Iomhar snatched the cloth from her, glancing behind him, evidently afraid of being seen. He shielded her from view with his height as he lifted the cloth to her face, cleaning it for her.

"You're looking after me again," she murmured softly.

"Little wonder there." He stuffed the handkerchief into his doublet before beckoning her to follow him. They wandered through the inn, heading toward the stairs.

"We don't have rooms."

"I've sorted them."

"What of Oswyn?" As she asked the question, she heard him.

"Kit? Iomhar? Drink before we lay our heads?" Oswyn called to the two of them.

"Not tonight, Oswyn." Iomhar waved off Oswyn before urging her up the stairs. "He shouldn't see ye. Not like this."

Kit chose not to look down at her doublet, for the way Iomhar was looking at it told her all she needed to know. She rushed up the staircase instead, peering round every turn in the wooden steps to ensure she wasn't going to meet anyone part way before she reached the landing. Iomhar urged her into one of the rooms and closed the door sharply behind him.

"Kit, tell me everything that happened," he said as he lit candles around the room, flooding the space with light.

Kit couldn't speak at first. She moved to the nearest glass propped on a cupboard at the side of the room. It was small, barely big enough to see her whole face, but the more she angled it, the greater she could see her body.

The cloth must have removed most of the blood from her cheeks, but there were some dried specks on the underside of her neck and around her lips from where she had bitten her attacker's hand. She wiped the blood away with her sleeves, then found a cut on her chin; around it, a purple bruise was beginning to bloom, like petals unfurling from a flower. Across her forehead, her hair was matted with sweat despite her body feeling cold and the front of her doublet bore a deep red mark, rather like a dark red rose had been imprinted on the surface, though it still glistened.

She said nothing, but she stepped back from the mirror and unbuttoned the doublet, throwing it to the side of the room in her haste to escape the blood. To her relief, the stain had not soaked through the heavy material onto her shirt below.

Iomhar snapped up the doublet and thrust it into a washbasin nearby that had already been filled with water by a maid, leaving it to soak.

"Kit, ye had nay choice. His life or yours, am I right?"

She nodded, wordlessly, knowing it was the truth.

"Has Walsingham never prepared ye for this?"

"What do you mean?" she asked, leaning against the wall as he passed a candle into her hand. She clung to it, as a small feeling of warmth.

"I mean ye are an intelligencer. There are some like us who meet death all the time." He held her gaze as his voice quietened. "It's not nice, but it is sometimes necessary."

"Tell me you have not done this?" she asked, feeling her voice begin to shake.

"Do not ask questions ye don't want to hear answers to," he said simply before turning to the tiny fireplace in the corner of the room and starting a fire, adding a candle flame to the wood that was piled ready to be set alight.

"I feel sick."

"Aye, many do."

She held one hand to her lips as the candle flame trembled in her other hand.

"Kit?" Iomhar's voice made her look down at him, seeing half his face cast in the light of the flames as he crouched by the hearth. "Ye could be dead had ye not done it."

"I know," she spoke hurriedly. "That does not make it easy to accept." He nodded understandingly before standing and pushing a chair forward, offering it to her. "You do not need to keep looking out for me." She motioned the candle in the direction of the chair.

"I do not need to, nay," he acknowledged with the smallest of smiles. "Ye rather I leave ye alone right now?"

"No." Her answer came fast as she sat down in the chair, leaning toward the fire. Iomhar sat down on the floor beside the fire, leaning against the stone hearth.

"What happened?" he asked, his voice much gentler now.

"He came at me. Through the darkness. Grabbed me and tried to stab me." She kept her eyes on the candle in her hands, trying to concentrate on stopping the trembling of the flame.

"Did he say anything?"

"Only similar to last time."

"Kit, ye didn't tell me he said anything last time."

"Didn't I?" she said, turning her gaze on him. "He said this was for justice. A message from someone I had never met."

"Ah, wonderful. Whoever wants ye dead is going about it in the most cryptic way."

"The gaoler in Richmond … you are certain that bolt was meant for me, are you not?"

"There isn't a doubt in my mind. If they can track ye between Alnwick and Newcastle, what's to stop them tracking ye from Richmond to here?"

"Yes. That makes sense." She slowly put the candle down. "This cannot go on though."

"What do you mean?"

"At some point, ye could run out of luck." The words were blunt, but they made her sit taller, thinking of how close that blade had come to her eyes that night. "We cannot let that happen."

"I will just have to keep watching over my shoulder."

"Then who's watching your front? Nay, Kit. There is more we have to do," Iomhar said firmly. "This ends now. They are not having the chance to come after ye again."

She smiled sadly. It was the first smile she had felt creep into her cheeks since the attack. It felt odd on her bruised jaw, knowing it was wrong to smile after she had stabbed someone, yet it came anyway, as a sort of glimmer of dark humour.

"We cannot control everything, Iomhar. Do you think it possible for us to stop them coming for me again? I am not so certain."

# CHAPTER 24

"Where is Oswyn?"

"Searching Newcastle. I told him to find every watchman that works in the town and see if they saw anything of Luca last night."

"Good," Kit murmured as she steered the mare that she was riding behind Iomhar, following him into a new town. "Where are we?"

"This is Morpeth." Iomhar held up a hand, showing they were stopping with the horses. "This is where we are staying now." He pointed a finger toward a building on the very edge of the town.

It was a noisy place, with the smell of manure so strong that Kit repeatedly hid her nose in her collar. The cattle that was being walked through the streets by the farmers were shivering, despite their thick woolly coats. The buildings were somewhat finer than in Alnwick, yet the town seemed scarred with buildings half destroyed and a garrison of men standing along the edge of the town.

"What happened to this place?" Kit asked as she climbed down from the horse, turning to look at Iomhar. He moved to her side and took the horse's reins from her.

"There was a battle between Scotland and England, under old King Henry when he was alive. Aye, the place is battle wounded well enough." He took the horses to the end of the road and delivered them to a coaching inn where a stable boy awaited him, leaving Kit in the middle of the road.

She was unsettled, looking at every face nearby, searching for any sign of the Scottish unicorn tattoo or that brown and grey whiskered face that haunted her. Each sound made her flick her head behind her, even the cows mooing at the sun, pulling against their restraints. When a farmer dropped a bucket on a cobbled wall, she whipped round, so certain for a minute that a pistol had gone off.

"It was a bucket," Iomhar said as he reached her side.

"I know." Kit stood a little taller, attempting to hide her unease.

"Nay one will know ye're here, Kit. It's safe." He pointed toward the house ahead of them, urging her to go in first.

The half-timbered building was at the edge of a street, protected on one side by the garrison of the town with a high stone wall. The house had large eaves, overhanging the street, with windows so small that it had to be dark inside. Kit pushed open the door, finding the rooms dusty and disused with a cloth thrown over a table and set of chairs. Iomhar strode in behind her and removed the cloth, whipping it in the air and kicking up the dust.

"What is this place?" Kit asked, coughing around the dust as she took a second sheet off a cupboard on the far side of the room.

"My brother once made use of it. Niall sent me the address this morning. He said it was the safest place he knew."

"You told him what happened?" Kit asked, darting her head around.

"Aye." Iomhar shrugged. "Out of everyone I know, I trust Niall the most in this world." He moved to a window and lifted a woollen covering, stuffing the border tartan plaid into a gap as he pointed out of the glass. "Take a look at what he has sent for us."

Kit moved to his side, peering out of the window to see there were two soldiers sat nearby wearing Scottish uniforms, watching the streets avidly. One held a pike in his hand and a crossbow at his belt, the other carried two pistols.

"Soldiers? What for?" she asked.

"To guard ye."

"Guard me?" She jumped back. "I do not need guarding." Iomhar simply raised his eyebrows before turning away.

"Iomhar, I am not someone to be locked up and protected."

"I never said ye were, but I don't see the harm in two more pairs of eyes watching over ye when someone wants ye dead. Do ye?" His penetrating gaze made her turn away, tossing her bag down into the nearest chair and sitting down beside it.

"This is pointless."

"Ye are going to argue with me now?" he asked as he sat down on the opposite side of the table and pulled out a slip of parchment. It took a few minutes for him to prepare the inkwell and quill, using a small knife to whittle the shaft into a nib.

"We should be searching Newcastle for Luca. You and I both know that."

"Do ye really think we will find an assassin by searching the streets?"

"Well … no." Kit had to accept it. "He is hardly going to hide just in any shadow or nook he finds. He will have had a plan."

"So what is the harm in waiting here?"

"Because we are doing nothing!" Kit said loudly, sitting forward in the chair and slamming her palms down on the table. Iomhar took hold of the inkwell, stopping it from shaking and spilling ink over the rim.

"I am doing something," he said as he began to write. Kit sat back in her chair, wanting to argue with him, but deep down, she knew it was futile. With no leads of where to search for

Luca, they had little information to begin their next search. Instead of arguing, she kept glancing at Iomhar's letter to see that he was writing to Walsingham.

"Taurus?" she asked, pointing out the name at the top of the letter.

"Aye," Iomhar said, not looking up from his letter. "He needs to know someone is after ye, Kit."

"Do not tell him that." Kit hurried to her feet, reaching forward to take the letter from him, but he held out a hand, stopping her from doing so. "He will think I'm not capable of looking out for myself."

"What do ye care what he thinks? Would ye not rather be alive?"

"You know what I mean."

"Nay, Kit. I do not." He turned, taking the letter far out of her reach and bending his head down to finish.

Kit felt the fury swell within her. She debated walking around the table and snatching the letter from him for good.

"Take it from me now and I'll simply write another when ye fall asleep."

"Pox on you," she muttered, walking to the window, knowing she had been defeated. She peered beyond the border tartan out to where the soldiers were sat guarding the house, watching the people walk up and down.

She would not be defeated by this. Come what may, she was sent here for a task, and she would accomplish it.

"*It's what we are, Kit.*" She could still remember Walsingham walking around her in Seething Lane in one of her lessons with his chin tilted high. "*We are here for one purpose only. To protect England. What are we without that, hmm?*" His eyes had turned on her then, expecting a reply. She had nodded in answer.

Kit reached beneath the collar of her doublet, pulling out Luca's rosary beads and fiddling with them as she thought of how Walsingham would respond to Iomhar's letter.

"Not well," she whispered to herself, knowing it for certain. He would be furious when he learned of Luca's escape.

Thinking of Walsingham brought another thought to mind, it was of the imagining she'd had of being under the water as a child, with a figure leaving her there and another coming to rescue her. Perhaps she had created this version of Walsingham reaching down and pulling her from the water.

"Was it my imagination?" she whispered, keeping her eyes on the guards out in the road.

"Hmm?" Iomhar looked up from his letter. "Did ye say something?"

"No," she said hurriedly, not looking back at him. She had never told anyone about the dream, she did not think it wise to speak of it now.

She continued to fiddle with the rosary beads, thinking on Iomhar's words and fearing how long she would have to wait in hiding. If she was going to find the man who owned these beads, then she would have to be certain that it was safe for her to be outside of these walls.

"What if he comes for me again?" Kit asked.

"Then we and the soldiers will be waiting for him," Iomhar said distractedly, still writing his letter.

"No, Iomhar, you do not understand." She turned to look at him, waiting for him to lift his eyes from his letter with the peregrine falcon quill, speckled with grey dots, hovering in the air. "What if we make it happen?"

He slowly lowered the quill to the table and leaned on the wood, staring at her with lifted eyebrows. "Go on."

"We could set a trap."

"And use ye as the bait? Nay," he dismissed the idea at once, picking up the quill once more.

"Why not?"

"Because such traps are risks. Ye want to stand outside and wave your arms, advertising to a murderer to come and kill ye? Aye, sounds mightily clever," he added sarcastically.

"I will not die. Besides, risking my life is my decision, is it not?" she asked. He finished his letter with a flourish and pushed it away, waiting for the ink to dry.

"It will not work."

"Why not?"

"To begin, nay one knows ye are here. He will not trace ye here."

"How can you be so sure?"

"There are only a handful of people who know where we are." Iomhar pointed at the two of them. "Us, Niall, and Oswyn. The soldiers out there don't even know who they are guarding."

"You told Oswyn we were here?"

"Aye, but I didn't tell him exactly why." Iomhar looked down as he pulled out a red wax stick from his bag. Using a tinder box, he lit a candle, waiting for the wax to melt. "If the man attacked ye does die, we do not want anyone coming to ye for the crime, do we?"

Kit looked sharply away, peering out of the window again as she chewed the side of the mouth. "Would they hang me?" she asked, her voice quiet.

"Walsingham would not let that happen."

Kit felt the nausea swell. She could be a killer, and the guilt would forever be there on her shoulders. She pictured it rather like a shadowy figure that lurked behind her. She could feel it on her shoulder, but every time she tried to look it in the eye, it moved.

There was a sound beyond the window. She recoiled, jumping back, watching as two farmers argued, in a heated debate, one angry at the other for colliding with his cart.

"I cannot live like this," she murmured, turning back to see Iomhar was melting the wax, preparing to seal his letter. "Let's set a trap for him."

"I don't remember saying aye to that."

"Well, I'm saying 'aye'." She mimicked his Scottish accent, pulling the smallest glimmer of a smile from him as he looked up at her from the wax. "I will not live in fear, Iomhar. Neither will I let myself be scared enough to hide indoors forever more. We set a trap."

Iomhar let the red wax drip down on the seal, but he left no imprint, leaving it blank and untraceable to any messenger who carried it. The candle hovered in the air for a minute as he looked back to her.

"If we do this, we do not tell Oswyn."

"Why not? Do you still distrust him so?" she asked. He stayed perfectly still, not moving an inch as the candle beside him flickered.

"I can well believe your attacker following ye to Northumberland, and to Alnwick, but to Newcastle? Nay, there are only a few ways ye could have been traced there. Either Oswyn told someone, or one of the guards who saw us leave from Bamburgh Castle informed your attacker."

"Surely the latter is more likely. Oswyn works for Walsingham."

"Think that if ye like."

"You simply don't like the Northumbrians."

"I am not as biased as ye think. I do not like Oswyn. I have met many a man here so far I can respect." Iomhar shifted in his seat, uncomfortable.

"So, you agree? We will set a trap?"

"Nothing I can say will persuade ye otherwise, will it?"

"No," she said simply.

"Aye, as ye wish." He murmured with a sigh, "but we do this carefully. I have a feeling Walsingham will send me to the Tower if anything happened to ye."

"That's the only reason you want me alive?" Kit asked with a smile, watching as he chuckled softly.

"There may be another reason." He didn't elaborate though and blew out the candle in his grasp.

# CHAPTER 25

"Any sign of him?" Kit asked as she led the way to Morpeth church. It was Sunday morning, with the church bells ringing loudly in the air. Either side of her, Iomhar and Oswyn walked forward, ready to attend the service.

"None, pet," Oswyn said, shaking his head. "The watchmen saw nothing, neither did the dockmaster or the boatmen. Even the garrison watch did not remember seeing him walk through the city walls. Aye, maybe he never made it to Newcastle. I'd wager good money that Luca is far away from Newcastle by now. Probably on his way to whoever he was sent here to kill."

"Shh," Iomhar said with a wave of his hand, pointing to the crowds around them that were also heading to church. "We do not want every man here to know our business."

Kit nodded in agreement, walking forward and lifting her head to peer over the crowd of heads all moving toward the church tower. With the spire standing tall and reaching to the sky, it was the highest building in town, practically cutting through the grey clouds. With each head turned in the direction of the spire, it would have been easy to spot any man looking in Kit's direction, but there was none.

"Are you well, pet?" Oswyn asked, elbowing her side. "You are shivering."

"Cold, that is all." She folded her arms across her body, holding the thick material of the doublet close to her chest as she looked to Iomhar.

They were waiting for someone to move toward her. The night before, Kit had put together her plan, and despite Iomhar's objections, she hadn't let him protest for long.

"This is a bad idea," Iomhar whispered to her.

"All clouds bring not rain, Iomhar," she said, using a phrase she had often heard in London. He nodded his head slowly, but still kept his eyes on the crowd around them. "Let us just hope the gossip you spread is heard by the right man."

"Hmm, I hope not."

"What are you two whispering about?" Oswyn asked, turning his gaze on them.

"The church service," Kit answered before Iomhar could. The closer they moved to the church door the more edgy Kit grew.

Two nights ago, she had insisted Iomhar tell the soldiers that were sent by Niall to spread the news she was hiding in town, and to spread it as far and as wide as possible. Uttered in a tavern, it would surely be only a matter of time before all knew of it in town. All they needed was for the news of a woman that dressed as a man staying in Morpeth to spread beyond the town's walls.

"What makes ye think he will attack here?" Iomhar asked as he held open the church door, urging her to step inside.

"When else will he have the chance?" Kit whispered. "We must all attend church. If he hears I am in Morpeth, then he knows I will have to come to church."

Kit was aware of Oswyn following them into the church, looking between them with a suspicious gaze. She chose not to answer his curiosity and turned away, sitting in the nearest pew. Iomhar and Oswyn sat down beside her, where Iomhar's cloak fell down by his knee, revealing that he had worn his weapons belt beneath his cloak. The glint of the pistol in the sunlight streaming through the stained-glass window made Oswyn flinch in his seat.

"You brought a pistol into a church?" Oswyn hissed in a mad whisper. "Have you no respect, man?" His voice was hidden by the conversation of others as they hurried into the church.

"I am an intelligencer. God will appreciate that being unarmed is a risk I cannot take."

"This is the house of God, Scot."

"Be quiet, Sassenach, or someone will hear ye."

Kit elbowed Iomhar in the side, making a beckoning gesture with her hand. He nodded slowly, and reached under his cloak, pulling out the dagger she had asked him to carry for her that morning. She bent down and slid the dagger with its small scabbard into her boot, leaving only the handle sticking out of the leather. It no longer held bloodstains, but the weapon itself made Kit stare a little longer at the steel handle, thinking of when she had used it last.

"It's beginning," Iomhar said, clearly urging Oswyn to be silent as the vicar started the service.

It did not take long for Kit to feel eyes on her. The more she looked around at other faces, the more she felt it.

When the first prayer began and they all stood to their feet, bowing their heads and closing their eyes, Kit used the opportunity to search the pews. Her eyes danced across farmers and housewives, as well as seamstresses, laundry maids, and scholars. At the far end of the church, the local baron had a private pew for his family, separated by some distance from the rest of the congregation. Beyond this pew, there was a shadow beneath the stained-glass window, of someone hiding from the light.

Kit angled her head, trying to see the figure better. He moved forward, as if sensing she was trying to see him, and his eyes met hers.

He was more hunched than she could remember, with the wider girth suggesting that beneath his shirt and doublet was a heavy bandage, but the eyes were the same, as was the tattoo she could glimpse at the top of his neck and the woollen cap that was bundled in one of his hands.

"Iomhar," she whispered, nudging him so sharply in the ribs that he exhaled suddenly.

"Ye trying to injure me?"

"Look." She urged him to follow her gaze. "He's alive. Let's move. Now."

"Kit, let's think about this a little more — ow!"

Kit turned and elbowed Iomhar to be silent as others stood from their pews and began to make their way to the church door as the service came to a close.

"I look forward to the day ye can just tell me to be quiet," Iomhar said, rubbing the sore spot on his ribs.

"Do you want everyone to overhear what we are about to do?" she whispered. "Now, draw Oswyn away."

"Kit, wait!" Yet she didn't, but walked off, listening to him as he mumbled behind her. "Why do ye always have to act on your impulse?"

"It's kept me alive so far," she murmured in return though she was not sure he heard her.

She circled the pews as people inched toward the church doors, watching out of the corner of her eye as Iomhar turned Oswyn away from her and urged him to exit the church at his side. For this to work, it was imperative that Kit's attacker thought she was completely alone. She was careful not to look round for him, fearful that it would make her plan obvious.

In the busyness of the church, no one seemed to look her way as she carved a path along the edge of the stone room, heading toward a staircase in the corner. She pushed open a small wooden door and stepped beyond onto a set of spiral stairs that descended quickly. She and Iomhar had come to see the place the day before, scouting out the perfect corner with which to trap the attacker. The crypt she reached was dark and so far removed from the main atrium of the church that she doubted anyone would have cause to come to such a place after the service.

"I am alone. Come and find me," she whispered as she stepped out through a second door, into the crypt.

It was not the largest of rooms. Vaulted with a low-lying stone arch ceiling, bordered in grey gargoyle faces that led down to graves on either side, it offered the perfect corner to trap any animal or man. Kit moved to the centre, looking between the two graves that were lit by small windows placed in the top of the wall. Below ground level, the room could have been lit by two candles and been brighter.

It didn't take long for Kit to hear footsteps on the staircase, of boots softly scuffing the stones. Flicking her head to the side, hearing someone as they approached, she stared at the burial that was far ahead of her. This effigy was shaped like a knight, with its stone armour still intact. Kit inched toward it, reaching for the dagger in her boot and hiding it within the stone fingers of the figure. She had just released him when the door creaked open behind her.

"Ye could have killed me, wee gowk." The insult was familiar to her. Kit turned round to find her whiskered attacker advancing toward her, with one of his hands placed to his side, covering up the exact place where she had plunged the dagger.

Kit didn't know whether to sigh with relief that she was not a murderer, or curse that her aim hadn't been better.

He flung open his doublet, revealing that he had worn his own weapons belt to church that day. He pulled out a small billhook, not dissimilar to the one he had held when he had attacked her by the river. Closing the door to the staircase behind him, he jammed it shut with a loose cobblestone that he kicked beneath it.

"Ye cannot escape now."

Kit pretended to be even more afraid than she felt. It was not difficult, her temptation to breathe quickly she gave way to, and she backed up toward the effigy of the knight, until she collided with it and yelped. The man advanced, lifting the billhook high within his hand.

As he reached for her with his free hand, taking hold of her arm, she reached behind her and snatched the dagger from the effigy's fingers, bringing it sharply round her body. She cut across the man's arm, forcing him to release her. He yelled in pain, looking down at the long scratch-like wound on his forearm. His face turned red, with spittle forming around the edge of his lips as his eyes flicked up in her direction.

"Ye trying to kill me one stab wound at a time?"

Kit hurried round him, heading for the door. She only had time to kick the cobblestone away from the bottom of the door before she felt his hand on her neck, jerking her backward. She lifted the dagger and brought it down sharply toward his thigh behind her. He managed to avoid the blow, but only just. As he lifted the billhook, hovering with the curved blade over her face, Kit struck out a second time, aiming for his hand. She sliced through his fingers before he could bring it down, compelling him to release her and drop the billhook.

She spun round, backing up as he gathered himself. Kit was vaguely aware of the sound of a door opening, but she didn't pay attention to it. She was too busy watching the man stalking toward her with a dagger in his hand.

When she collided with the second grave in the crypt, she lifted her weight upon it and kicked out, connecting with his already cut fingers and his dagger clattered to the floor beside the billhook. She had the advantage and lifted her dagger up. She could cause a real wound, one so deep that it could kill him. He was unarmed, unprotected, and unshielded. It would be all too easy to stop him from coming after her again. Yet Kit couldn't do it. Her hand hovered in the air with the dagger, never quite bringing it down toward him.

It gave him the time he needed to recover, collecting both the billhook and the dagger from the floor. He only took one step when the cocking of a pistol made them both freeze.

Kit flicked her eyes behind the man, seeing Iomhar had descended the staircase and had his pistol ready, pointing it directly at the man's head.

"Drop them," Iomhar instructed. The man darted his head round, his nostrils wide with heavy breathing, appearing ready to continue the fight. "I will not miss at this distance." Iomhar took another step forward and pressed the barrel of the pistol flush to the man's temple.

At once, the billhook and the dagger dropped to the floor, the blades slipping between the gaps in the cobbles.

# CHAPTER 26

"Why?" Kit was the first to speak. She was perfectly still as she stood in the middle of the dungeon cell, staring at her attacker.

The whiskered man looked up from where a gaoler was seeing to the irons around his wrists and ankles, fastening him to the wall.

"Speak, man," Kit ordered, stepping closer toward him. Yet the harshness of her tone was not enough to break him. He merely rested back on the wall, leaning slightly, as if trying to protect the wound she had caused him earlier that week. "Why come after me? Who sent you?"

"He will not talk easily, Kit," Iomhar said, walking around her and heading straight for the prisoner. As the gaoler stepped away, Iomhar took hold of the prisoner's collar and jerked it downward, revealing more of the tattoo upon his neck. In the light from the lanterns, the lines upon his neck seemed to shine. "Gunpowder and urine?" Iomhar asked with a clear sneer. "I hear it's painful."

The prisoner smiled a little as he lifted his eyes to meet Iomhar's.

"Worth the pain, aye." The Scottish accent was thick, but a little different to Iomhar's own.

"Where is he from?" she asked Iomhar, watching as he pulled more of the man's collar away to reveal all of the imprint across his neck.

"With that accent, Glasgow." Iomhar returned his attention to the man, holding him still as he examined the mark.

"Have you met Lord Egbert Ruskin?" Iomhar flinched at her words, but it had the response she had so desired. At last, the prisoner returned her gaze. He leaned forward off the wall and spat in her direction. She only had to step back to avoid it, watching as the spittle landed between the flagstones in the floor. "I will take that as a yes," Kit murmured. "Did he send you?"

"Wants justice. For his wife's death."

The words rang clear, making Kit's hands curl over her belt and rest near the weapons she carried. A confrontation with Lady Ruskin a few months ago had led to the staunch Catholic taking her own life.

"He thinks I killed his wife?" she asked, her mouth turning dry as the thought aligned itself. Iomhar looked to her, that same panic she imagined in her own eyes was reflected in his. "I did not hurt Lady Ruskin." Kit turned her eyes on the prisoner. "What gave Lord Ruskin the conviction that I did?"

"All know what happened in London. Even if ye didn't wield the blade yourself, ye are the reason she is dead. Are ye not?" The prisoner's question made Kit stiffen, thinking of how she had tussled with Lady Ruskin, trying to get the dagger from her. If it had gone differently, if she had managed to take hold of that blade, then it was true Lady Ruskin might still be alive.

"Ye cannot hold her responsible for what Lady Ruskin did to herself." Iomhar's words were cold and quiet as he released his hold on the prisoner. "Yet there is nay point in persuading ye of that, is there? If Lord Ruskin thinks it, nothing will stop him."

Kit turned in a quick circle, running her hands through her short hair before she looked back to the prisoner. "How did you find me?"

The prisoner said nothing though a small smile curled up one side of his lips, revealing a rather wicked grin.

"When you caught me in Newcastle," Kit urged him on, "how did you know I would be there? Did someone tell you where to find me? One of the gaolers from this castle? Or another?"

"There will always be men loyal to Lord Ruskin's cause," the prisoner said, jerking his chin high in pride.

"Ye mean loyal to Mary Stuart, do ye not?" Iomhar asked, earning a dark gaze from the prisoner. "Care to tell us your name?"

The man slowly shook his head and looked down to the stone floor; apparently, he was finished talking.

Kit nodded her head at Iomhar and stepped out of the cell, followed closely by him. They watched as the gaoler began to pull out the padlocks, for this time Kit wanted to be certain everything was done right. She wasn't prepared to see another prisoner escape Bamburgh Castle.

As the barred door closed, Kit looked away, unable to keep staring at the face of the man. She could hear him though. He tested his chains at first, pulling on the irons to see how far he could stretch them. When the gaoler warned him off, he simply pulled all the more.

"Aye, let him burn out his strength," Iomhar said after a minute of watching him try.

"Do we have a name for him?" one of the gaolers asked nearby.

Kit didn't answer, but she felt Iomhar at her side fidget, searching through the pockets of the jerkin they had taken off the prisoner.

"Nay name," Iomhar said eventually, "but there is this." Rather than presenting it to the gaoler, he passed it to Kit instead. It was a strip of parchment, long and thin, and embossed on the top in thick black ink was the familiar shape of the unicorn, the Scottish Royal symbol.

"What is this?" she asked, taking it from him.

"A message, perhaps. Aye, from someone else who works for Ruskin, nay doubt."

Kit turned the scrap of parchment over, finding a long list of numbers and letters on the other side.

"Code. Can ye decipher it?"

"We will see." Kit pocketed the parchment and walked forward, away from the cells. She felt Iomhar behind her, hurrying to keep pace with her, though he said nothing for a minute, not until they were out of the dungeons of Bamburgh Castle. Once they were in the courtyard, Kit paused, glancing back to the corridor they had just exited. "Is this a safe place to keep him? The last man we put here escaped."

"Men will work hard to flee a man like Luca. He is valuable to them. That man in there..." Iomhar paused and shook his head. "He isn't so important. They will not take the risk to free him. They'll simply send another after ye."

The words made Kit recoil and walk across the courtyard, heading for where they had left their horses in the stable.

"Kit?" Iomhar called after her. "Are ye well?"

"Well? Perfectly well," she said with thick sarcasm. "How would you feel knowing that you may have caught one killer, but another will come after you at any moment?"

"I know, aye. It was a foolish question."

"The word is stupid, bampot."

"Ye are fond of our Scottish insult, are ye not?"

"It suits you well," Kit said with triumph as she descended the track toward the stables. She didn't get far before she felt Iomhar take her arm, turning her round so that she was facing him. "What is it?"

"Kit, be serious a moment," he pleaded with her, his expression bearing only darkness with a scowling brow. "We cannot stop these men coming after ye. We may have delayed it for a while until they realise this man is in a dungeon, but it will not be long."

"If you are trying to cheer my spirits, you are failing." She tore her arm out of his grasp and hastened down the last of the path, walking straight into the stable. The mare that had been saddled for her earlier that day was chomping on straw and neighed in objection as she took hold of the reins and pulled her away.

"I am not trying to cheer matters. I am being practical." Iomhar took hold of the reins on the other side of the horse, pulling the mare to a rather ungainly stop.

"Iomhar, release the horse."

"It's a good way to get your attention."

"You are insufferable sometimes."

"Thank ye," he said, acting as though she had given him a compliment. "Kit, if another comes for ye, ye cannot do what ye did today."

Kit froze in her tussle with the reins, peering over the saddle of the horse to Iomhar on the other side. "What do you mean?" she asked.

"Ye know what I mean. Ye hesitated with that blade. I saw it. In that hesitation, he could have killed ye."

"He did not."

"He could have done." Iomhar's voice grew louder as he leaned over the saddle, pinning her to the spot with the strength of his green gaze. "Do not hesitate again. If it means saving your own life, sometimes ye have to be willing to take another's."

Kit felt a shuddery breath escape her as her fingers trembled around the reins. She clamped down on the leather, trying to stop any hint of those shakes. She couldn't look at Iomhar again, only at the horse as it snuffled toward the ground, preparing for their ride.

"Kit? Can ye do that?" Iomhar asked.

"We will see." She spoke harshly, wanting an end to the matter. Iomhar wandered off, releasing the reins of her mare and muttering something under his breath as he collected his own steed, but she didn't ask him what he was murmuring about. She was too busy climbing into the saddle and thinking on what he had said.

She had come close to killing the man in that dungeon twice. Once with the wound to his side and that day his life had only been spared by her hesitation. Kit knew Iomhar was right. Sometimes it took a hard decision to preserve one's life over another, but each time she thought of death, she saw Lady Ruskin in her mind, capitulating forward down to the cobbled ground with that dagger plunged so deep in her stomach that no hint of the blade could be seen, only the hilt.

"I am not sure I can do that to another," Kit whispered to herself as she steered the mare forward, leading the way out of the stable.

# CHAPTER 27

"Iomhar? This just arrived for you." Oswyn passed a letter into Iomhar's hands as he stepped through the door of the house in Morpeth. Kit looked up from where she was sat in a rickety chair, bobbing her knee up and down restlessly. "What's wrong with you, pet?" Oswyn asked, walking past Iomhar and coming to her side. "Where did you get to after church?"

"Somewhere not nice, Oswyn. Let us leave it at that." She tried to smile, but the effort hurt her cheeks and it soon faded, leaving her leaning forward with the same restlessness to her leg bobbing repeatedly.

"Well, I think I have something to cheer you up." Oswyn sat in the chair beside her and reached into his doublet, pulling out a small muslin cloth and handing it to her.

Kit took it slowly before unfurling the muslin. The smile that took up residence in her face was a genuine one this time.

"Marchpane. My favourite. Thank you, Oswyn." She tucked in eagerly, finding she needed that taste of sugar, anything to distract herself from the knowledge that Lord Ruskin wanted her dead. Across the room she grew aware of Iomhar watching the two of them. She looked up, meeting his gaze. "What is wrong?" she asked. He slowly shook his head, flicking his gaze to Oswyn.

"Ye bootlicking today, Oswyn?" he asked, scoffing.

"He did something kind, Iomhar. Leave him be."

"Aye, I did. Thank you, pet." Oswyn looked mightily pleased with himself as Kit offered him a small chunk of the marchpane. She kept shovelling bites in her own mouth, unable to stop herself.

"How did ye know it was her favourite?" Iomhar asked, walking toward the window to use the last light of the day as he broke the wax seal on his letter, opening it wide to read.

"I noticed how much she enjoyed it when I served it before at dinner."

"Well remembered," Kit said, stopping Iomhar before he could say anymore. Iomhar turned his eyes on the letter in his hands as Kit offered another piece to Oswyn. "Any news on Luca?"

"None," he said with a sigh. "I have asked all the watchmen from not only Newcastle, but the ports, Alnwick, even here in Morpeth, but no one has seen an Italian. You would think he would stand out, be easy to find."

"He's hiding well." Kit paused with the marchpane and reached below the collar of her doublet, pulling out Luca's rosary beads and fiddling with them.

"Why do you keep wearing those, pet? If the wrong person sees you, they'll think you a Catholic."

"He wanted them so badly," Kit murmured, more to herself than to Oswyn. "When we were in the dungeon, he could not stop staring at them. I find it hard to believe he merely wanted them to pray."

"These things mean a lot to Catholics. Can I see them?" Oswyn asked, holding out his hand. Kit removed the rosary from her neck, ready to pass them into Oswyn's hands when a string of curses erupted from Iomhar's lips across the room. It made her hesitate in the air with the rosary, even as Oswyn reached out, trying to take them.

"What is wrong?" she asked, lowering the rosary and looking to Iomhar.

"For the wee man's mercy." Iomhar turned round and threw down the letter, letting the parchment slap so loudly against the table that both Kit and Oswyn jumped in their seats. "It's from Taurus."

"What can he have to say?" Kit asked, standing to her feet. She threaded the rosary back around her neck and carried the marchpane with her as she crossed to the table.

"He was answering my letter. That bloody, self-righteous —"

"Iomhar," Kit's voice held a warning tone, but it only earned a dark gaze from Iomhar as he slid the letter along the table toward her to read.

"Your wish to never hear a bad word said against that man has to end, Kit. It's a fool's resolve." He walked away, rubbing his hands over his face and the scars on his cheek.

Kit picked up the letter, taking it toward the window to read what Walsingham had written.

*How dare you ask such a thing of me, Blackwood? You two are the ones who have lost Luca, you will both stay there until he is found again. Return and you may visit the Tower for your failure. You've let him go once, any more slips and I'll be forced to wonder just who you are supporting in this war of ours.*

*As for your request to send Kit home alone, I cannot allow it. As far as I'm concerned, if she is in danger, then with you watching over her is the best place she can be. In London, it is all too easy to see someone stabbed in a dark street at night.*

*Finish this. Do not return to London until you have Luca.*

Kit slowly lowered the letter down to the table, unsure where her sudden anger was pointed at. She resented Walsingham's words, refusing to allow them to go home without seeing the task done, but there was another matter that bothered her more.

"You asked him to call me home?" Kit asked, almost choking on the last of her marchpane as she lowered the muslin cloth to the table beside the letter.

"Aye, I did."

"Iomhar! That was not your decision to make."

"Clearly." He gestured down at the letter. "What was I supposed to do, Kit? Ye have someone running round trying to kill ye, they know exactly where ye are, and now Walsingham insists on keeping ye in this danger. Does that not sound odd to ye?"

"Wait ... someone is trying to kill you, pet?" Oswyn asked, leaning sharply forward in his chair. "I thought you said the attack at the river was a thief. What have I missed?"

"Much," Iomhar said simply, turning in a quick circle again.

"What is the point in keeping secrets from him now?" Kit asked, motioning madly in Oswyn's direction.

"Still don't trust me, Scot?"

"What do ye think?" Iomhar said with derision. "Do not be angry with me, Kit." He walked to the other side of the table and rested his hands upon it, nodding his head down at the letter. "Ye would have done the same. The safest place for ye at this moment is somewhere they do not know how to find ye."

"Well, that is just not possible, is it?" Kit snatched up the letter. "Taurus has given us our orders. We are to stay here until the task is done. We find Luca."

Iomhar said nothing for a minute, but the anger was plain to see with the skin around his scars turning red and the sinews in his neck growing taut. "Would ye do anything Taurus asked of ye, Kit? Even if it means dying for it?" His question made her back up from the table.

"Oh, my, that was an intriguing question." Oswyn chuckled to himself. "It is like watching my brother and sister-in-law argue, they have much the same arguments, bickering all the time."

"Be quiet, Oswyn," Iomhar said sharply. "Kit, think about this." Iomhar had clearly decided to ignore Oswyn completely, shifting his gaze back to Kit. "Ye want to stay alive? Then at least go into hiding."

"Hiding? No."

"Kit, think a little more before ye answer." He demanded of her, rounding the table. "I saw ye in that fight today. Who knows how it would have ended if I had not come when I did?"

"I have survived two of his last attacks without your help. I did not need any assistance."

"Attack? Fight? What did you two do today whilst I went back to Newcastle?" Oswyn asked, yet neither Kit nor Iomhar looked his way, they continued to glare at one another, with neither blinking.

"Kit, all I am asking is ye think about defying Taurus. This one and only time. We cannot be certain we can keep ye alive otherwise."

"You wish me to abandon our task and run and hide?" she asked. "No. I will not do it."

"Why are ye always so loyal to him?"

"Because I owe him that much."

That image was clear in her mind of Walsingham being the one to reach into the water and pull her out, when she was a very small child. It could have been a creation of her mind, but it could also have been real. What if it was all true?

"What do ye owe him, Kit?" Iomhar asked.

She couldn't explain the memory to him, not when she was so unsure whether it was real at all. "I was a foundling, Iomhar," she said. "I could have died on the street before I was ten, many did."

"Not this again." Iomhar sighed and walked away from her.

"Yes, this again," she said, following him around the room. "I owe him because he is the reason that I am alive now. Who cares if I have to risk my life in order to do what must be done? I am lucky to have made it this far."

Her words brought silence to the room. Iomhar stayed firmly turned away from her as she stared at his back and Oswyn's eyes flicked between the two of them. The silence was eventually broken by a whistle from Oswyn.

"So, I am struggling to follow matters a little here, but aside from the fact it is clear you two have been keeping secrets from me, it seems we have a resolution. Kit is not going home but staying here. Looks as if we need a new plan. How shall we find Gregorio Luca now?"

"Aye, we need to think of something," Iomhar said distractedly, still not turning to look at Kit.

"Wait, that is it?" Kit asked. "You are not going to argue with me anymore?"

"What would be the point?" He shrugged and turned for the door.

"Where are you going?"

"To see someone. Someone who may be able to help us find Luca."

"You are determined then now?" Kit asked in confusion, walking toward the door and blocking his escape. "Less than thirty seconds ago you were telling me to go home, now you're all set to find Luca again. What changed?"

"It's the only way I'll get ye away from the border, is it not?" he asked, raising his eyebrows. "If we find Luca first."

She had nothing to say. She stared at him, dumbstruck, before he reached behind her, coming much closer than she had anticipated as he turned the door handle and flung it open. She was forced to scamper out of the way and give him his escape, where he closed the door quickly behind him, leaving her alone with Oswyn.

"So, that was interesting," Oswyn muttered as he sat back in his chair. "Something you want to tell me, pet?"

Kit looked at him, making a quick decision. Iomhar might not trust him, but right now, he was just about the only help they were going to get.

"Hope you are ready for a story, Oswyn."

"There is one thing I do not understand."

"What is that?" Kit asked, not looking up from the rosary beads. She was fiddling with them as she stared at the scrap of parchment that they had taken from the prisoner, emblazoned with the emblem of the unicorn. Sat at the table within the small house, darkness had fallen beyond the windows and Iomhar still hadn't returned.

"Why did you not tell me any of this before?" Oswyn asked as he slid the second of two candles toward her, lighting the area around her as she turned over the parchment, staring at the code on the other side.

"Iomhar does not exactly trust you," Kit said with a small smile.

"What changed your mind enough to tell me tonight?" Oswyn asked, gesturing toward the muslin that he had brought the marchpane in. "Was it the marchpane, pet?" He smiled with humour.

"My trust is not bought so easily." She laughed and shook her head, but the laugh died quickly as she returned her gaze to the code. "Call it the realisation that if you did have anything to do with telling this prisoner where to find me, why would you do that? If you worked for Lord Ruskin, Oswyn, you have already had plenty of opportunities to kill me yourself."

"Aye, that is a fair argument to make. So, I am free from your suspicion? At last!" he declared happily and clapped his hands together. "Though it still feels a little weird to think you ever suspected me at all."

"Apologies for that."

"Any luck with the code?"

"None." Kit shook her head and pulled the parchment nearer to her as she fiddled with the rosary. "It's a cipher, but in order to decipher it, I effectively need a key."

"A key? Like a lock to get in a door?"

"Basically, yes." Kit drew the candle closer to the parchment, watching as the light that fell upon the yellow sheet danced in the shuddering flame. "Each number and letter stands for something else, but without a clue of what they stand for, it's hard to find your way into the cipher. We have to start by looking for patterns." She pointed out the repeating numbers and letters on the parchment, certain that there had to be a way into it somewhere. "It's no use," she said, sighing and sitting back.

She looked to the closed door, yet it stayed firmly shut.

"You know something, pet. It does not matter how many times you look at that door, it will not make him come back any faster."

"I was not looking that much," she said in objection, yet Oswyn laughed at her, standing to his feet.

"Aye, sure you weren't. I'll get us something to drink. Maybe that will help you relax and stop watching the door."

She shrugged off his words and turned her focus back down to the cipher. As she fiddled with the rosary, looking at the pattern in the cipher, she began to see a commonality, but not in the cipher, in the rosary. Turning her focus completely on the rosary beads and holding it up in the candlelight, she observed each wooden and glass bead. They seemed to be in a sort of pattern, with a couple of wooden beads placed together, and then a few differently coloured glass beads too. It could have just been the decoration, nothing important in it, yet the more she looked at the beads, the more she was certain it meant something.

Kit abruptly stood to her feet, making Oswyn jump as he retrieved a bottle of beer from a bag. She walked past him, collecting parchment and a quill before she returned to the table. She performed the most common way to decipher any code she had come across, guessing that the colour bead that appeared most must stand for the commonest letter in the alphabet, *E*.

It didn't take long to decipher. Once she had applied the letter *E*, it was clear two smaller wooden beads together stood for spaces in what was an entire message. The code revealed itself to her by guessing a few different possibilities.

*Open me.*

Kit dropped the quill and reached for the cross at the end of the rosary beads, aware that Oswyn had come up behind her, peering over her shoulder to see what she was doing. It took some effort, turning the wooden cross pendant back and forth to figure out how it would open, but eventually she found it. Where the string connected with the top of the cross, there was a small latch that could be slid across. When she pulled on the string, separating it from the cross, it came out with a small strip of parchment attached to the bottom.

"How did you do that?" Oswyn asked behind her. She didn't answer, she was too busy unrolling the parchment to read the message that had been left for Luca to find: *Meet me at Lindisfarne Priory. A week before Yuletide.*

"Look." Kit pushed the parchment into Oswyn's hands. "He's meeting someone. They arranged to meet at Lindisfarne."

"A week before Yuletide. We do not have long then." Oswyn fumbled to hold the parchment as he placed down the bottle of beer.

"Only two days."

# CHAPTER 28

"Lindisfarne. Aye, it makes perfect sense," Iomhar said as he took the note from Kit's hands, reading the scrap she had found. "What about the other code? The one we took off your attacker?"

Kit produced the slip of paper, reading 'Morpeth'. She had deciphered it in the early hours of the morning. "It was a message, telling my attacker where to find me."

"I knew it. Lord Ruskin has men in Northumberland. Looking for ye."

"Where have you been?" she asked.

"Meeting someone."

"You have been gone all night." Kit pointed out of the window to the rising sun. Iomhar smirked as he sat down beside the fire she had lit, leaning against the wall of the fireplace hearth with his rear on the floorboards. "What amuses you?"

"If ye wish Oswyn to stop making jests at our expense, then ye shouldn't say things like that. It sounds rather like ye were worried about me, Kit."

"I am simply worried about our task. That is all."

"That was a lie. Ye and I both know it."

"Stop arguing with me and read the note again." Kit ended the conversation. She was not willing to discuss it anymore as she took the chair nearby. Her nerves were on edge, and she had barely slept. "Two days, that is all we have to wait in order to find him at Lindisfarne."

"So it would seem," Iomhar spoke quietly, his gaze firmly on the note in his hands.

"Who did you see?"

"The last person I saw, Kit," Iomhar said and flicked his gaze up to the ceiling, where Oswyn was still sleeping on the floor above. "I do not particularly want to share it with Oswyn that my brother isn't far away."

"Do you still not trust Oswyn?"

"Perhaps a little." Iomhar lowered the parchment in his hands. "Not enough to give him that information though."

"You told me. You even took me to meet Niall."

"Aye, I did." Iomhar turned a rather piercing gaze on Kit, making her shift uncomfortably in her seat.

"What did he say?"

"I asked him if he knew where Lord Ruskin is now. The man is something of a ghost. If King James's men could get their hands on him in Scotland, they would, just as any man working for Walsingham here in England would too. He is a danger to both monarchies. My bet is Lord Ruskin is hiding somewhere near the border, somewhere he thinks nay one will look."

"Why are you trying to find him?" Kit asked.

Iomhar shifted where he was sat, throwing another log on the flames and making the sparks dance. "I'm always trying to find him, Kit. Until I have an answer from him on what happened to my father."

Kit flinched in surprise. Iomhar so rarely spoke of what had happened, only ever talking to her of it once, that she leaned forward out of the chair, desperate to hear a little more.

"You are certain that Lord Ruskin was there when your father died?" she asked softly.

Iomhar turned a rather hardened glare on her, making her retreat back in her chair. "That is not a conversation for today."

"It never seems to be a conversation for today."

"Ye wish to know my secrets, Kit?"

"Oddly ... yes," she said, adopting a bolder voice. "I do not know what's on your mind half the time. What if what happened between Lord Ruskin and your father is relevant to what is happening now?"

"It's all related, Kit. I'm sure of it."

"Then tell me what happened."

"Ye want my secrets? Very well. Tell me first why ye are so loyal to Walsingham." His question made her stand to her feet and walk away from him, crossing the room quickly to where she had begun preparing some food before he returned through the door. "See? That is the response I have every time I ask that question."

"I have told you why. He took me in. Raised me. That is all you need to know." Kit took a copper bowl full of water back to the fireplace and placed it upon a grate, ready for the water to boil. The action brought her close to Iomhar, sat beside the fire.

"Nay. It is more than that."

"God have mercy. What more do you need?" she said, loudly. "I trust the man. That is all there is to it."

"Why?" Iomhar's voice was startlingly calm compared to her own tone. That image was back in her mind of the hand reaching through the water, pulling the smaller version of herself to safety. "Tell me your secrets and I'll tell ye mine."

Kit felt unable to take her eyes away from him. The words were on the tip of her tongue for the first time ever, to talk of that memory, to tell him everything of it. Revealing that this was why she was always so afraid of water, that she was certain someone had left her there in that water, and that maybe, just maybe it was possible Walsingham was the one who pulled her free.

A sound made her whip her head round, breaking the connection of her gaze with Iomhar's to see Oswyn standing in the doorway, yawning and looking between the two of them with bleary eyes.

"Interrupting something, was I?" he asked with a smile.

"No." Kit stood, hurrying to finish preparing the food. "We were just speaking of Lindisfarne. That is all. We need a plan."

"Aye. First of which, I had an idea last night." Oswyn came so close that she was startled, backing away toward the table as his hand took hold of the sleeve of her jerkin. "All this has to go."

"What?" she asked, glancing down at her clothes.

"Someone is trying to kill you. Aye?" The words were spoken plainly. When she didn't answer, he turned his head to Iomhar, looking for his answer instead.

"Aye," Iomhar said with a firm nod.

"Then let's not make the task easy for them. A lass dressed as a man is an easy thing to spot. At least, it gives them something to look for. You want to outwit whoever is after you? Change."

"This is how I dress."

"Does that matter if it means saving your life?"

"Oswyn is right." Iomhar's voice was firm, as if calling an end to a matter. "Kit, we need to get ye a gown."

"I look ridiculous."

"Nay, ye do not."

"I do." Kit shifted in the clothes, looking down at what she was wearing. Oswyn had found her a gown to wear; the cheapest thing he could find. Made of wool dyed pale green, it was loose fitting, hanging down to the ground with a loose skirt. The stays beneath were lighter than Kit had worn before, without whalebone and made only of reeds, but she still shifted uncomfortably, lifting the skirt a little as she walked to try and give freedom of movement.

"Ye're still wearing your boots?" Iomhar hissed in her ear as they walked toward the stone dock.

"Yes. The slip-on things Oswyn found would have been useless. They would have dropped off the moment I started running."

"They would have kept ye hidden."

"No one is going to be looking at my feet."

"Aye, I can agree with that." Oswyn's voice made her look ahead, seeing he had a rather mischievous smile on his face. "Look at the way she is dressed! No man will be looking at her feet."

Kit glanced down at the deep neckline. "Where did you find this gown? In a brothel?" she called ahead, trying to pull her sleeves down over her hands as her fingers trembled in the wind.

"I had to be inventive," Oswyn called back.

"Here. Wear this." Iomhar dropped something on her shoulders. She looked up to find a sheepskin shawl. She wrapped it round her shoulders and her chin, bracing herself against the bitter wind that was picking up off the ocean and buffeting them atop the stone dock.

"Where did you find this?" she asked.

"I came across it." Iomhar's answer made her smile a little, glancing back along the dock to see there was a fisherman sleeping on the dock beside his own boat. The sheepskin shawl he had been using as a blanket before was gone.

"Impressive," Kit murmured, wrapping the shawl tighter. "Where is this island then?"

"Wait a little more for the light to lift," Oswyn called to the two of them. He stopped on the very edge of the dock, looking out toward the ocean.

Kit paused at his side, peering to the horizon where the night was lifting. Midnight blue began to mix with a deep amber, the colour of falling leaves in autumn, signifying the sun was on its way. It was slow, but the more the orange hue grew in the distance, a lump formed.

A flat ridge above the ocean peaked around two stone buildings before cantering down to the ocean. As the sun rose, the light reflected off the buildings upon the island, making them appear yellow. Holy Island had appeared.

"It is a distance. We will need a boat." Kit looked round, marking the empty fishing boats.

"No. No boats." Oswyn shook his head.

"What? I may not be the strongest of swimmers, but I think even Iomhar would struggle to cross that." She waved a hand at the island in the distance.

"We wait until tonight. For the tide to go down."

"Ah, I see." Iomhar stepped forward, peering down off the stone dock. "There is a causeway."

"Aye." Oswyn nodded. "We wait for the right moment, and we can cross on foot. We'll be there at night, waiting for Luca to arrive tomorrow morning."

"He may already be there," Kit pointed out.

"Then we'll be there early to find him."

Kit chewed her lip, moving to the edge of the dock and peering over to the rocks beneath. The ocean was so high it was hard to imagine it being low enough for them to walk the distance to the island. She could imagine being caught in a rising tide. With the woollen dress, she wouldn't stand much chance of fighting the pull of the ocean. She breathed deeply, trying to dispel the image as she watched Iomhar move back away from the edge.

"We'll have to wait for sunrise. Even if we find him earlier."

"What do you mean?" Kit asked.

"We need to know who sent that note to Luca, do we not? Who will be there waiting for him in the morning?" Iomhar's tone was cold as he turned on his heel and walked off across the stone dock, not bothering to wait for Kit and Oswyn.

"Pet, you two had an argument?" Oswyn whispered, nudging her with his elbow.

"We are always arguing."

"I had noticed. No, I meant something more than the usual." He gestured after Iomhar again.

Kit watched Iomhar for a few minutes as he disappeared off the other end of the dock, uncertain what to make of his behaviour.

"He will be fine." Kit shrugged, moving past the matter. She didn't have time to find out. They had to prepare for their crossing and wait there for Luca to appear. "Anything else we should know about this place? Lindisfarne?"

"Few people there. It's mostly fishing cottages. Anyone new will stand out, that's for certain. That reminds me of something else." He held a hand toward her. "Those daggers you've hidden in your boots, they'll have to go."

"What? I am not leaving unarmed." Kit's voice was high-pitched. After what she had been through, there wasn't a chance she was going anywhere without those daggers.

"The man that attacked you is in a dungeon, aye?"

"Aye." Kit mimicked his Northumbrian accent, making his whiskered face smile.

"Then what harm is there in it?" Oswyn asked. "You walk and lift your skirt up round your ankles; people can see the boots. One glimpse of a dagger hilt in those boots and your attempt at hiding will be thwarted. You want to stay hidden? You have to appear like any other lass."

"Why can I not just be a lass that happens to have daggers in her boots?"

"How many lasses like that do you see round here?" He gestured to the fisherman's dock behind them. It was still early, but a few had risen, with ladies amongst them. Some were sorting fish from early morning catches, others were washerwomen, carrying baskets of linens toward the river that ran into the ocean. "What do you see?" Oswyn's words made her shift on her feet.

There was not a weapon amongst them, unless one of the washerwomen was planning to use a basket as a weapon, that was her only line of defence. Kit grunted and lifted a foot onto a stone ridge within the dock, flipping up her skirt to retrieve the daggers.

"Do not lift it too high, pet."

"You are the one who found this ridiculous dress. I would much rather wear hose."

"Aye, but some fishermen are looking this way."

"Then without a weapon to hand, I'll have to use my fists to defend myself." Kit snatched the daggers out one at a time from each boot and thrust them toward Oswyn. He quickly added them to his own weapons belt, chuckling under his breath. "Better?"

"Aye, much better. You look like any other lass now."

"As undefended as one too." She turned round and walked off the dock, hurrying after the retreating figure of Iomhar.

"This way." Oswyn beckoned the two of them forward. Kit

stepped off the track road, with her boots practically sinking into the wet sand, the colour of burnt candle wax, that was quickly rising over the toes of her boots.

"This is not a causeway."

"It will do." Oswyn strode forward with Iomhar following closely behind.

The causeway was merely mudflats, pockmarked by retreating waves and stretching out toward the lump of an island far ahead. Iomhar and Oswyn were making quick progress, their boots splattering in the wide puddles and kicking up yellow and black bladderwrack.

Kit went to follow, with the land falling away behind her and the flat ocean stretching out either side, but the long hem of her dress kept getting caught in the shallows of the ocean, slowing her feet and weighing her down. She lifted the skirt higher, but it was already heavy from the water, dragging her down again. In the distance, the sun was beginning to set, bouncing off the shallows of water that were dappled across an old path. Either side of the muddy path, rocks were covered in dark green seaweed, making the ground slippery under foot.

"Ye coming, Kit?" Iomhar called to her.

"I am hardly taking my time about this!" she snapped, trying to keep up, but the dress continued to drag her down. They hadn't reached the halfway mark when Iomhar and Oswyn stopped, looking back to her. "You should have just let me wear the doublet and hose."

"Aye, and watch ye be killed? Nay thanks." Iomhar returned, reaching toward her.

"What are you doing?"

"Ye walk the whole causeway this slowly and the tide will be above the path before we're halfway across."

"I'd like to see you do it in a gown."

"Aye, I would probably be just as slow."

"I am fine. I do not need any help. Iomhar!" Yet her reprimand did nothing. He lifted her clean off her feet, an arm under her back and his other under the crook of her knees. "What do you not understand about the words, I don't need any help."

"Aye, shall I put ye down again and watch ye walk across as the tide rises?" he asked with a smirk on his lips, clearly knowing she would like that possibility even less. She looked around at the ocean, remembering the last time she was in its depths, and elbowed him in the chest.

"Walk on, then."

He did as she asked, shaking his head as Oswyn laughed up ahead.

"She talks to you like you're a pony pulling a cart."

"I had noticed."

Kit kept looking down at the shallows as they walked across, noting when they reached the middle of the causeway that the water reached Iomhar's knees, and Oswyn's hips. Had she still been walking she would have been in danger of being washed away by the waves thanks to the gown.

"This is why gowns are a foolish idea," Kit mumbled as Iomhar walked on, splashing through the water.

"Aye, I agree with ye."

Kit glanced ahead, checking Oswyn was enough of a distance away before she muttered her thoughts to him. "You going to tell me what's on your mind?" she asked.

"Always wanting to know my secrets, Kit." He shook his head as they reached the other side of the causeway.

"At some point, one of us has to start telling the other our secrets."

"I suppose so." He put her down on the rocks that lined the beach of Holy Island, leaving her to clamber up the seaweed-covered stones. She streaked ahead and, though her boots slipped beneath her, she reached out with her hands, grasping on and not letting her body fall back down the embankment of rocks. Oswyn and Iomhar were not so good at climbing, and both kept falling into the crevices between the stones. Kit paused, reaching back around to Iomhar and offering him her hand. He looked up to her with raised eyebrows.

"You help me, I help you. It is a fair deal, is it not?" she asked, waving the hand toward him another time.

He smiled and instantly took her hand, letting her steer him up the rocks. It was slow progress, with her having to instruct him where to put his other hand so he didn't fall back down again. When they reached the top, they clambered onto a road, both peering over the edge to see Oswyn was struggling.

"Ye want to know what's on my mind?" Iomhar asked, breaking the silence and turning his gaze to her. "Very well. Have ye thought of who could be meeting Luca at the priory?"

"Any number of Catholics." Kit shrugged.

"Aye, but one man was seen near the border, going into the very castle where Luca was hiding three weeks before he arrived. And we know the same man knows ye are here and has sent a killer after ye. That is nay coincidence, is it?" he asked.

"You mean…" Kit trailed off as Iomhar lifted a finger to his lips, urging her to be quiet as Oswyn clambered over the last of the rocks. *Lord Ruskin.*

Kit understood his quietness now. If they were about to find the man Iomhar had been looking for, it begged the question what would happen when they found him.

"This way." Oswyn heaved himself onto the path and pointed ahead, leaving Kit and Iomhar to follow behind. In the distance Kit could see two buildings, far on the southern and eastern points of the island, a good distance away.

"What are they?" she asked, pointing to each one in turn.

"The one with the burning torches is the castle. Aye, guarded and bears canons. Built by old King Henry to keep out the Scots. Like him." Oswyn gestured in Iomhar's direction. "So it is not doing a very good job, in my opinion."

"I am nay invader." Yet Iomhar's words seemed to go unheard.

"That's the building we want. On the other side of the island, far away from the fort." Oswyn pointed toward the second building. "The old priory. Ruined and disused. If Luca is meeting a Catholic on this island, where better than a disused Catholic monastery?"

Kit nodded, following him as the path curved down. In the last light of the day, the cold was picking up, making her wrap her sheepskin shawl tighter around her shoulders as the priory came into view. It was on the southernmost tip of the island. Unlike the fort on the eastern side that was built on a hill, the priory was on flat land, with many stones taken, merely a ruin of what the priory must have once been. It appeared like a rabbit warren of stone walls and arches. As the sun was setting, the darkness across the priory began to spread, casting long shadows from the arches and stacked walls.

"Many a place a Catholic could hide in there," Kit muttered, striding ahead of the others and leading the way.

# CHAPTER 29

Kit's feet were impatient, striding out across the path that led to the priory. In the walk from the far north of the island, the sky had turned black, and the moon had risen. A half crescent, it cast the land in a misty white glow, not quite clear but murky. The walk was longer than Kit had expected, making her pace faster and prompting Iomhar and Oswyn to hurry along behind her.

When they reached the middle of the island, the tall trees and mounds of earth covered in seaweed fell away, revealing signs of living. On her right-hand side, the cambering rocks tapered, revealing small cottages built on the very edge of the island. Beyond them there was a wooden dock, barely appearing safe to stand on. In the wind and hissing waves, it creaked, making the wood crack every now and then. Fastened with ropes to the little dock were fishing boats, some so small they could only have been designed to get to the mainland and back again. They were visible in the moonlight only by the white light shimmering off the water around them.

"Iomhar?" she called behind her, urging him to catch up. When he reached her side, she gestured to the boats. "That is how we can get Luca back to the mainland, rather than having to walk him across the causeway."

"Ye'd rather not do that again?" he asked. She turned to him, knowing he was probably holding a smile, but she couldn't tell through the dim light.

"I do not fancy waiting here all night for the tide to go out again. Do you?"

"We will wait until whoever he was meeting appears."

"And what if the tide is still in then? We need a way off the island. Quickly."

He agreed with a nod. Behind them, Oswyn was making slow progress. Iomhar turned his head, beckoning Oswyn forward. "Taking your time?"

"Look." Oswyn pointed to their left, urging Kit to look the other way.

There was a small village in the middle of the island; full of stone cottages, each built with just one floor and a thatched roof that bristled in the persistent wind. A few candles were placed in windows, showing people lived inside, but not a face moved to the windows to watch them pass. Kit pulled the shawl on her shoulders higher, tempted to hide her face in case anyone did peer out of the windows.

"We cannot make much noise," Iomhar whispered, looking between the two of them. "We do not want to give anyone a reason to search the priory."

"We should be more worried about *them* searching the priory." Oswyn pointed beyond the village, out to the east side of the island.

Kit faltered in her pace, looking to the castle mounted on a hill. It was closer now than when they had first stepped onto the island. Circled with stone walls, creating tall battlements, it was hardly a thing of beauty, more of necessity. The fort had clearly been built for a purpose with the buildings merely block shaped with an oval embankment. Atop the battlements, burning torches were fixed in place. At this distance, it was impossible to tell if there were any figures in that torchlight, wandering to and fro, keeping guard, but Kit knew they would be there. No fort would be safe without their guards, especially at this time of night.

"That is supposed to keep the Scottish from invading?" Kit asked, curling her nose. "It seems too small to stop a fleet of ships."

Iomhar turned toward her, shaking his head. "Canon, Kit. Ye don't need an army to stop a navy, just the right weapons. I'd wager they have everything from canons to these." He tapped the pistol at his belt.

"Then we don't give them a reason to follow us. We do not want them to shoot and then ask us why we are here." Kit moved off to the right, heading toward the priory, but using a bank of trees as a shield. Iomhar and Oswyn followed, masking themselves from any guard who might have been looking their way from the castle's curtain wall. Kit knew they were probably too far away for any guards to see them, but she wasn't going to take that chance.

The further south they moved on the island, with their boots squelching in grass that was dampened by errant high waves, the more sheltered they were from the castle's view. Between the trees and the rocks that edged the ocean, they walked along a thin strip of land, leading out to the priory.

"Wait here a moment," Oswyn pleaded, holding his hand outward to stop the two of them moving any further. They were standing in the shadows of the priory, each stone archway and wall that remained appeared white and grey due to the light of the moon.

"Why are we stopping?" Iomhar asked impatiently.

"We do not know who is in there waiting for us." Oswyn gestured madly to the priory. "Luca may be alone, but he may also have company. Maybe you should wait here." He nodded his head at Kit.

"This is not the time to be protective." She shook her head.

"What if whoever wanted you dead has sent another after you? What if they are here now?" he asked, waving a frantic hand.

Kit didn't flinch or cower. She held her ground, merely adjusting the sheepskin shawl upon her shoulders to ward off the chill. "Then they will simply have to try again and be frustrated when they fail." She was not going to wait behind. She walked straight to the priory, moving so fast that she left Iomhar and Oswyn walking behind her.

"Do not tell her what to do," Iomhar muttered to Oswyn.

"Why not? Because she doesn't listen?"

"Would you two stop?" Kit called to them distractedly. When they fell silent, she hurried forward, stepping beyond the first tall archway of the priory. Rounding the corner, her feet slowed a little, finding much of the building still remained.

It was easy to see where some of the stones had been taken over the years to build cottages and the castle on the island, leaving behind spaces and patches of moss in nooks. Kit walked along a wall beside her, discovering what appeared to have once been living quarters. Moving down a corridor that only had one of its walls remaining, she found discarded beer bottles on the floor, with some of the glass shattered. She stepped over the broken glass as Iomhar approached behind her.

"Luca, do ye think?" he asked, nudging some of the glass away with the toe of his boot.

"No. It will be the people from the village." She dismissed the idea quickly. "Luca will try not to make his presence so obvious." She walked on through the corridor until she found individual chambers. "Did you say monks used to live here?"

"Aye. Before King Henry's time."

"You can tell." A couple of the rooms were still intact, though barely bigger than cupboards. Without windows, it would have been a dark and lonely place to lay their heads.

"Well, he's not sleeping here."

"How can ye tell?" Iomhar asked.

"No windows. He would choose somewhere with an exit." She gestured to the blank wall ahead.

"Kit? Iomhar?" Oswyn's voice called in a rather loud whisper.

They turned, leaving the half-ruined corridor of the quarters to follow his path. He was striding out across an open lawn. On one side, the sea rolled in, dangerously close. So much so that Kit thought in the wildest of storms the waves must have struck the priory walls. On the other side, the rest of the priory stood, with these stone arches much taller and wider, dominating the dark sky above them.

"Look." Oswyn gestured down to the ground. It was difficult for Kit to see what he was pointing at. Squinting in the light of the moon, she could just about see footprints in the earth before a gatehouse. They were large footprints and could have belonged to anyone, yet Oswyn strode in anyway.

"Stay close." Iomhar beckoned to Oswyn.

"You telling me what to do now?"

"If ye fancy wandering off and meeting an assassin alone, by all means, walk to your death."

"Aye, aye, I'll stay close," Oswyn said impatiently, waiting for the two of them to catch up.

This part of the building was still standing, enclosing them within dark walls that had a few holes where windows used to be. Kit led their path, searching every nook she could find. She had her head bent down to the floor, analysing what was once an old fireplace when a smell caught her nostrils. She sniffed rather loudly, standing straight.

"What is it?" Iomhar asked, moving to her side.

"Fish."

"Aye, to be expected on an island, isn't it?" Oswyn said drily.

"No. Cooked fish." She explained, following the scent and walking away down a corridor. She was aware of Iomhar following behind her, urging Oswyn to keep up. The corridor disappeared at one point, being nothing more than a few stacks of rocks either side, then it appeared again, enclosing her from the light of the moon. She stepped through an open doorway, finding the door was still in its place, but barely hanging on its hinges, with the door cracked in two, unusable.

The scent grew stronger, making her nose curl as she looked around the room. A giant fireplace opened up on one side of the room with half its chimney piece missing. Above the hearth, there were holes in the stones where iron hooks and fastenings had once been placed. Within the fireplace, there was a lonely pan, crusted with blackened scales on its surface.

Kit crouched down toward the fire, placing a hand over the pan to feel it was still warm.

"The old kitchen." Oswyn's voice moved around the room. "Not much left, is there?"

Kit glanced back to see he was right. Barely anything remained of what must have once been a busy kitchen, feeding hundreds of monks. There was a stone table opposite where Kit knelt with marks upon the surface, worn from years of use.

"What ye found?" Iomhar called to her.

She moved her hand from the pan and hovered it over the fire beneath, seeing there were still some orange embers within the grey ash. "Someone has been cooking themselves a supper.

Recently. The last hour or so." She lifted the pan, showing it to Iomhar who sniffed it, recognising the fishy scent.

"He's here." He stood straight, looking around the chamber. "Nay one from the village would come here just to cook fish."

Kit nodded in agreement, standing straight and moving to the side of the fireplace. There was a blanket screwed up on the floor, torn and tattered, in the border tartan pattern of small grey and white squares. "This is where he sleeps." She kicked the blanket to the side, trying to see if it was hiding anything beneath. "It must be the warmest room here."

"Then where is he now?" Oswyn said a little too loudly. Iomhar waved a hand in his direction, silently urging Oswyn to be quiet.

"Maybe he is preparing for midnight," Kit murmured as an idea occurred to her. She turned her head in Iomhar's direction, watching as he froze at her words. With half his face lit by the moonlight that streamed through the open chimney, she could see the way his eyebrows raised.

"Are ye thinking…?"

"What do most Catholics do when no one is looking?" Kit asked, moving back to the doorway and stepping out, prompting the others to follow.

"Midnight Mass." Iomhar hurried to answer her question. "We need to find the church."

Leaving the corridor, they found what appeared to be an inner courtyard. On both sides they were flanked by half fallen down walls, all too high to clamber over, meaning the only way in and out of the courtyard were the few doorways that remained. Kit wandered through pillars of stones scattered around the courtyard, moving toward a building that mostly remained on the far side. The familiar transept structure with a half-remaining spire on its eastern roof told her she had found the church. Elbowing Iomhar, she caught his attention, pointing at the church. He nodded, creeping toward the wall of the building. High above both of their head heights, there was a space in the wall, with still a few shards of stained glass poking out from the stones. The more Kit gazed at it, the more she was convinced that there was some kind of light beyond, flickering against the glass.

She pulled on Iomhar's arm, urging him to be quiet with a finger to her lips and pointed at the window. He nodded once, showing he understood. She thrust the sheepskin shawl into his hands to carry for her and took hold of the skirt of her gown, wrapping it tightly around her legs.

"What are ye doing?" Iomhar asked in a whisper.

"We both know you cannot climb up there."

"Be careful with that skirt," he warned. "Ye'll make Oswyn happy." She rolled her eyes as she began to climb, being careful to keep the skirt around her knees. Clambering up the wall as a squirrel would, with quick hands, she reached the empty window where there were the remains of the stained glass and peered over the edge.

Within was the priory church, but a ruin of what it had once been. There were no decorative items, nothing at all, no ostentatious glory that the Catholics were so fond of, only an empty stone floor. A flicker of light urged Kit to trace an orb around the church. A single candle had been lit and a figure carried the candle forward, down the aisle of the church between where pews would have once sat. With a hood hanging over his face, it was impossible to see who he was.

He stopped walking when he reached a stone altar and placed the lit candle against a second, creating two orbs in the dim room. With care, he moved them to either end of the altar, then he reached down, pulling a satchel bag off his shoulder. Slowly, he lowered the satchel to the altar, delving inside and making things clatter, metal items struck together, before he pulled out a cross. As tall as Kit's forearm and heavily bejewelled with a golden surface, it practically gleamed in the yellow candlelight. The darkened figure placed the cross in the middle of the altar then stepped back, discarding his satchel to the side.

He receded down the steps that led to the altar and stood before it, bowing his head and clasping his hands in prayer.

"Well?" Oswyn hissed from down below.

She waved a hand in his direction, urging him to be silent, never taking her eyes off the figure. To her relief, he hadn't heard Oswyn, and was absorbed in his prayer. After another minute of silence, with the only movement the flickering of the candles in the wind, the figure raised his head. He reached for the altar, retrieving a lantern from the foot of the steps. Pulling back the small glass doors, he lit the candle within using his other flames and placed the lantern at the end of the steps, casting his figure in a brighter orange orb.

Kit was now able to see more of him, with the black cloak and the tanned hands. He was familiar to her, but she couldn't be certain it was Luca, not until he reached up and pulled the hood of his cloak down from his face.

"Luca," she muttered to herself. He stepped forward, moving to his knees and bowing his head in prayer, clasping his hands in front of his chest. He was muttering loudly, speaking such prayers in Italian that they sounded more like incantations to Kit's ears.

Kit scrambled back down the wall, turning to face Iomhar and Oswyn who were waiting for her expectantly. "He's there," she whispered, "but…" She held up a hand, stopping Oswyn from interrupting her. "It is odd. He has a satchel with him. We took everything off him when we found him."

"Perhaps he visited a merchant." Oswyn shrugged, clearly seeing nothing troubling in the idea.

"How would he do that when we left him with no money?" Kit asked.

"Whoever helped him escape may have given him money."

"And no one would think it odd in these parts that an Italian man wanted to purchase a Catholic cross? He has one. Made of gold and precious stones. That is not just expensive but hard to find." She shook her head, unwilling to believe it. "No. He has friends. Someone who must have given him the satchel."

"Let's find out." Iomhar nodded his head toward the church.

"There are two entrances. One through the vestry." She pointed behind her, toward where one of the doors opened up into the southern transept of the church. "The other using the main door. Iomhar, you take the vestry. If I go in alone, he will think he is safe, then you can take him from behind."

Iomhar nodded, needing no more instructions. He passed her the sheepskin shawl as he hurried away, heading toward the open doorway of the vestry.

"What of me?" Oswyn asked.

"Follow me in after Iomhar has him. We want Luca to think he's safe to catch him by surprise." She tugged on his arm, urging him to follow.

Hovering in the doorway, she peered back into the courtyard, seeing Iomhar in the distance, his silhouette just about visible. He nodded once to her and disappeared inside.

In the antechamber of the church, Kit waved a hand at Oswyn, urging him to stop and not make another move. He bristled where he stood, restless, clearly not liking being given the order, but he obeyed. Kit wrapped the shawl around her shoulders and tiptoed toward the back of the church, stepping into an archway. Without a sound, she crept further into the atrium, closing some of the vast distance between her and Luca.

Something scraped under her foot. She looked down, seeing there were errant stones between the flagstones, and she had brushed one of these small pebbles with her buckskin boot, making it echo around the church.

Luca's head snapped up from where he was bent forward, kneeling in prayer.

"Good evening, Luca," she called to him.

# CHAPTER 30

Luca scrambled to his feet, kicking the flaps of his cloak away as his eyes found Kit in the shadows. She stepped forward, into the light cast from his lantern and candles, watching as his gaze wandered up and down the gown she was wearing.

"*Donna?*" He appeared almost doubtful he recognised her at all.

"Who are you waiting for, Luca?" she asked slowly. "Who is coming to meet you?"

He backed up further, colliding with the altar where he had laid out his wares. The enamelled cross in the centre, flanked by the two candles atop adorned brass holders, wobbled. He knocked the cross over in his panic to reach for the leather satchel. He dived his hand inside as Kit moved further forward, pulling out a thin basilard and pointing it in her direction.

"Someone has been buying you gifts," Kit murmured as she moved toward him, flicking her eyes to the doorway to the vestry in the church far behind Luca. She could see a shadow moving in the doorway. Iomhar was ready. "Where did you get all this?" she asked, gesturing to the altar pieces.

"Do not take another step, *donna*." Luca moved forward, swiping the basilard in the air. "You know I can use these weapons. Leave now if you wish to live. Go."

"I cannot do that, Luca." Her plain words riled him further. She held her ground, lifting her chin a little. He breathed deeply, his nostrils widening like a bull's as he stepped forward, lifting the basilard another time.

The shadow in the doorway moved and Iomhar stepped forward, barely making a sound as he lifted the rapier from his belt, emerging far enough into the room to creep up on Luca and place the tip at Luca's back. The assassin froze with the basilard in the air, his face turning pale as he realised the trap that he was in.

"Lower the weapon," Kit ordered. Luca did nothing at first. His eyes became slits as he glowered at her. Iomhar turned the hilt of the rapier in his hand, making the threat clear. "Put it down on the floor."

Luca followed her instruction this time, tossing the basilard to the floor with barely restrained frustration. Behind Kit, she heard a sound of footsteps. Oswyn stepped into the room, picking up the basilard and adding it to his weapon's belt.

"Kneel. Place your hands on your shoulders." Iomhar pushed Luca in the back for good measure, forcing Luca down to what was once a set of steps leading up to the stone altar. Now decrepit, only a few steps remained with tufts of grass showing through the stone slabs. Luca lifted his hands, crossing them over his chest and placing them on his shoulders, as Iomhar returned his rapier to his belt. He reached for one of the lengths of rope in his belt, unwinding it, ready to tie Luca up.

"Oswyn, we will need to bring the boat round," Kit said, looking back to him. Yet Oswyn appeared not to have heard her. He was staring straight at Luca, his scrawny face even more pursed than normal. "Oswyn?" Kit's harsh voice captured his attention this time, making him dart his head toward her. "We need the boat."

"A minute more. I want to make sure this isn't a trap." He stepped away from Kit, walking around the remains of the church. Kit frowned, watching him as he inspected every nook of the church walls. Where old ornaments used to rest, there were now only shadows, and the spaces where stained-glass windows once sat were shrouded in the darkness of the night.

"Who gave ye these things?" Iomhar asked, gesturing to the ornaments on the stone altar and the satchel bag. Luca didn't respond. He stared forward, straight at Kit, with his hands restless on his own shoulders. "Who gave ye them?" Iomhar snapped again, elbowing Luca in the back to encourage an answer from him. Luca barely winced at the pain as he held onto Kit's gaze.

"The bag was waiting here for me. Someone knows how to greet a Catholic priest."

"Are you a priest?" Kit asked, somewhat doubtfully. "From what I hear, your Catholic God is no more impressed with a murderer than a Protestant God."

"You think I am a murderer, *donna*?" he scoffed, shaking his head as Iomhar finished unwrapping the rope. "This is war. I am a soldier of God."

Kit lifted her eyes, finding Iomhar had paused with the rope and was staring at her in equal wonder. "This is not war." She shook her head. "Do you see a battle around you?"

"Battles are not always fought on fields. They are fought in the shadows, in corners of buildings and in alleys that few people walk down. I am no murderer. Every death taken was for God, for His purpose, He will see that." Luca tipped his chin higher, the resilience making the skin around his eyes and leading up to his bald head taught. "As He will see every Protestant burned for their faith."

"He's talking like old Queen Mary," Oswyn called from the other end of the church. He advanced toward them quickly, his boots scraping the stones beneath his feet. "What is the point in taking him back to land? We should see the end of him now."

"What?" Kit asked, stepping in Oswyn's way, forcing him to stop short to avoid colliding with her. "What did you mean by that?"

"I mean no good comes from allowing a murderer to live. Kill him. Throw him in the ocean. Have done with him. No one would ever know and this country would be free of him."

"That's murder, ye tadger," Iomhar called from where he stood beside Luca, not letting him move an inch. "Ye want to be sent to hell as he will be?" He gestured down at Luca.

"It is not murder."

"You are starting to sound as mad as Luca." Kit tapped Oswyn around the arm, trying to bring some sense to him. "No. Luca will only die at the hands of a trial. Not by our hands."

"Agreed," Iomhar called to the two of them. "Oswyn. Come tie him up." Iomhar held up the rope for Oswyn to take.

Oswyn seemed to mutter something under his breath, something unintelligible to Kit, as he walked around her, reaching for the rope. He took it from Iomhar and bent down to Luca, ready to tie his hands as Iomhar turned away, picking up the satchel bag and searching the contents.

"You will not take me." Luca's words were sharp, but quiet, making Kit think for a minute it was but a hiss on the cold wind off the sea, then she heard Oswyn yelp. Luca was on his feet, trying to run.

"Stop him!" Kit ordered. Oswyn was ahead of her. He grabbed hold of Luca's cloak, dragging him backward, and snapped one of Kit's daggers out of his belt, placing it firmly at Luca's neck.

"Do not move again," he drawled the words in Luca's ear, making the assassin lean back, tipping his head on Oswyn's shoulder to try and escape the blade.

"Tie him up so he cannot do it again," Iomhar said, looking up from where he was rifling in the bag.

"Anything?" Kit moved to Iomhar's side, though she kept flicking her eyes to Luca and Oswyn, checking that Luca wasn't going to make another escape attempt.

"Grass stains, damp..." Iomhar shook the material of the satchel. "Aye, it could have been hidden out here in the priory for a few days before he arrived. I can believe it well enough."

"Who would leave it?" Kit mumbled. "Whoever was coming to meet him, perhaps?"

"You going to tell us that, killer?" Oswyn asked, his grip on Luca tightening so much that he grimaced.

In answer, Luca firmly clamped his lips shut. Kit moved away from Iomhar's side, moving to stand in front of Luca and Oswyn, watching the two of them together. Luca no longer fought Oswyn's grasp, but that didn't seem to make a difference. Oswyn was keeping Kit's dagger so close to Luca's throat that he was in danger of slicing it.

"Oswyn, careful with that blade," Kit snapped in his direction, watching as he twisted, holding the blade close to Luca's throat. "We need the man alive, remember?"

"Aye, I remember, pet." Oswyn looked discomforted at the idea as he forced Luca down onto his knees, still holding the blade in front of his throat.

"Kit?" Iomhar said slowly as he paused his search of Luca's bag to stare in Oswyn's direction.

"Yes?"

"Why does Oswyn have your dagger?"

"He was worried someone would see it," she said hurriedly.

"Who would see ye here, Kit?" he asked plainly, gesturing around the room. Kit frowned, turning her eyes back on Oswyn. She was unarmed, and for some reason, Iomhar was intimating Oswyn had purposefully made it the case. Her eyes rested on Oswyn, watching as he bent down over Luca.

"Oswyn. Give me the dagger." She stepped forward, ready to take his place. "I can take Luca now."

"No further, Kit." Oswyn ordered, holding the dagger even closer to Luca's throat. The assassin tipped his chin back, trying to get as far away from the blade as possible.

"Oswyn?" Iomhar stepped forward.

"Not another step." Oswyn's eyes shifted between the two of them, forcing them to stop. "I have orders. Luca is not to make it out alive. Not with you two."

"What? Taurus's orders were to arrest him. Not to kill him, you fool." Kit stepped forward again, but the yelp that escaped Luca's lips showed the dagger was being pressed against his skin.

"Stop there, Kit." Oswyn's words and the yelp forced her to a halt.

"This was not what Taurus ordered."

"I did not say they were Taurus's orders, did I?" he asked.

"Whose orders then, Oswyn?" Iomhar demanded, reaching into his belt. "Ye are a traitor, aren't ye?" He lifted the pistol from his belt, pointing it straight at Oswyn's head.

Oswyn darted his head toward Iomhar, the lips flattening at the sight of the barrel of the gun. "You would not do it."

"Do ye want to find out?" Iomhar asked.

Oswyn slowly released Luca, stepping back enough to allow him to scramble forward on his knees. Iomhar advanced toward Oswyn, trying to get a rope from his belt with his other hand when Oswyn sharply brought up Kit's dagger, knocking the pistol away — it went off, shooting somewhere into the ceiling and casting dust from the stones around them.

"Get him, Kit," Iomhar called to her as he snatched Luca away.

Luca stumbled to his feet, trying to run for the archway leading out of the priory church, but Iomhar tackled him, knocking him to the floor.

Kit turned her focus on Oswyn. He was trying to run past her to get to the vestry door, holding out the dagger in her direction. Seeing her own blade turned on herself, Kit refused to be injured by it.

He made a dive for her, trying to catch her in the arm, but it was a feeble attempt, making it all too easy for Kit to dodge the blow, stepping to the side. She reared forward, grabbing hold of the wrist that had her dagger, and bent it backwards, forcing him to cry out and drop the weapon.

Oswyn grasped for his weapons belt, taking hold of the second dagger she had given him, as Kit used his arm within her grasp to vault him over her shoulder. It was an ungainly and difficult move, but he was shorter, and without such a strong footing on the ground, he flipped, landing with a loud crack on the stone floor. Winded on his back, he huffed into the air as she snatched the dagger from his fingers. She kicked away her first dagger, pointing the second straight at Oswyn's chest, refusing to let him move.

"Who gave you the order?" she asked, beckoning her hand toward Iomhar across the room. "Rope!"

"In the middle of something!" he called back. She barely flicked her eyes in his direction to see him wrestling. Luca was reaching up toward the altar, trying to grab something off the surface to use as a weapon, but Iomhar wrenched him back down to the floor, standing above him.

A kick against Kit's ankle showed Oswyn was trying to escape. She bent down, reaching for him as he leaned up toward her, trying to get the dagger off her. She curved it back in his direction, wounding him across the arm. The blade cut a slit through the sleeve of his doublet, slicing the skin with a slither of blood following behind.

"Argh!" he cried out in pain, falling to the floor with his back curled up, rather like an insect hiding for cover.

"Rope, Iomhar."

"Give me another minute."

It only took a few seconds for a rope to be thrown her way. She caught it from the air, wrapping it round Oswyn's wrists. He yelped from the way she heaved at his injured arm.

"Who gave you the order, Oswyn?" she demanded. He turned his head away from her, clearly not intending to give an answer. "It was an order to silence Luca if we came near him, wasn't it? You were afraid his tongue was loose." The look on his face answered her question. "Were you ever Walsingham's intelligencer? Or did you change allegiances later?"

"I follow orders. If you found Luca, you couldn't hear what he had to say."

"Even if that meant killing one of your own?" Kit asked, baffled. "You couldn't risk him talking. Iomhar? Did you —"

"I heard." Iomhar's voice urged her to turn her head to see he had Luca bound up in so much rope that more rope was visible than the tunic and cloak he wore beneath. Iomhar grabbed the ropes fastened at Luca's back, using it like the harness on a horse, dragging him to his feet. "Clearly, he could tell us something interesting."

"The boats," Kit murmured. "The one by the beach in the village."

"We'll take them both back with us, Oswyn as well as Luca." Iomhar dragged Luca past her, shoving him into the archway. "I'll go first. Ye have him?" he asked, pointing down to Oswyn.

"He cannot put up any more of a fight." She took hold of the rope around his wrists, heaving Oswyn to sit up against the wall behind him.

Iomhar nodded as he picked up the lantern Luca had been using, holding it out ahead of him as he dragged Luca through the priory. Kit heard Luca's complaints, throwing an increasing number of Italian curses on Iomhar's head as they faded through the stone walls. With Oswyn secured sitting against the wall, she bent down, adding a second rope to his wrists.

"So?" she asked, holding his gaze. "Were you ever really loyal to Walsingham?" He grimaced, trying to clutch onto the wound on his arm, but failing with how tightly she had bound his hands together. "What changed your mind?"

"They pay well."

Kit scoffed, barely able to believe what she had heard. She stood to her feet and moved back to the altar, snatching up Luca's bag that Iomhar had been searching through. She emptied it onto the altar, mixing it with the other things Luca had already discarded there, trying to find if there was anything useful. There were muslin clothes bound around lumps of manchet bread, and flagons that had once held small beer.

She continued to shake the bag, trying to urge more out, when metal clattered together. She dropped the bag, finding three more basilards had fallen onto the altar, each one with the grooves upon the blades stained dark red. Kit gulped at the sight before lifting the basilards and throwing them back into the bag. She tossed it to the side. They could come back for the bag another time. What was important was to get Oswyn and Luca off the island first.

"On your feet, Oswyn." She turned to face him.

"You could have killed me, Kit." He glared down at his wound, accusingly.

"You were about to kill a man." She pointed out the irony, though he didn't seem to appreciate it. "Up. We need to move you to the boat and out of here before Luca's man arrives." She bent down at Oswyn's side, taking hold of his arm and trying to jerk him to his feet. Oswyn stood on half bent legs, trying to bend over his wounded arm as he growled through gritted teeth at the pain.

"You have cut deep. I could die with this."

Peeling back part of his doublet, she examined the wound. He wouldn't die, that was clear. It would simply need a few stitches to close the wound. "Stop moaning. Stay standing." Yet her order did no good. As she released him, he slid back down to the floor. "I don't want to have to carry you."

There were footsteps behind her. Kit flicked her head to the side, listening. It couldn't have been Iomhar, he did not have the same gait and he would surely not leave Luca unattended.

The steps grew closer. When they reached the archway leading into the church, Oswyn made a small whimpering sound.

Kit slowly turned round, peering through the orange lantern light to see there was a figure standing in the shadows. He was tall, broad too, with his eyes flitting between where she stood and Oswyn in the corner, then he took one more step forward, casting his face into more of the lantern light.

"Where is Luca?"

# CHAPTER 31

Kit said nothing for a minute. She stared at the stranger, wondering if her eyes were deceiving her in the torchlight, yet the figure didn't disappear. He stayed exactly where he was, staring back at her.

He was more advanced in his years, yet not old, his figure was too young and the lines on his face had not yet formed deep crevices. The fair hair on his head was coiffed beneath a woollen cap that was embroidered finely, far too finely for a common man. The cloak around his figure draped low, hiding where his hands rested.

"Do not…" Oswyn's voice murmured from the corner.

Kit flicked her eyes his way to see he was speaking to the stranger, slowly shaking his head from side to side.

"Be quiet, Ingleby." The stranger spoke calmly, yet the instruction was clear. He would not be happy with a refusal. His voice was unusual, rather raspy without much tone. Oswyn was hunched over his wound, closing his lips as he tried his best to pull apart the ropes Kit had used to tie his wrists.

"Who are you?" Kit asked, looking straight at the stranger.

He stepped toward the altar of the priory church, out from the shadows, beneath what was left of the stone arches above them.

"I was about to ask the same." The man smiled at her, there was nothing happy in his expression, more like he couldn't believe his luck. "A lass here? Must be Miss Kit Scarlett."

Kit bristled, taking a step back. She reached for the daggers she had taken off Oswyn, whipping round to face the stranger again with her hands outstretched.

"Not what I was imagining." The Scottish accent was clear, making Kit watch him all the more.

"Who are you?" she asked again, yet to no avail. He took another step forward, his hands still hidden beneath his cloak. She was not prepared to let him reveal a weapon. She strode toward him across the room, meeting him in the middle and pointing the daggers directly in the middle of his chest. "Did you come for Luca?"

"I did." He peered past her toward the altar, where the blood splatters on the stone floor glistened in the torchlight. "Is he alive? Luca?"

"He's —"

"Be quiet, Oswyn." Kit warned him. She could hear Oswyn trying his best to break the ropes still, but she didn't turn to face him. She never took her eyes off the man before her. "Give me your name," Kit ordered of the stranger.

He shook his head slowly, turning his gaze down to the point of the dagger at his chest. His movements were quick. He swiped up a hand from within his cloak, knocking her dagger away with another blade. By the time she brought her second one up, lunging backward to ensure she had her balance, he pulled out his other hand, bearing a pistol.

In the torchlight, she couldn't see the detail. Only that it was another wheellock pistol, like Iomhar's, with white decoration shining in the dim light. The barrel was pointed straight at Kit's chest.

"Put the dagger down." His voice was soft, yet the deepness of it held danger. When Kit didn't move, he lifted his finger over the trigger. "Put the dagger down and untie his ropes."

Kit didn't consider defying him. If she did, there was nothing to stop him burying a bullet in her chest and leaving her for dead. She flicked her eyes to the archway behind him, but with no sign of Iomhar, she had no choice. She lowered the dagger at her side.

"Drop it to the floor."

She did as he asked, listening as the metal clattered against the stones. He waved the pistol in Oswyn's direction, hurrying her to the task. Kicking the hem of her gown out of the way, she moved slowly to Oswyn's side and bent down toward him, untying the ropes. She was aware of Oswyn's eyes on her, his face contorted in pain.

"You will live," she murmured. "It is not a fatal wound." Something in his expression changed. Something she couldn't quite fathom.

"Up, Ingleby." The stranger barked the words, ordering him to stand.

Kit stepped back, giving Oswyn the room to move forward. He bent down as he walked, clutching the wound on his arm. When he reached the stranger's side, he hovered beside him, looking back to Kit.

"There's another here. We must go. Before he comes back." Oswyn's voice was harried, betraying his panic.

"Another minute more." The stranger kept the barrel of the gun trained in Kit's direction.

"No. No, we must go. Now." Oswyn pulled on the stranger's arm, urging him to flick his head in Oswyn's direction, causing the short fair hair to dance around his temple. With the cloak now a little open, Kit could see the weapons belt that sat on his waist, and an elaborate doublet, embroidered in the finest detail. Whoever the man was, he had wealth, that was clear.

"Start walking, Ingleby." The stranger delivered his final order before taking a step forward, lifting the pistol from the centre of Kit's chest, to point at her head.

She backed up, going so far that she collided with the altar, clattering against it and sending the few ornaments that Luca had lined up there flying.

"No. No, you do not need to hurt her." Oswyn pulled on the stranger's arm. "The threat is enough to get us out of here."

"I was thinking of more than just hurt." The stranger didn't take his eyes off Kit. His finger hovered over the trigger.

"No. Do not kill her. You don't have to do that." Oswyn grew agitated, pulling on the stranger's cloak so much that the latter shoved him away, pinching Oswyn's wounded arm and making him cry out like a wounded animal.

"Shh!" the stranger snapped. "Do ye want the other one to come running?"

"You do not have to do this, man."

"It will be quick." The stranger advanced toward Kit.

She panicked, with flailing arms she reached behind her, grabbing hold of anything she could find. Her fingers latched onto the enamelled cross, snatching it up from its fallen position. She spun round and threw it in his direction.

She knocked the pistol flying, out of his hand where it soared behind him, landing on the floor near to her daggers. The stranger backed away, baffled, reaching for the pistol another time. Yet Oswyn reached it first. He kicked it in Kit's direction.

"What are ye doing?"

"You don't need to kill her." Oswyn grabbed the cloak of the stranger, shoving him toward the archway, urging him to flee.

Kit reached down, picking the pistol hurriedly off the floor. By the time she had the pistol in her fingers, there was nothing but shadows left in the archway, betraying which way the stranger and Oswyn had gone.

"God's blood!" she muttered angrily, running after them. With one hand she had to grab the skirt of her gown, hitching it high to allow herself to sprint away, whilst the other clutched tightly onto the pistol, keeping it outstretched in front of her. She followed the shadows and the sounds of running footsteps all the way down the enclosed passage of stone, coming out into the inner courtyard. Stone pillars stood around her, like people, their shadows confusing her in the moonlight, making her dart the pistol from side to side, frantically preparing to shoot them all.

The sound of footsteps had stopped, urging her to halt in the middle of the courtyard, peering at all of the pillars. It was just possible that she was not alone. The stranger and Oswyn could have been in the courtyard still, hidden behind one of the pillars. She looked to the bases of each pillar and the shadows, trying to see if any shadow was wider than another in the moonlight.

She found one. Where the shadow was not only wider, but moving, perhaps shaking a little and bent forward, betraying the shape of a figure clutching his arm. It was Oswyn.

Kit moved toward it, creeping on the tiptoes of her boots, being careful to keep the pistol outstretched in front of her at all times. Yet there was a sound behind her, of a small stone being scattered beneath someone's boot. She veered round, swinging with the pistol, just as something loomed toward her, tall and dark.

She tried to yelp as a hand went over her mouth, backing her up until she collided with one of the pillars. Her back and the top of her neck struck the stones, stinging with pain as she tried to focus on the figure before her. It was the fair-haired stranger. This close in the moonlight she could see his eyes were pale blue, with a milky tinge to the whites. He gritted his teeth as he took hold of her hand, trying to snatch the pistol from her grasp.

Kit bent her wrist back, trying to keep the pistol away from him for as long as possible before she bit into his hand. He grunted in pain against his gritted teeth, releasing her mouth and reaching for the pistol with both hands. It gave her freedom of movement. She used her free arm to elbow upwards, catching the man in the jaw and forcing him to rear back on his heels, staggering away and releasing her hand.

She lifted the pistol, aiming it at him, remembering what Iomhar had said. Sometimes, it was down to Kit to survive. She remembered shooting the tree trunk in Iomhar's garden, the bullet firing far off into the distance and missing the bark entirely. She peered down the barrel of the gun, using the light of the moon to aim. She'd shoot his arm, anything to keep him alive and stop him from running. The stranger backed up, bumping into a stone pillar before he rounded it, just as she fired.

The shot ricocheted loudly, echoing across the stones of the priory. Kit didn't even see where the bullet landed, but it was clearly not in her target, for he was still running.

"This way." He had grabbed hold of Oswyn and was dragging him across the courtyard, their figures disappearing through a gap in the wall ahead, out of the courtyard.

Kit checked the pistol, but with the bullet gone, and no powder hidden within the folds of her gown, it was useless to her now. She held the pistol down at her side, preparing to use it as a missile if it came to it and ran ahead, following the stranger and Oswyn.

She tracked them through the old refectory and the gatehouse, listening to the way their footsteps thudded against the earth and what was left of a stone floor. On the other side of the gatehouse, the lawn stretched out. Made of flat land, rimmed with rocks, the dark ocean was ahead, with the silhouettes of the stranger and Oswyn running toward it.

"I need a weapon," she muttered to herself, hurrying after them. "Iomhar!" she called loudly into the night, trying to peer round the priory for any sign of where he would be with Luca, but there was nothing and no one, only empty grass and tall stones. "Iomhar!" she barked again, but still there was nothing.

Looking ahead at the lawn, she could see the two figures were running toward the ocean with purpose. On the other side of the rocks there was a shallow beach, the shingle appearing white in the moonlight. Upon the slither of white, there was a boat, a small thing made of wood with no sail, easy to hide within the tall waves of the North Sea.

"No," Kit said harshly to herself, setting off in a run toward the boat. Her feet thudded against the earth so hard that pain ricocheted across the arches of her feet and up her ankles. The more she ran, the closer the two figures grew in the distance and the more frantic their movements became. When she reached the rocks, Oswyn pulled on the stranger's cloak, pointing back toward her.

"She's back!"

"Give me that." The stranger snatched an oar up from the boat and walked across the beach, lifting it high in Kit's direction. She dropped the pistol, knowing it would do her no good now and felt around on the edge of the sand, looking for any rock she could find. Sand dug its way under her fingernails, just as she latched onto stones.

Spinning round on her feet, she launched them in the stranger's direction. The first hit his oar, making him stumble with it, but the second hit his chin, drawing blood. He lifted a hand, touching the cut. With a stiffened body, he lowered his palm enough to see there was blood on his fingers.

"Now! We must go," Oswyn called to the man. He had pushed the boat a little out to sea, so that there were shallows of ocean between them. He clambered into the boat, using just the one oar to push himself further. "You want to be stranded?"

The stranger reached toward Kit. He tried to hit her with the oar, but she jumped out of the way. Yet with his second strike, she was not so lucky. It rammed her shoulder, knocking her into the shingle, where sand filtered into her mouth. With her face on her side, from one eye she could see his silhouette lifting the oar over his head again, clearly aiming to finish the job he had started.

"There is no time!" Oswyn barked from the ocean. The stranger hesitated. It was enough for Kit to recover herself a little, pushing herself up on the sand. She grabbed another rock, this time aiming for his hand only. It struck perfectly with his knuckles, forcing him to drop the oar.

Kit snatched it up before he could, standing to find he was running back to the boat. He splashed in the shallows with great strides, hurrying to climb into the vessel. Kit went to follow, but she was too late. With their one oar, they were pushing themselves far out into the ocean, out of distance.

She came to a halt, with the hem of her gown dampening in the shallows and the salted water rising around the ankles of her boots. She backed up quickly, taking herself out of harm's way and onto the stones as the boat began to sail into the ocean. Oswyn used the one oar to push them away, paddling on both sides of the boat interchangeably, just as the stranger stood at the very tip of the boat, cupping his hands over his mouth and calling back to Kit.

"Give my regards to your friend!"

Kit veered back, uncertain what he meant by the words as he sank down into the boat. She watched them retreat, going from a boat on the water to nothing but a dot in the distance.

"Kit? Are ye here?" a voice called far behind her.

She turned, scrambling back up the rocks and onto the lawn, waving in the direction of the voice.

"Over here," she shouted. She could see a shadow moving from the gatehouse of the priory, hurrying toward her. It was Iomhar, running without anyone at his side. "Where is Luca?"

"Bound up well. He cannot escape those ties. Why didn't ye follow? Where is Oswyn?" he asked, looking around her. She pointed out to the ocean, gesturing to the dot on the waves.

"It seems whoever was sent to meet Luca tomorrow morning came here early. He took Oswyn with him. Oswyn must have been their spy."

Iomhar's body went stiff as he stared after the boat, his eyes practically glowing in the moonlight. "Who was he? The other man?" he asked impatiently.

"I do not know."

"Nay?" he asked, moving past her, his stride betraying his anger as he hurried to the stones she had just traipsed across and jumped down onto the shingle. "Did he not give ye a name?"

"No name."

"What did he look like then?" He waved a hand toward the ocean. "Give me a description, Kit. Anything!"

"Tall, as tall as you." She gestured toward him. "Scottish accent. Raspy voice. Fair hair, well dressed, blue eyes, pale complexion." At her words, Iomhar's body had gone very still, saying nothing as he waited for more. "A crooked nose too, rather like a kestrel's beak, pointing back toward his face." Kit took a step forward, waiting for Iomhar to return his eyes to her. "He said to give you his regards."

"Kit, ye do not realise who ye just met." Iomhar strode back across the stones, stopping when he was just a metre in front of her. "That was Lord Ruskin."

# CHAPTER 32

The silence stretched out as Iomhar rowed the boat across the slip of ocean toward the mainland. Kit was glad not to be walking the causeway this time. With the night thick and the tide high, the causeway would have been impossible. Using a lantern they had found discarded in one of the boats on the shingle, Kit held it high above the boat, so Iomhar could use the light to row. Kit kept swinging the lantern behind her, looking toward Luca who was sat beside them, his entire body bound in rope as he was slumped forward.

The only sound that disturbed the silence was the splashing of the oars striking the surface of the ocean, and the occasional hiss of a wave brushing the sides of the boat. The hissing of the waves grew louder the closer they came to the shores of Northumberland. Kit lifted the lantern higher as she saw a beach stretch out behind Iomhar's head, pale yellow in the moonlight.

"Do you know this place?" she asked as the boat began to skid along the beach, coming to a firm stop.

"Ye know it too. Take a look that way." He pointed toward a castle in the distance further south on the shore. Kit recognised the castle as Bamburgh, the same dungeons where they had held Luca captive. She bristled at the sight, looking down as Iomhar jumped out of the boat and pulled it further onto the beach.

It seemed Luca had never gone to Newcastle after all. He merely may have said that to distract them all, meanwhile he had taken the road to Lindisfarne.

"Stand." Iomhar took hold of Luca's bound arm, urging him to his feet. Kit took Luca's other arm, forcing him up as she too climbed out of the boat, holding the lantern out in front of them. It was difficult, with the gown flapping loosely around her ankles, but eventually they strode across the sand together. They didn't stop, not until they were at the back of the beach, where the sand cantered up into a bank of dunes. She released Luca's arm as Iomhar forced him to sit down on the beach.

"Do not think of moving," Iomhar warned. Luca didn't argue. He didn't make a sound and laid back on the sand, betraying his exhaustion.

Kit moved away first, taking a few steps from Luca and inching toward the ocean. She beckoned with a nod of her head, prompting Iomhar to follow. He did, reaching her side as they both looked out to the ocean together, their voices muffled by the waves as she placed the lantern down by her feet.

"What do we do with him then?" Kit asked, wrapping the sheepskin shawl around her shoulders as the wind rushed toward them off the waves.

"What do ye mean?"

"If we take him back to Bamburgh Castle, he could escape again. We still do not know who helped him out of the dungeon."

"Nay, but I did lose track of Oswyn shortly before Luca vanished. He could have looped round from the castle path."

"Oh." Kit nodded, putting together the pieces in her head. "He may have stolen a uniform, crept in. He could have been the guard that passed me in the corridor. The light was dim, and his hat was pulled too low for me to see his face."

"Aye. He may have been given orders to get Luca out of there. Explains why Oswyn was so keen for torture, does it not? He simply wanted to stop Luca from talking." He paused, letting the thought hang morbidly in the air for a moment. "We could take Luca to Bamburgh, but under torture…" He grimaced, shaking his head. "As we said before, Kit, I don't think he would tell us anything. Nothing true or useful."

She made a noise of agreement and looked behind her, to where Luca was almost asleep on the sand.

"He believes he's doing God's work, doesn't he?" Kit asked, earning a slow nod from Iomhar. "No man who believes that would tell us anything under torture." She winced, not liking the idea of seeing any man suffer torture regardless. "If we want him to tell us anything about Lord Ruskin, or who he was here to kill in the first place, then we need to find another way to make him speak."

"Aye, ye are right." Iomhar shifted on the sand, moving his weight between his feet. "About Oswyn…"

"Do you want me to tell you that you were right?" she asked, tilting her chin up to him in a challenge. "You just didn't like him because he was Northumbrian, that doesn't mean you were right."

"I didn't like him because I couldn't get on with him. It had little to do with him being Northumbrian in the end. Though, if we are keeping track of things, I was right in one regard."

"What was that?"

"He could not be trusted."

"Very well! You were right. Is that what you wanted to hear?"

"Very much. Thank ye," Iomhar said triumphantly. Kit was startled by the smile that emerged on her cheeks, shaking her head in amusement.

"This is not helping us right now."

"Perhaps not, but it makes me feel a little better."

"He was not as bad as you think," Kit murmured, chewing her lip in thought.

"What do ye mean? He seemed pretty awful to me. Trying to kill one man on his side, simply because he was afraid of Luca talking."

"Iomhar, he stopped Lord Ruskin from shooting me." Kit's words made Iomhar fall still and his eyes widen.

"Why?"

"I do not know." Kit shook her head. "Maybe in the end, he could not bring himself to see a woman die."

"He liked ye. It may have been that."

"Or … maybe he was returning a favour," Kit muttered quietly, thinking about the moment she had told Oswyn he would not die of his wound. She had told him he would survive, that was all he needed to hear. Perhaps he felt he had to repay that debt.

"Nay. I do not think he could do it. Couldn't bear to see ye killed,"

"Why?"

"He was Lord Ruskin's spy, aye? Ruskin could have ordered him to kill ye any moment. Ruskin wants ye dead, does he not? I can understand why Oswyn would not hurt ye when I was around. He would dispel his illusion as an intelligencer for Walsingham, but alone? Nay. He had plenty of opportunities that he didn't take. He could not kill ye, Kit. That is all."

Kit thought on the words for some minutes, thinking of the man who had brought her marchpane. It was odd to think that when it came to her, she was the line he would not cross. A traitor, but he had decided on his own principles somewhere along the way.

"When someone searched my room … do you think that was Oswyn?" Kit asked. "You thought so at the time."

"Aye, it makes sense now. Perhaps he was looking for those rosary beads. Trying to hide the message within, so we would never find Luca. Did he never try to take the beads off ye once he realised ye were wearing them?"

"Yes. Once." She remembered the way she had almost handed the rosary over to him, and how much he had grabbed at the air, trying to take it from her, but she had been distracted. "Oswyn can wait for another day. We have another of Lord Ruskin's spies to deal with now." She gestured back to Luca, making Iomhar nod in agreement. "We both think torture would be useless."

"Aye. Taking him to Bamburgh, that is what they will do. It was Walsingham's order."

"Exactly. Is there anywhere else we could take him?"

"We could take him to the border."

"What?" Kit asked, snapping her head toward him away from the ocean.

"It is an option." He shifted between his feet, not appearing particularly comfortable with the idea. "Niall could find a prison for him. At least there, he wouldn't be tortured. Well, I do not know if King James would permit it or not."

"Scotland." Kit toyed with the idea for a minute. "It's too risky."

"Why?"

"Because if Luca was working with Lord Ruskin, then he has more Scottish allies. We cannot be certain where those allies are. What if they are in the very prison that we take him to?"

"Aye." Iomhar rubbed his face, scratching the burn mark and the scar on his cheek in thought. "Whatever prison or dungeon we take him to, we run the risk of someone breaking him out. Then he can accomplish his mission and murder whoever he came here to kill."

"The safest thing would be to get him out of England and Scotland, back on the continent."

"What would Walsingham say to that?" Iomhar asked, looking down at Kit.

"Probably a few curse words. What safer way is there to do it?" Kit asked, shaking her head. "As long as he's here, awaiting the trial Walsingham wants for him, he could escape again."

"I cannot pretend I like the idea of Luca escaping a court. Not after all the deaths he's been linked to, but aye. Maybe that justice can wait for another day. We need to get him off these shores." Iomhar turned, looking back at Luca. "We need to convince him that going back to the continent is his only choice." With the way Iomhar was angled, she could see the burn mark and the old scar across his cheek clearly. Kit was unsure what made her say it, as she tilted her head, analysing the scar in detail, but she couldn't stop herself.

"It's been mentioned before that Lord Ruskin gave you that scar." She lifted a hand and pointed at the mark on his cheek. He jerked back to face her, stepping slightly away from her reach. "What happened, Iomhar?"

He sighed and faced the ocean. "The last time I saw Lord Ruskin, I tracked him to a road out of Edinburgh, found him alone, without his soldiers. The day my father moved Mary Stuart out of Lochleven Castle, Lord Ruskin was there waiting for him with his men. They attacked out of the blue. He was supposed to be my father's friend, yet he was the one in charge the day my father died. When I found Lord Ruskin in Edinburgh, I wanted to know the truth. Was Lord Ruskin following orders that day? Who did the deed? Who struck my father with the blade that killed him?" Iomhar kept his voice level, though his eyes never moved from the ocean, not once slipping back to Kit, even when she recoiled at the mention of a blade. "Needless to say, Lord Ruskin was not happy at being accosted. He said I was all wrong at first, that he had not been leading the soldiers that day, but he had. I have found many to confirm it. The argument grew into a fight, and he left me this to remember him." He raised a hand, gesturing to the scar. "He was aiming for my eye."

"God have mercy," Kit muttered.

"Aye, maybe God was there that day to stop it from being any worse." Iomhar looked to her at last. "It was clear to me what happened. Lord Ruskin would not tell me the truth, which means there is something he cannot face. He talked a lot in the end of how he was the one in the right, freeing our rightful queen. Pah! Mary Stuart hasn't been queen for years. Yet he went on and on, refusing to tell me what happened. Either he knows who killed my father and is protecting them, or he did it himself."

"There's no justice. Not until you have an answer from him."

"Exactly." He lifted his hand, gesturing in her direction.

"Revealing your secrets, at last!" she said with humour, pulling the smallest of smiles from him.

"Does that mean I get to hear one of yours now?"

"Maybe." She bit her lip, looking up at him. There was something she could tell him. It would be a way to explain her fear of water, but now? "Not now."

"It is never now, is it?"

"Iomhar." Her sombre tone caught his attention. "I will tell you something. I promise. First, how do we make him leave?" She pointed back toward Luca. When no idea came, she looked down at her feet on the wet sand. She could see shapes in the sand, where sea worms had wriggled through the earth. The way the casts of their bodies showed they had escaped toward the ocean offered her an idea. "Maybe there is a way to make a deal with him."

"What deal?"

She beckoned Iomhar to follow her. She moved back to Luca and sat beside him, pulling on his ropes and urging him to sit up. He blinked, bleary-eyed, waking up from his exhausted sleep.

"What, *donna?*" he said, spitting in anger with his words.

"I have an offer to make you, Luca." At her words, Iomhar crouched down on Luca's other side, his dark hair whipped by the wind as he watched her with wary eyes. Luca turned his face toward her, that look of anger fading into one of curiosity.

"I have no choice but to listen. Do I?" he asked, clearly trying not to sound too interested.

"You stay here, you will die. You know that as well as I." Her words made Luca's glare harden.

"I have survived thus far, *donna.*"

"I am talking of facing a court. You are an assassin, are you not? Your weapons are bloodstained, and goodness knows how many know what you have done on the continent." She kept her voice calm, watching as Luca appeared to listen to her more and more. "Our courts are not forgiving, no matter what the crime. A man responsible for one death will face the noose. How many deaths have you seen?"

Luca flinched, just as Iomhar did on his other side.

"He deserves punishment, Kit. I will not argue against that." Iomhar's voice held a warning tone.

"I agree with you." Kit nodded, keeping her stare straight. She and Iomhar both knew that Luca wouldn't stay in prison long enough to see a trial, he would be broken out to do his deed, but she didn't have to let Luca know that. "But it doesn't help us to see that punishment done today."

Luca sat up a little straighter, wriggling against the rope bindings that were cutting across his tunic and the woollen black coat. "You would release me?"

"This is my offer." Kit held his gaze. "If we put you on a boat back to the continent, you would escape our courts here."

"For what? What reason, *donna*, would you do this?"

"Tell us why you were sent here. Who did you come to kill?" she asked.

The corner of his lips smiled a little, as if humoured by her words. "You think I would tell a Protestant what will bring about the coming of the rightful religion?"

"Do you wish to die at the end of a noose?" she asked, watching as his lips flattened together.

He looked away from her, turning his gaze down toward the sand. Silence fell between them. The only sounds were the soft hiss of the waves nearby and the cawing of wading birds.

"Perhaps he would sooner die for his cause than tell us." Iomhar's words broke the silence, making Luca wriggle beneath his bindings.

"I did not say that."

"Ah, or he has had a change of heart." Iomhar smiled a little at Kit before returning his gaze to Luca. "What do ye have to tell us?"

"I need to know you will keep to your word first." He looked between the two of them repeatedly. "Take me to a ship. Put me on it and I will tell you all, but not before."

"That is fair. We have a deal, Luca."

# CHAPTER 33

Kit pulled the cloak hood over Luca's face, hiding him from view.

"Can you change your accent?" she asked, resting her hands on the weapons belt around her waist. She was glad to be back in her hose and doublet, no longer in the pale green gown.

"No," Luca said, with the Italian accent still strong.

"Well…" She paused, grimacing as she looked toward the captain on the deck of the ship at the end of the dockyard. "Tell him you're a merchant then."

Iomhar appeared at their side, thrusting some parchments into Luca's hands. "This will get ye to Brittany." Iomhar urged him to pocket the papers within the folds of his cloak. "From there, ye are on your own to find your way home."

Luca nodded, showing he understood. "You will not give me a weapon to defend myself on my journey?" he asked, looking between the two of them.

"We are not giving you a way to kill another." Kit spoke in a harsh whisper, so full of venom that the words hissed.

"You are righteous for a Protestant." Luca seemed amused by the idea, smiling a little, before he glanced at the ship behind him.

Kit followed his gaze, looking toward the dockyard. Made of stone and timber, it stretched out across the estuary that connected the two sides of the busy town of Newcastle. There were many ships readying themselves to set sail, the largest of which was a passenger ship set for Brittany, with its sails being unfurled and its crew running about on deck.

"You have held true to your word." Luca turned back to the two of them, his wide eyes betraying his surprise.

"Then hold true to yours." Kit kept her voice level, waiting for him to speak. He nodded ever so subtly before he stepped toward the two of them, pulling his cloak hood slightly forward, as if to stop any passers-by from hearing his voice.

"I was sent for your queen. Elizabeth."

Kit felt a deadening in her stomach as her hands balled into fists.

"Why?" Iomhar asked. "There are constant plots against her head. Why did they send ye?"

"They were tired of the plots going wrong. They wanted someone who could be certain of the task." Luca went onto explain. "The plan has three masters. The man you saw last night is the first."

"Lord Ruskin," Iomhar mumbled the name, with barely concealed hate.

"That is right." Luca gestured toward him. "The other two, I do not know their names."

"Then ye are giving us nothing!" At Iomhar's outburst, Luca lifted a hand, quelling his anger.

"I can give you more." Luca assured him. "Their plan was to kill your queen and break Mary Stuart from her house arrest. They were to march on London where one of the privy councillors would put her forward as the next queen."

"Wait ... the privy council?" Kit repeated the words. "The second of these three men. He is in the privy council."

"*Si*. The third I do not know, but I have read codenames for both men."

"Give us the names," Kit pleaded.

Behind, they were interrupted by catcalls. The captain of the ship was ordering the final preparations, shouting toward the dock to ensure any passengers were on board.

"Time to go." Luca stepped away, Iomhar went to grab his arm, but Luca stepped out of reach. "Patience."

"Patience? What does he mean by that?" Iomhar cried as he and Kit ran after him.

Luca was the faster runner and clambered up the board to the ship, waving his papers in front of him. Kit was ready to follow when a sailor blocked her way.

"Where are your papers?"

"I have none."

"Then you are not climbing aboard this ship." The sailor turned his back on her, urging her away as he strode onto the deck and lifted the board connecting the ship to the dock. "God's wounds!" she cursed, hurrying to Iomhar's side who was calling up to the ship.

"Luca!" he shouted.

Luca turned on the deck of the ship as the anchor was lifted and it began to drift away from the city. He leaned over the bough of the ship and called to them.

"The Rose and the Lily."

"What did he say?" Iomhar turned his head to Kit.

"They're the codenames, Iomhar. For the second and third man. The Rose and the Lily."

# CHAPTER 34

"I'm looking forward to being warm again." Kit blew on her gloved hands, trying to bring some heat to them as she threaded the horse's reins over her wrist.

"Ye would suffer in Scotland at this time of year."

"Northumberland is bad enough for me. I'll take your word for it when it comes to Scotland." Kit turned her eyes on the horizon ahead. They had long left Newcastle behind and were riding far from the border, heading along Hadrian's Wall to meet the main road leading down through to York, and then on to London. Around them, the skeletal trees shivered in the breeze, each twig like bony fingers beckoning them to hurry. That breeze made Kit turn up the collar of her doublet and pull her hat down a little more. "How long do you reckon it will take us?"

"Two days. Maybe more. We'll change horses in York," Iomhar called to her, slowing his horse so she could catch up. She moved her mare to ride alongside his steed, with the wall stretching beside them, staying around the level of their ankles upon the saddles. "We will head to Seething Lane first."

"We have to tell him."

"What? Tell Taurus we let Luca escape? Aye, that sounds wise."

"Not in so many words."

"It would be better to say he escaped back to the continent. Do not let Walsingham place any blame on our shoulders, Kit. We can say Oswyn helped him."

Kit shifted uncomfortably in her saddle. They had the information they needed; deep down, she knew she had accomplished her task, but it was the first time she had ever defied an order of Walsingham's. The only time she could ever remember deciding that he was in the wrong. "I mean we have to tell him what Luca said. About the second and third man, and the codenames. There is a chance he may have heard of the codenames already."

"What if Walsingham is the second man?"

"Iomhar!" Kit snapped the word, turning her head toward him to see him sitting back in the saddle with open palms, looking at her in equal wonder.

"All we know is there is a man in the privy council that wants to put Mary Stuart on the throne. Lady Ruskin said as much, now Luca has too. That man could be any of the privy council. Ye cannot be sure it isn't Walsingham."

"Of course it is not him! You think he would have so many intelligencers running around trying to protect Queen Elizabeth otherwise?"

"Well, perhaps we are just good for keeping up an illusion of loyalty."

"No. No!" Kit spoke with vehemence. "That is not Walsingham. You may not know the man at all, but I do. I've known him for years, been by his side since I was no taller than his kneecap. I am telling you. His life is keeping Queen Elizabeth safe. He sees no other purpose for his life."

Iomhar stared back at her, saying nothing, only returning the heaviness of that glare.

"Is that not enough for you?" Kit asked. "My belief in him?"

"Nay." His answer made her flick her head away again, staring at the undulating hills. They urged the horses to descend the hill, following the path of the wall down to where a well sat in a nook, with a sycamore tree beside it that had grown so tall it practically filled the sky above them.

"Have you not heard the way he talks? How passionately he speaks?"

"He could be a good liar."

"He is a good man. I know it."

"Because he took ye in and raised ye? Hmm, I've been thinking about that." Iomhar grabbed hold of her reins, pulling the horses to a stop.

"What are you doing?"

"Getting your full attention." He tugged on the reins a little more, forcing her to look straight at him. "A man took ye in as a wee lass and raised ye to work for him. He made ye his intelligencer. Gave ye no other option for a life, did he?"

"He gave me a life." Kit practically barked the words, but it didn't take the anger out of Iomhar's face.

"He said he raised ye, but he could have raised ye like family, couldn't he? He could have raised ye alongside his daughter."

"Something tells me his wife and real daughter would not have taken kindly to him raising a redcap."

"Redcap?" Iomhar repeated, refusing to let go of the reins of her horse, even when she tugged on them.

"It's what his wife thought I looked like when he first brought me home."

"So what then? He kept ye in Seething Lane, raised ye to solve codes, taught ye to fight, and none of that seems odd to ye?"

"He was giving me a way to protect myself, that is all."

"He carved ye into being nothing more than a servant to him!" Iomhar practically shouted the words to be heard over her. She stilled, abandoning her attempt to pull back the reins as she stared at him. Iomhar shook his head, evidently trying to control his temper. "Have ye never thought of it like that?"

"Never." Kit breathed for a minute, thinking over the words, then an image appeared in her head, the one of Walsingham reaching down to pull her out of the water. "And I will not start thinking it now."

"Why not?" Iomhar asked, his voice as quiet as hers.

"Because I still trust him."

"Why? There must be something more to this, Kit. Give me a reason to trust him too, and I will, otherwise…" He released her reins, holding up his hands, showing his meaning. He would never trust Walsingham.

Kit stared forward, bracing herself against the wind as it rustled up the valley. She climbed down from the horse, wrapping the reins around a nook in the wall before she walked to the well nearby. Iomhar watched her, until she beckoned to him, urging him to follow. When he joined her at the well, she pointed down at the water within.

"I told you I would tell you a secret, as you told me one."

"Aye. Ye are choosing this moment?"

"I can continue keeping my secret if you like?" she teased him, making his lips curve into a small smile.

"Go on." He urged her.

"I was going to tell you why I do not like water." She pointed down at the well again.

"Ye are telling me this just to avoid talking of Walsingham anymore."

"I'm not. It connects."

"Very well." Iomhar bent over the edge of the well, looking down into its depths. "How does it link?"

"Ever since I can remember I've had this dream. For a while I was convinced it was a memory, and then I started to doubt myself. Whilst it always begins the same, each time I have the dream, I see a new version, as more things are added." She gestured to her head; unsure she could trust her own thoughts. "In the first dream, I'm small, perhaps nor more than three or four, and I'm under water." She gestured down at the well.

"Ye are certain of your age?"

"Not exactly. I see small hands reaching toward the surface ... stockings falling off my feet... It sounds about right." Her palms felt clammy despite the chill as she prepared to tell him more. She had never uttered these words to anyone. "I'm drowning in the dream, Iomhar."

He looked up to her from the well, his expression contorting and furrowing his brow. "Is that how the dream ends?"

"It used to. With just me struggling under the water. Then something changed." She cleared her throat, feeling the nerves prickling her skin as she bent over the edge of the well, peering down at the water below. It was just about visible, with the surface glistening. "I saw a figure. A woman, I think. She is standing over me when I am in the water."

"Does she pull ye out?"

"No. She just stands there. It's as though she's watching me, then she walks away. She leaves me there." Kit looked up from the water to find Iomhar staring at her, his body perfectly still.

"Are ye certain this is a dream, Kit?"

"No. It could be a memory. I used to think it was."

"What do you think it is now?"

She stood straight, bracing both palms against the wall of the well and shifting her focus completely to Iomhar.

"The last time I had this dream, I wasn't asleep. I was in the water, and I cannot really explain the feeling. It was as if the cold of the water reminded me of that moment, and then I saw something else happen. A second figure came along, reaching down toward me. I think he was pulling me out of the water. No, I do not think it, I know it."

"He? Who is he?"

"Walsingham." Her simple word made Iomhar's posture sink as he leaned completely on the side of the well.

"That would explain a lot."

"Does it? I feel it explains nothing."

"Is this why ye trust him so much? Ye think he saved your life?"

"No. That is not what I'm saying." She pulled off her cap, pulling on the tendrils of hair in frustration. "I cannot be certain it is a memory; it could just all be in my imagination. I trust Walsingham because I have known him for as long as I can remember. I know who he really is, even if you do not. So much do I trust him that I may have invented a world where he saves me from my worst fear." She gestured down into the well again, pointing at the water.

"Aye, very well."

"What? No more questions? No more words on why I am a fool to place my trust in the man?" she asked in disbelief as he shifted to face her, crossing his arms.

"Nay. If ye trust him that much, then fine. I will not query it again."

"Good." She turned on her heel, heading back toward the horse.

Kit knocked on the door of Seething Lane, looking around the timber courtyard behind her as she waited for it to be answered. Iomhar was standing a little behind her, his eyes darting around the same space, barely able to settle.

"Ye warm now?" Iomhar asked, glancing at her with a small smile.

"I'm less cold."

"It's practically hot," he jested, pulling a rather reluctant smile from her.

"Well, we cannot all be built to bear the Scottish winters."

"There now."

"There now what?" she asked, angling her gaze toward him.

"I've been trying to get a smile out of ye since we left the border. It has taken a while, but I've finally done it."

She tutted at his efforts, turning to the door as it was answered. The familiar face of Doris appeared, with the eyes that were alight with energy and the grey hair stuffed under the white muslin cap.

"Kitty!" the housekeeper cried, stepping out of the door and wrapping Kit in such a tight embrace that she was nearly knocked from her feet.

"Doris, are you well?" Kit asked in panic. "Last time you hugged my like this you were trying to hide me from Walsingham's rage."

"You have been gone for weeks." She parted from the embrace, looking up at Kit with a smile. "I kept asking Walsingham if you would be back in time for Yuletide but getting an answer out of him was like taking blood from a stone. Impossible!"

"I'm back now." Kit offered a smile as she peered around Doris' shoulder. "Is he here, Doris? We need to see him."

"He's here. Best you go up and see him, Kitty. Be warned though, oh, he's in a foul mood today." She stepped back and ushered Kit forward with a wave of her hand. When she saw Iomhar, she hurried to curtsy, before retreating into the kitchen.

"A foul mood," Kit murmured as the two of them walked down the corridor.

"Aye, he'll be in a worse one soon enough." Iomhar's words prompted her to glance his way. He did not appear as apprehensive as she felt, fidgeting with her own hands until the palms were clammy beneath the covering of her gloves. Iomhar was calm, striding forward as if they were to deliver some menial report, rather than the news that they had let an assassin go.

They creeped up the wooden stairs, with their feet so loud on the steps that they creaked, forewarning Walsingham of their approach before they even had to knock.

"Come!" Walsingham barked from inside. "I pray whoever you are that you bring good news."

Kit stepped inside first, turning to face Walsingham who was pacing his chamber, with so many papers in his hands that he struggled to carry them all. He glanced up, distractedly, then did a double take when he saw Kit's face.

"Kit?" He practically dropped the papers, hurrying to place some of them on the desk behind him whilst others drifted to the floor. "Let me look at you." He moved toward her and took her shoulders. The touch was such a shock that Kit froze, aware that Walsingham was looking her over. The last time he had done such a thing she was a child and had gone clambering across rooftops to escape her lessons. He had gazed at her for many minutes then, checking she was well before he reprimanded her. "Well, you look unharmed." He allowed himself a small smile. "Iomhar's letter left something of a fright here." He released Kit and sent a glare Iomhar's way.

"Aye, so ye wish me to keep it a secret the next time someone is trying to kill your favourite?" Iomhar's dry humour wasn't helping. The smile vanished from Walsingham's face and Kit sent Iomhar a warning glare. "The man who tried to kill her is locked up in Bamburgh Castle now."

"Good, that is good news. But ... why are you both here?" Walsingham stepped back and glanced between the two of them, his chin jerking so quickly that the few grey hairs that were left on his head trembled with the movement. "You are supposed to be in Northumberland."

"There was nay cause to keep us there anymore," Iomhar explained and moved to the nearest seat. He sat down heavily and yawned, betraying their exhaustion after so long a journey.

"We have news." Kit kept her focus on Walsingham as she spoke, wary of how he would react. "News of Luca."

"And? Is he with you?" Walsingham glanced behind them, as if he expected them to trudge Luca into Seething Lane. "Did you take him to the Tower?"

Kit fidgeted with her gloves, adjusting the grips around her wrists as she thought of what to say. The silence that fell between the three of them was so uncomfortable that she looked to Iomhar. He seemed to understand she wanted help for he sat forward.

"I'll tell him, Kit," he said slowly. Kit backed up, increasing the distance between Walsingham and herself. "Luca is gone."

"Gone? What do you mean gone?"

"You could have said it a little gentler than that," Kit protested, tapping Iomhar around the arm as she stopped by his chair.

"Better to deliver the wound fast than to see it drawn out and bleeding for long, Kit." Iomhar shrugged, clearly not minding the turmoil he had now delivered to Walsingham.

The older man started shaking his head, returning to his desk and clinging to the edge as if it was the very thing that kept him standing on his feet.

"You mean we have an assassin on our shores? Free to do as he wishes?" Walsingham looked to Kit so sharply that she was tempted to flinch. "Kit! Tell me the meaning of this?"

"He is not on our shores," Kit continued, speaking quickly this time. "He escaped and has fled to the continent."

"This is madness. Pure madness!" Walsingham rounded the desk and reached for a cup on his desk, knocking back the contents. Judging by the scent of spices in the air, it was some sort of cinnamon-laced wince. Kit glanced at Iomhar who bore the same look of worry in his own expression. "I ask you both to find one man. That is all! One man."

"Aye, simple task indeed when he's a killer."

"Iomhar," Kit warned him to be quiet, standing on his toe.

"Ye didn't want to tell him yourself."

"I've changed my mind." She strode away from Iomhar and reached Walsingham's desk, seeking out his gaze. "Not all is lost, Walsingham."

"How can you say that? Pah!" He scoffed and rounded the desk, coming to face her. "In the time you have been gone, we have made little progress. The intelligencers I sent to watch the privy council have found nothing. If there is someone leaking information on the council, then we have not found them. The one hope I had on the two of you was clearly equally fruitless. You may have found that Henry Percy was hiding Luca, and he is on his way to the Tower now, so that I may talk to him alongside his father about that family's allegiances, and whether it is to our crown or the Pope, but what more have you done? You might as well have packed Luca's bags for him and waved him off yourself!" He practically shouted the words in his anger, prompting Kit to hang her head, fearful the truth would be read on her face, that they had as good as waved goodbye on the docks to Luca.

"We have something to show for it," Kit said, her quiet voice somehow breaking through Walsingham's fury. His body stiffened, though the redness of his face did not fade as his eyes fixed on her, unblinkingly. "There is much you need to know."

"Aye, we have a tale to tell ye about your friend, Oswyn Ingleby," Iomhar called from his seat. "Some friend."

"What do you mean?" Walsingham asked distractedly, his hands hanging limp at his side.

"We shall tell you all, but first let me tell you the good news – what we discovered from Luca." Kit paused, waiting until she had Walsingham's full attention. "Luca gave us the codenames of two men in England, working to free Mary Queen of Scots. They are working alongside Lord Ruskin." She hesitated, watching as a muscle in Walsingham's jaw ticked at the man's name. She knew how he had fretted over Lady Ruskin's involvement in the last plot against the queen. "Their names are the Rose and the Lily."

Walsingham backed up a little, his brow creasing in thought. He collided with his desk and sat on the edge, his chin drooping forward.

"Two spies?" he whispered, almost fearful of hearing the truth. "What does this mean?"

"It's confirmation of what we feared. One of these men sits on the privy council." Kit waited until Walsingham lifted his chin again. "Maybe the men you have sent to watch the privy council have worked in vain, but we have confirmation of it regardless. We now know a betrayer who wishes Mary Stuart on the throne sits close to the Queen of England."

"So ... your commission was not a hopeless one, eh?" Walsingham's lips quivered into the smallest of smiles before it vanished. He was clearly not convinced of his own words. "I fear what this means for us now. This spy on the privy council, we must be prepared for when he chooses to act."

A solemn quiet air descended on the room. Walsingham walked away from Kit and sat down behind his desk, prompting the chair to creak. He said nothing for a minute but stared at the wood ahead of him.

Kit took the seat beside Iomhar, hoping that she could find some comfort, but she sat on the very edge, restless, struggling to find that peace.

"I knew he would not be happy," Kit mumbled, quiet enough that only Iomhar could hear her.

"We know something we didn't know before," Iomhar said, his voice a little louder than her own, enough for Walsingham to hear. "Aye, and ye are alive. I'd call that a success, wouldn't ye?"

"Yes, you are alive," Walsingham called from his place at the desk. He revealed the glimmer of a smile that made Kit's spine at last soften. "And I must praise you both for one thing at least. Luca is no longer on our shores. The danger he threatened, at least it is past. For now." He sniffed audibly and sat forward. "You two should rest, before I have need of you again."

# A NOTE TO THE READER

Dear Reader,

Thank you for taking the time to read the second in the series of Kit Scarlett's adventures.

The inspiration for Kit's tale comes from a longing to see more stories where women are at the centre of a tale that is truly adventurous. We know from hints of this time period that there was the occasional woman doing espionage, but with Kit, I've taken that idea and thrown her completely into this world. Not only is she a spy, fighting to defend her Queen in one of the most turbulent times of history, when there were often assassination attempts on the Queen's life, but Kit is in the deep end. It is her responsibility to see that the Queen stays safe.

Naturally, at times, fact is played with a little and people are invented. The purpose of this book is to entertain after all, so I hope I have indeed done that, and you have enjoyed this story as much as I did writing it. This is a created world, where a woman walks freely dressed as a man, saving lives and even the country, but who knows? This is a world of shadows, where intelligencers operated in the dark and, for all we know, a woman like Kit may have truly existed.

Reviews by readers these days are integral to a book's success, so if you enjoyed Kit's tale I would be very grateful if you could spare a minute to post a review on **Amazon** and **Goodreads**. I love hearing from readers, and you can talk with me through **my website** or **on Twitter** and follow my author page **on Facebook**.

I hope we'll meet again on Kit's next adventure.

Adele Jordan

**Sapere Books** is an exciting new publisher of brilliant fiction and popular history.

To find out more about our latest releases and our monthly bargain books visit our website: **saperebooks.com**

Printed in Great Britain
by Amazon